Emily Harvale lives in East Sussex
You can contact her via her website
Google+ or Pinterest

Author contacts:
www.emilyharvale.com
www.twitter.com/emilyharvale
www.facebook.com/emilyharvalewriter
www.facebook.com/emilyharvale
www.emilyharvale/blog
www.pinterest.com/emilyharvale
www.google.com/+EmilyHarvale

Scan the code above to see all Emily's books on Amazon

Also by this author:

Highland Fling

Lizzie Marshall's Wedding

The Golf Widows' Club

Sailing Solo

Carole Singer's Christmas

Christmas Wishes – Two short stories

A Slippery Slope

The Perfect Christmas Plan – A novella

Be Mine – A novella

***

The Goldebury Bay series:

Book One – Ninety Days of Summer

Book Two – Ninety Steps to Summerhill

Book Three – Ninety Days to Christmas

Ninety Days

to

Christmas

Emily Harvale

ISBN 978-1-909917-10-1

Published by Crescent Gate Publishing

Print edition published worldwide 2015
E-edition published worldwide 2015

Editor Christina Harkness

Cover design by JR, Luke Brabants and Emily Harvale

Acknowledgements

Goldebury Bay is loosely based on my home town of Hastings as you'll know if you follow me on social media. Hastings is a beautiful seaside resort on the East Sussex coast of the UK. It has many tourist attractions, several of which are similar to those in my fictitious resort of Goldebury Bay. However, the attractions in this book are purely fictional and therefore, should not be confused with any real tourist attractions either in Hastings or in any other resort.

My special thanks go to the following:

Christina Harkness for editing this novel. Christina has the patience of a saint and her input is truly appreciated.

My webmaster and friend, David Cleworth who does so much more for me than website stuff.

Luke Brabants and JR for their work on the gorgeous cover. JR is a genius in graphic design and Luke's a talented artist. Luke's website is: http://www.lukebrabants.com

My fabulous friends for their support and friendship.

My Twitter and Facebook friends, and fans of my Facebook author page. It's great to chat with you. You help to keep me (relatively) sane!

And finally, you – for buying this book. Thank You. It really means a lot to me. I hope you enjoy it.

Note from author

Hello!

I just wanted to say a few words before you get into this book, the third in the Goldebury Bay series. Each book stands alone, so you don't have to have read the first two books before you read this one but it will make it easier for you to understand what's going on and who all the characters are, if you have.

The lunar eclipse mentioned in this book is real, so in the early hours of the 28th of September 2015, the moon (which is a Harvest moon and a Super moon to boot!) will look like a massive, red ball. It's definitely visible from the U.K. but you may need to Google it to see if it's visible from elsewhere. I'll be staying up to watch it, weather permitting. I'm a bit of a star-gazing nerd, so I'm rather excited.

As the title of this book suggests, it tells a story leading up to, and finishing on, Christmas Eve. Like all my books, it's wonderfully romantic and somewhat light-hearted. Friendship is an important part of all my stories and the friendship between Cleo, Poppy, Sophie, Thaddeus and Oliver, in this series, is very special to me. I hope that comes across in all three, Goldebury Bay, books.

Well that's enough from me, except to say a big thank you for buying this book. I hope you enjoy it.
Love,

Emily xx

This dedication is not mine. It's by Sheila Moore, one of my newsletter subscribers, who won the chance to dedicate this book to her family, friends and anyone else she chose. Over to you, lovely Sheila...

To my darling husband, Donald Moore for being my hero during our thirty-two years of marriage. To our daughter, Yvonne, the best daughter ever, our wonderful son-in-law, Roger Staples and our grandkids, Linden and Jeanetta. And I mustn't leave out our two pooches, Ralph and Beadle. I love you all. XXX
Thanks Emily. X

Chapter One

She was stuck. There was no doubt about it.

No matter how carefully Poppy twisted or turned her body, the hem of her figure-hugging dress was just out of reach. Every move she made, however slight, was accompanied by a ripping sound. It was as if an invisible security guard had leapt up and grabbed it.

The hem must have caught on a nail. Or perhaps a sliver of wood from the edge of the 'Keep Out' sign attached to the railing she'd just clambered over. Whatever it was, she couldn't risk causing more damage to the dress. Sophie would kill her. She'd been the one who'd paid the deposit and it was a fortune. Although Sophie *had* a fortune, so it was probably a drop in the ocean to her but that wasn't the point. You didn't let your friends pay for your mistakes and Poppy couldn't afford to pay for this one.

She peered into the fading twilight but there was no one in sight. Not even Toby Blackwood. The only sounds were the waves swooshing over the pebbles on the shore several feet away and the occasional caw from a passing gull.

Where were all the bloody dog-walkers when you needed one? Probably up at Summerhill enjoying themselves, along with everyone else in Goldebury Bay… apart from her.

'Sod it!' she said.

Why hadn't she listened to Cleo and Sophie and stayed at the party instead of doing what she always did? Act on impulse.

And now she was stuck.

Because of Toby Blackwood.

If he hadn't behaved so mysteriously, she wouldn't be in this predicament. When he'd stopped mid-sentence, apologised, hastily removed his iPhone from his pocket and glanced at the screen, he looked as if he'd just been contacted by the Almighty himself. Poppy's inner radar had beeped. When he apologised again and said he had to go, should she have simply smiled and let him? That's what any sane person would do – or so her friends had told her.

'Why does it matter who texted him, or why he's rushing off?' Sophie had asked as they watched him pick his way through the throng of party guests. 'You only met the guy tonight.'

'So what?' Poppy replied. 'Didn't you see us? We've got chemistry. He's the man of my dreams and I knew it the minute he smiled at me, took my hand and led me to the dance floor. It's destiny.'

'Hmm,' Cleo said. 'Sounds more like insanity to me but if it *is* destiny, what're you worried about? He took your number and said he'd phone.'

'But why did he leave like that? One minute we're here, getting a drink and chatting with you two and the next he's racing off into the night as if his life depends on it. And why be so secretive? He could've said: "Sorry, that was my Gran. She's on her deathbed and needs to see me right this second," or something like that.'

'Yes,' Sophie said. 'Because an old woman on her deathbed is bound to be texting people, isn't she? And even if she had, why should he tell you? Do you tell total strangers who you're getting texts from?'

'Perhaps it was his wife,' said Cleo.

'He doesn't have a wife, *Miss Merrifield*. I asked him.

Don't look at me like that. I wanted to know if he was available. So I asked.'

'Well, there you are then,' Sophie said. 'He's just not available tonight. Leave it at that and wait for him to call.'

But Poppy didn't like mysteries. She'd had enough of those to last her a lifetime since she and Cleo had come to Goldebury Bay. She wanted to know who had texted him. She wanted to know where he was going. She wanted to know everything about Toby Blackwood – and she wanted to know it now. Because Toby Blackwood was the man for her. She was sure of that.

And it had nothing to do with the fact that all her friends were in relationships except her. Or that she was desperate for a man. Or that Christmas was only ninety days away and that number one on her list of New Year Resolutions had been: *be in a relationship before Christmas.* Although all of those facts had possibly influenced her a little. Especially the last one.

No, it wasn't really any of those. It was the man himself. To say Toby Blackwood was drop-dead gorgeous was the understatement of the year. Like saying caviar was fish eggs.

And he wasn't merely gorgeous. He was kind, considerate, funny… and good in bed. Well okay, she didn't know if he was good in bed but you can get a rough idea by the way someone dances with you. The way they hold you in their arms. And she may have only spent twenty minutes in his company but you can tell a lot about a person in twenty minutes.

Or less.

Poppy could tell a lot about a person in twenty seconds… and she didn't *always* get it wrong.

She'd got it wrong with Geoff Hadleigh though. Badly wrong. But that was another story. And it wasn't the first

3

time she'd fallen for the wrong guy. She wasn't going to make that mistake again. Neither was she going to waste time planning a cosy, romantic Christmas with Toby Blackwood only to find out he was a serial killer or something. And he could be, despite Cleo telling her not to be "a complete, bloody idiot". Geoff had turned out to be a criminal so was it such a stretch of the imagination to wonder if someone as gorgeous and seemingly perfect as Toby Blackwood, was also involved in some nefarious activity?

No it wasn't, in her opinion. So Poppy had ignored her friends and gone with her gut. She was going to find out for herself... even though she'd told Cleo and Sophie she wouldn't.

But now she was stuck.

Could she reach one of the high-heeled sandals she'd thrown, along with her clutch bag, onto the concrete balcony before climbing over the railing separating it from the raised walkway?

Her bag was of no use because her smartphone was on charge at home. She didn't think she'd need it at *Sophie Summerhill's and Thaddeus Beaumont's Moving in Together Party* (which she still thought was a crap name for a party but when she'd said as much and they'd told her to come up with something better, she couldn't.) But her sandals... She might be able to use the heel to free herself and with the added length of the shoe, she wouldn't have to twist so far round and risk tearing the dress further.

She stretched out her leg and pointed her toes. Despite the situation, she grinned. It was probably a good thing no one could see her. She must have resembled a demented ballerina with her dress hoisted up around her bottom and the copious, gossamer folds of the overskirt scrunched up under the crook of one arm like a gigantic, displaced, tutu.

4

'Bugger!' The sandals were an inch or so too far.

She heard footfall on the concrete steps and cringed. That would be Toby and despite the fact that he'd have his back to her whilst he climbed the steps, he'd turn to his left at the top and then – unless he was half-blind – he'd spot her. The railing separating the walkway and the balcony was about thirty feet along from the large, wooden, double doors but he couldn't really miss her. Even in the fading twilight, she stuck out like a sore thumb.

She needed to think of a suitable explanation and she needed to think fast. She took a deep breath and twisted her head in his direction. But when he reached the walkway, the man who turned towards her wasn't Toby – although there was a vague resemblance. He stopped in his tracks and stared at her with a look of haughty bemusement on an otherwise handsome face.

Unable to think of anything else to say, Poppy said: 'I'm stuck. Or at least my dress is.'

The man's expression changed to something akin to amused indifference. He tilted his head to one side and a mane of reddish-brown hair flopped across his forehead. As he shoved it back, Poppy thought she saw a flash of irritation.

'So I see.' His voice was as smooth as glass. Cut glass.

Poppy assumed he'd offer to help her as any decent man would but he remained exactly where he was. Not even his pristine white shirt or charcoal-grey suit – both of which looked designer – moved an inch, despite the cool, evening breeze heading in from the sea.

And that was odd, because it was making the waves of gossamer material forming the bulbous overskirt of her dress, flutter and lift, revealing more of her than she'd like a total stranger to see. She'd had to slide the dress up in order to climb over the railing and when the hem caught, the dress had ridden higher. The overskirt was the only thing preserving her modesty and if the breeze grew much stronger, she'd be showing this man her knickers.

And they were lace.

White lace.

Not that that mattered. You didn't want a total stranger to see your knickers, no matter what colour they were.

'Are you drunk? Or on some sort of hen-night dare?'

'No!'

'Then, this may be a silly question, but why were you climbing over the railing in the first place? The 'Keep Out' sign is there for a reason.'

Poppy felt her cheeks burn, and more so when she noticed his cool gaze – which she could see even from this distance – travel the length of her body.

'I know the owner,' she said, tugging at the folds of material flapping around her thighs like the wings of several crazed butterflies. That was a stupid thing to say but she couldn't think of anything else. And that was also odd, because she wasn't usually lost for words. Her friends were always telling her that she often had far too much to say.

'Oh? Then why didn't… *the owner* invite you to use the door?'

Poppy didn't like his tone. It was a reasonable question but it was irritating nonetheless.

Should she lie? Should she say she was meeting Toby but as the place was in darkness, she'd climbed over the railing with the intention of looking through one of the windows?

Arranging to meet someone in an abandoned building just as it was getting dark sounded pretty dodgy even to her. And Toby may have been coming here to meet this man, so the guy would probably guess she was lying.

She only knew Toby was headed to the derelict

Goldebury Bay Yachting and Sailing Club because she saw him exchange a brief word with Thaddeus before dashing out. When she'd quizzed Thaddeus about it seconds later, he'd told her Toby had asked him the quickest way there. She'd thought about it for as long as ten seconds and then, despite Cleo and Sophie's less than enthusiastic response, she'd scurried away from the fancy dress party to see what Toby was up to. She'd trotted down the ninety steps from Summerhill, each of which was lit with coloured lights, to the cove below and jogged along the promenade to the long-abandoned building.

When she arrived, it seemed she'd beaten him to it even though it shouldn't have taken him longer than five minutes to drive here. Maybe he'd entered via the side door. But wasn't that boarded up? And if he was inside, surely there would be a light of some kind. A torch beam at least. Unless he really was up to no good.

After a moment's hesitation, she'd tiptoed along the concrete walkway towards the balcony at the front of the building which faced the sea. There were floor to ceiling windows at the front and Poppy knew they weren't all boarded up. It wasn't the first time she'd climbed over the railing onto the balcony. She and Cleo had done it last summer when they found out about the smuggling.

'Well?'

The man sounded a little impatient but the breeze had picked up and Poppy was having difficulty keeping hold of the billowing overskirt. She looked back at him and was furious to see he was staring at her thighs.

'When you've quite finished ogling my body, perhaps you'd actually come and help me!'

He raised his brows. 'It's a long time since I've had to come to the rescue of a damsel in distress.'

Despite his comment he didn't move – unless you

counted the twitch of his lips.

After a second or two, Poppy said: 'Today would be nice.'

He completely ignored her sarcasm.

'Well?' Poppy demanded.

'Well what?'

If only she could reach her sandals… she'd throw them at him. He was blatantly raking over every inch of her, with eyes that from here, looked the same colour as the incoming, cobalt tide, and similarly cool-looking. What was she? Some piece of artwork or something, like the sculptures on display in The Artful Fisher gallery. From the look on his face, this guy couldn't seem to decide whether or not he liked what he saw.

'What do you mean, "Well what?" Are you going to help me or not?'

'Certainly.'

Still he didn't move.

'When exactly?'

'You asked me to help you when I'd finished ogling your body. I haven't quite finished.'

Poppy could feel her mouth drop open and she was sure her eyes were bulging in their sockets. Did he really just say that?

He was obviously a nutter… or worse. Wasn't that typical? No knight in shining armour for her. Just some bloody psycho who was probably going to murder her.

'Pervert! Don't you come near me. I'll call the police.'

'If you have a phone somewhere in that dress, I'd like to know where. But if anyone should be calling the police, it's me. I'm sure I don't need to point this out but you're the one who's trespassing.'

Now the bloody guy moves! 'Stay where you are,' Poppy said, wishing she could back away.

'You've got nothing to worry about from me, I promise you. And let's face it, I'm not the one dressed up as some sort of fairy tale princess and climbing over railings. I should be worried about my safety, not the other way around. Aren't you rather old to be playing dress-up?'

'Old? I'm not old! I'm thirty-three. And I'm Cinderella.'

She noticed the raised eyebrow and curve of his lips as he stopped a few feet away.

'Of course you are. Er. I may be wrong but didn't Cinderella leave a glass slipper – not her dress? Or is this the twenty-first century version of the fairy tale?'

'This is no fairy tale. And you're certainly no sodding Prince Charming. It's getting cold. At this rate I'll freeze to death, or turn into that snow queen woman from that film everyone keeps singing about, before you move a muscle to help me. And will you stop staring at my legs! You are a bloody pervert, aren't you?'

'No one freezes to death on the south coast of England at the end of September,' he said. 'And if you really want my help, may I suggest you stop giving me that icy stare and calling me a pervert. Just let it go.'

Was he making a joke? He wasn't smiling. There wasn't even the tiniest curve on his lips. Did he have kids? Was he married? She pitied his poor wife. Why was he looking at his watch? Was she boring him? It looked like a very expensive watch. Was he rich? Why was she asking herself all these stupid questions?

'Whatever,' she said. 'If you're not going to help me then will you at least have the decency to sod off? Oh! But lend me your phone first. I need to call someone who won't just stand and gawk at me.'

To Poppy's astonishment, he threw back his head and laughed. She couldn't help but notice the light from the waxing, gibbous moon, throw sprinkles of gold in his

9

lustrous hair – which was far too long. It skimmed his shoulders and kinked in one or two places as if even it felt embarrassed to show its true length. And as for his laugh... well, if he wasn't so bloody obnoxious, he'd be almost attractive just because of that.

'You're not doing yourself any favours with that attitude,' he said, finally. 'But I suppose you've come to expect men to do anything you ask them, regardless of whether or not you say please.'

'What's that supposed to mean?'

'Oh come on! You'd look gorgeous wearing a nun's habit – and you know it. Half naked, you make it difficult for a man to breathe. Any red-blooded male would do almost anything to see the rest of you.'

'What! I'm not half naked. I knew it. You *are* a sodding pervert.' She tugged at the layers of overskirt. 'Are you... are you actually suggesting some sort of sordid bargain? Well, you know what? You can bugger off!'

He tutted. 'One minute you want my help, the next you don't. You need to make up your mind. As for suggesting a bargain, sordid or otherwise, I've got more important things on my mind right now. I can't afford to be distracted by a beautiful blonde... half naked or not. So what's it to be? Do I stay or do I go?'

'I can't believe you need to ask. Mind you, I can't believe any of this conversation. Any decent man would've come over here and helped me the moment he saw I was in difficulty.'

'Well then, I guess I'm not a decent man. But you've got to look at it from my perspective. You're stuck, climbing over a railing – a railing with a 'Keep Out' sign attached to it, let's not forget. You're dressed up as Cinderella... apparently, and you're showing your white lace underwear to the world. Forgive me, but any sane and cautious man –

decent or otherwise – would wonder whether he were setting himself up for a law suit of some kind. Or prosecution. Or worse.'

Poppy's cheeks reddened at the mention of her underwear. This guy really was obnoxious. The problem was, unless Toby Blackwood finally showed up or someone was out for a walk, the only alternative to getting this guy's help, was to tear the dress. She really couldn't afford to do that. Although the alternative could prove to be worse.

'Oh, for God's sake,' he said with a sigh, before she could decide.

He covered the short distance between them and only then did Poppy realise how tall and athletically built he was. He wasn't muscle-bound but if there was so much as a millimetre of loose skin on him, she'd be amazed. This guy definitely knew what a gym was for.

Or perhaps he got his exercise outdoors. Judging by the dark tan on his face and the glimpse of flesh the open-necked shirt revealed, he was no stranger to the sun. Of course that might merely be from basking on a beach somewhere. Or a sunbed. But he didn't look like 'a sunbed' sort of guy and the tan looked real. As real as the Omega watch.

He took off his jacket and draped it around her shoulders. Poppy didn't say a word as he bent down behind her. She didn't even thank him for the jacket. It was as if she'd been enveloped in a heavenly cloud as traces of sandalwood, vanilla and neroli wafted towards her nostrils... and a hint of something else. Was that grapefruit? Or lemon? She closed her eyes and let the scent seep in.

'What did you say?' he asked.

He hadn't looked up but Poppy blushed anyway. She hadn't meant to sigh like that.

11

'Nothing. I… I was wondering how long it was going to take you to remove my dress!'

His head shot up and a seductive smile formed on his lips. His eyes didn't look quite so cool, this close up. In fact, they positively glowed with warmth.

'That rather depends on you,' he said.

'I meant remove it from whatever it's caught on, you bloody creep.'

As he held her look, her entire body quivered. She must be cold despite the jacket; there was no other reason for it. In any event, she hoped he hadn't noticed.

'So did I,' he said, finally looking away. 'I need you to stand still. Your hem's caught on a piece of wire from the 'Keep Out' sign.'

Poppy tutted. 'Sodding sign. How difficult can it be to free a dress from a piece of wire? If I could twist round that far without tearing it, I'd do it in a second.'

'You certainly know how to charm a guy, don't you? There. It's done. You're lucky. It's only a small tear. Someone who's good with a needle and thread will probably be able to mend it so that it's almost invisible. Or you could simply ask your Fairy Godmother. It's not quite nine. You've got three hours to spare.'

'Oh, how very droll. Um… thank you.'

'You're welcome.'

Poppy stepped away from the railing with an overwhelming sense of relief and wriggled her dress back into place, fully aware that he was watching her intently.

'I thought you had important things to do. I'm fine now. I don't need you anymore.'

His brows knit together. 'I said that I had more important things to think about – which is true. As for you no longer needing me… may I ask how you propose to climb back over the railing without getting stuck again? I

12

assume you *will* be climbing back over. Or are you intent on breaking into the building?'

'I wasn't going to break in. I was merely going to look through the window to see if my… if the owner's inside.'

'Of course. Because you said you know the owner, didn't you? May I suggest we both try using the door?'

'Why?'

He smiled sardonically. 'Because I find it easier than climbing over railings and scrambling through windows. Just a personal preference.'

'I meant, why would we both…? Oh!'

Before she could finish the question, he placed one hand on the top railing and leapt over to her side. Without a word, he swept her into his arms and deposited her back onto the concrete walkway before retrieving her bag and sandals and leaping back over with obvious ease.

'Yours, I believe,' he said, offering her the clutch bag and high-heeled sandals. 'But not glass. I'm a little disappointed.'

She took the bag and dangled the straps of the sandals on her fingers whilst using her other hand to slip off his jacket.

'And yours,' she said, looking up into eyes that appeared both teasing and inviting at the same time.

He seemed reluctant to take it and he stood so close that she could see the tiny sparks of devilment in his eyes; feel his warm breath on her cheek; smell the heady mixture of masculinity and aftershave.

'Poppy! What're you doing here?'

She turned and saw Toby Blackwood stepping onto the raised walkway at the top of the concrete steps.

'Oh! And Ryan,' he added. 'Have you been here long? Sorry. I forgot the plans so I nipped back to the car. Have you two met? That's a silly question. You've obviously met.'

Poppy glanced back at the man Toby had called Ryan. He looked annoyed.

'I thought it was just a line when you told me that you knew the owner,' he said in a low voice. He glared at Toby. 'Actually, Toby, we haven't. But clearly you two know each other. I suppose I should've guessed.'

'We met at my friends' party,' Poppy said, offering him the jacket again. 'I'm Poppy Taylor.' This time he took it without hesitation and Poppy shivered from the icy look he gave her. She slipped her sandals on, smiled briefly at him and then beamed at Toby. 'I'll get out of the way.'

'That's the first sensible comment you've made this evening,' Ryan said, drawing her eyes back to his face. 'I'm Ryan Blackwood, Toby's elder brother. It's been... enlightening. Toby and I have business to discuss so if you'll excuse us, we'll get on with it. Toby, do you have the keys? Or have you left those in the car too?'

Without so much as a smile, he flung on his jacket and marched towards the main entrance where its double doors were secured with a huge padlock.

'That was a bit rude, Ryan,' Toby said, but Ryan didn't respond. Toby gave Poppy an apologetic look and shrugged his shoulders. 'I've got to go. Will you be okay? Do you need money for a cab?'

She was still reeling from Ryan's comment.

'What? Oh no... thank you. I'm fine. I'm going back to the party. I just... came down here for a stroll and to get some sea air. Unfortunately, something very unpleasant came in with the tide,' she said, as Ryan who was waiting for his brother at the door, turned to face her. 'Or perhaps it wasn't the tide. Good night, Toby. I hope I'll see you again.'

'Definitely!' Toby said with genuine enthusiasm.

14

Poppy held her head high and sashayed towards Ryan. She'd show him his words meant nothing. She had to pass him to get to the steps and she hoped her expression was suitably contemptuous. She stopped right in front of him and looked him up and down.

'I don't suppose we'll meet again. People in Goldebury Bay are kind, good mannered and very friendly. It's clearly not your sort of place.'

She was two steps down when he replied: 'It's a pity some of them can't read. Where I come from, 'Keep Out' means just that.'

She stopped, turned and gave him her friendliest smile. 'If the residents of wherever it is you come from, are anything like you, I'm surprised you need a 'Keep Out' sign. I can't imagine anyone ever wanting to go in. Have a good evening, Mr Blackheart.'

'It's Blackwood.'

'Of course it is,' she said, trying to skip down the steps in a light-hearted fashion. She almost lost her balance when she heard Ryan's next words.

'You've only been in this place for one day, Toby. I seriously hope you're not thinking of seeing that woman again. You know what happens with women like that and I'm sure I don't need to remind you how important this deal is.'

Should she retaliate? Or should she wait to hear Toby's reply? She made it to the bottom of the steps and Toby hadn't said a word.

Perhaps he wasn't the man of her dreams, after all. Or perhaps he preferred not to discuss his love life with someone as obnoxious as Ryan Blackwood... even if the man was his older brother.

And what exactly did the ill-mannered pervert mean by: "You know what happens with women like that."?

15

Women like what?

How dare the arrogant jerk presume to know what kind of woman she was? He had no idea who he was dealing with. Well, she'd show him. And if he thought for one minute that he could stop her from seeing Toby Blackwood again, he had another think coming. Toby may be under his brother's thumb – but she could work on that.

She glanced up as she stepped onto the pavement but neither man was anywhere to be seen. They'd clearly gone inside.

So Toby and Ryan Blackwood were the new owners of the derelict Goldebury Bay Yachting and Sailing Club, were they? There'd been rumours that it had been sold but no one knew to whom. She couldn't wait to tell Cleo and Sophie.

And she couldn't wait to find out all about the Blackwoods, especially Ryan Blackwood. His last words had annoyed her and she was up for a challenge. Hadn't she read somewhere that you needed to know your enemies better than you knew your friends? Or was it: "Keep your friends close and your enemies closer"?

Ryan Blackwood may not be an enemy exactly but it felt as though he was going to be a serious problem. Whatever the saying was, there was no way she was going to be alone this Christmas. She had made up her mind the minute she'd met Toby Blackwood at the party: he was the man she wanted in her Christmas stocking.

And she was going to get him if it was the last thing she did.

Whether Ryan Blackwood liked it or not.

Chapter Two

'He sounds like a complete shit,' Cleo said when Poppy
returned to the party at Summerhill and dragged Cleo and
Sophie to one side. 'Well, not a *complete* shit. He did give
you his jacket after all, but did he really say all that?'

'Jacket or not,' Sophie said, grabbing a glass of
champagne from the tray of a passing waiter and handing it
to Poppy. 'I'm surprised you didn't thump him. I think I
would've.'

'I was very tempted, believe me. I'm really sorry about
the dress. I'll pay—'

'Oh don't worry about that. The thing's not made of
gold – or even silk, for that matter, so if they do charge to
replace it, it'll hardly break the bank. Consider it an extra
little pre-Christmas gift or something. Now forget the dress.
What did this Ryan guy look like? In spite of being a git, is
he as hot as Toby?'

'No he's… um… he's older.'

'Older?' Cleo repeated. 'What does that mean? How
much older? So old that he's not hot? Or so old that to call
him hot would be gross?'

'He's not old, just… older and yes, I suppose some
people would say he's hot.'

'How hot exactly?' Sophie asked. 'Hotter than Toby?
George Clooney's old and he's to die for. Does Ryan look
like him?'

'She said Ryan had reddish-brown hair,' Cleo said.
'George Clooney's hair isn't reddish-brown.'

Sophie tutted. 'I didn't say it was. But he can still look like George Clooney even if—'

'He doesn't look like George Clooney. Okay? He looks like Toby, only older, but I don't know how much older. A few years I would guess. He's got that 'air of sophistication' thing that always makes people look older. Ten years at most.'

'Ten years isn't that bad,' Cleo said. 'How old's Toby? A couple of years older than us I suppose, so that would make him about thirty-five and that would make Ryan... oh dear. Forty-five *is* old. You can't have sex with a forty-five-year-old.'

'George Clooney's older,' Sophie said, 'and I'd have sex with him. Well, I wouldn't now because I love Thaddeus, but if he'd asked me before I'd met Thaddeus, I'd have jumped at the chance.'

'Will you two stop going on about George Clooney! And it doesn't matter how old Ryan Blackwood is because I'm not planning on having sex with him. I'm not planning on doing anything with him... except perhaps wringing his neck. I don't fancy him. It's Toby I'm interested in. But anyway, Ryan would only be forty if he's ten years older... and forty's not that bad. If it were anyone other than repulsive Ryan, that is.'

'Are you telling us that Toby's only thirty?' Cleo sounded surprised. 'Since when've you been interested in toy boys?'

'Really?' Poppy said. 'Being three years younger hardly makes him a toy boy.'

Sophie shook her head. 'I'd have to go with Cleo on that. Men mature more slowly than women. If he's only thirty that makes him... about twelve. We could Google it. There's loads of stuff on the web about how immature men are.'

18

'Yeah, yeah. I don't care. It's Toby Blackwood I want and it's Toby Blackwood I'm going to get.' Poppy nodded towards the room Sophie and Thaddeus used as their study. 'That's what I was going to ask. Can we go into your study? I want to Google them and see what comes up.'

'Are you sure?' Sophie said. 'Toby should've told his brother to sod off when Ryan said that about you. He's not worth the effort if you ask me.'

'I agree,' Cleo said. 'But he was bloody gorgeous. If I weren't so crazy about Oliver I'd have given him more than a second look.'

'You keep your hands off him, madam.' Poppy nudged Cleo with her elbow and glanced back at Sophie. 'You'd be right, in the everyday scheme of things. But as I told you earlier, this is destiny.'

'And as I told you earlier,' Cleo said, 'it's more like insanity. Let's look at your track record. You're not exactly known for picking the right man, are you?'

'Oi! It wasn't my fault that Sophie came and took Thaddeus away from me,' Poppy declared, pulling a face.

'How many times are you going to hit me over the head with that? You told me you were just friends and that nothing was going to happen between you and Thaddeus. You even gave me your blessing.'

Poppy grinned and linked one arm through Sophie's. 'I know. I just enjoy teasing you about it, that's all. But I did really fancy him last year and if he and I hadn't become such good, bloody friends, I'd have definitely tried to get him into bed. Come to think of it, I think I did try but—'

'Okay,' Cleo said. 'So you did have good taste there. But what about Geoff?'

'I'm trying to forget Geoff.'

Sophie nodded. 'I think we're all trying to forget Geoff – and I've never even met the guy. If Thaddeus ever caught sight of him again, he'd be mincemeat.'

'And let's not forget the guys you dated in Gibraltar,' Cleo added.

'Old news.' Poppy switched the champagne glass to her other hand and linked her free arm through Cleo's, propelling both friends in the direction of the study. 'Come on. I know I've made mistakes in the past but this time it's different. You'll see. And the sooner we do this research, the sooner I'll have a boyfriend of my own.'

'I'm not sure it works like that,' Cleo said.

'I just need to find the skinny on repulsive Ryan and figure out why Toby looked like he was about to have his balls removed when his brother asked him such a simple, albeit very sarcastic, question about whether he had the keys or whether they were in his car.'

'Who are you?' Cleo said. 'What's this "skinny" business and the sudden interest in... research? Don't tell me it's true that you've been spending time with that bastard, Timothy Richards? I heard you were having coffee with him the other day in Betty's Pantry but I didn't believe it. Now I'm not so sure.'

Poppy felt guilty for a split second. 'I was fed up... and Betty was out of carrot cake. I had to do something to cheer myself up, so when he came in, I asked him if anyone had broken his nose recently. Oddly enough, the guy offered to buy me a cup of coffee and... well, I had nothing better to do, so I thought I may as well annoy him for half an hour.'

'Consorting with the enemy,' Sophie said, glancing over her shoulder. 'Don't let Thaddeus hear, or Timothy may end up with a broken nose for a second time.'

'He couldn't hit Timothy for buying me a coffee. That would just be mean. Although it would be quite amusing... and rather gallant, in a creepy sort of way. I should've brought Timothy to the party as my date.'

20

'What did you talk about?' Sophie asked, ignoring the remark.

'I asked him why he was still hanging around now that Hermione and Jeremiah have been sentenced and I suggested that he might like to go and finish writing his book somewhere else. Like Timbuktu.'

'You do know that's a real place, don't you? And it has an airport.'

'Yes, Cleo, I do. Well, I didn't know it had an airport but that's not the point. It's the sentiment behind it. I did add that another planet would be preferable, and one inhabited by creatures like the ones in those *Alien* films would be even better. He simply smiled and told me I say the sweetest things.'

'That's typical of him,' Sophie said. 'He only hears what he wants to hear.'

'Ooh. He did say he's got an agent for his 'toilet roll of a book'. My words, not his. He called it a blockbuster. Mind you, curry night at The Dead Llamas, Horse or Hamster busts all blockages, so perhaps I wasn't far off.'

'You must stop calling The Dalai Lama's House of Heaven such awful names,' Cleo said, even though she was smiling. 'The owners are here tonight and they'd be very upset if they heard you call their restaurant The Dead Llamas, Horse or Hamster.'

'My tummy's very upset after one of their curries but they don't seem to care about that.'

Cleo sighed. 'No one forces you to go. Or to eat the phaal. If you can't stand the heat, stick to the vindaloo. That's hot enough for most people. And don't make any toilet jokes about going... or the vindaloo, either.'

'Who? Me?'

'Does that mean his book will be coming out soon?' Sophie asked, obviously trying to change the subject.

'Are we still making toilet references?'

'No, Poppy, we're not,' Sophie said.

'Spoilsport. I suppose if the agent can sell it, it will. He told me there're a few publishers interested and he thinks there'll be a bidding war. He offered to buy me champagne instead of coffee, once he's got the contract.'

'I hope you told him where to shove his champagne,' Cleo said.

Poppy cleared her throat. 'Let's get back to the matter in hand, shall we? Have you got the key to the study, Sophie?'

'It's not locked.'

Poppy glanced at Cleo. 'Is she for real? Doesn't she know that every newspaper for miles around has been full of stories about the Summerhill treasure? Look at all the people here. I've met at least four people tonight I've never seen or heard of before – and that doesn't include Toby... or repulsive Ryan.'

'Excuse me. I am here, you know. So what? The treasure's not in our study. You know that as well as I do.'

'I have to agree with Poppy,' Cleo said. '*We* know that. But other people may not. Do you really want strangers to go rifling around in your drawers?'

'I wouldn't mind a certain person rifling around in my drawers, if you get my drift.'

'I think the whole of Goldebury Bay gets *your* drift, Poppy,' Cleo said.

'You're getting to be a bit of a grump, lately, Cleo. What's up? Is it because you've put on a few pounds? I told you your bum doesn't look big in the delightful Cleopatra outfit you're wearing.'

'And you also told me that if I was really worried about the size of my arse, I could come wrapped in a carpet because it worked for the real Cleopatra, and Oliver could roll me out when we got home. Why would I be grumpy when I have such caring friends as you?'

'Search me. I was only trying to help. Will you be able to squeeze through the doorway to the study?'

Cleo sneered. 'Let's do this. The sooner you get yourself a man, the happier I'll be. You won't have so much time to make fun of other people once you're having sex again.'

'Should we really be encouraging her to get involved with Toby?' Sophie said to Cleo, opening the unlocked door to the study. 'The brother sounds like a real piece of work and we know what she's like.'

'Oi!'

'That's true. World War Three could kick off in Goldebury Bay. But there's no harm in looking them up,' Cleo said. 'And I'm quite keen to find out more about them, aren't you? I mean, how did they get their hands on the old sailing and yachting club, for starters? Lots of people have been interested in it over the years, including Oliver's uncle Ben. Didn't Toby say he's a property developer, or did I imagine that? What're they planning to do with it? Perhaps we can find some information about other developments they've done. And didn't he come with the Mayor tonight? Perhaps he has friends in high places. Not that the Mayor of Goldebury Bay can do much for him.'

'But that's a good point,' Sophie agreed. 'And yes, he did come with the Mayor. We do need to find out what they're planning to do, especially as the building's not that far from Summerhill. We don't want a tower block suddenly appearing beside our cliff and overshadowing our cove. But I don't think this Toby guy is the one for her, do you? We need to find you a nice man, Poppy. One like Thaddeus or Oliver. Toby's gorgeous-looking, I'll give him that, but looks don't maketh the man. He might look like a dreamboat but all boats can get holes and some handle well

23

in stormy seas whilst others sink to the bottom and take you with them.'

Poppy glanced at Cleo and they both looked at Sophie.

'One of GJ's sayings?' Poppy asked. 'You're a Goldebury Bay local already.'

Sophie grinned. 'Miff's. She was telling me that the moment she saw GJ she knew he was the man for her even though one of the Beaumonts – who was drop-dead gorgeous, obviously – wanted to *court* her. I forget which one. Thaddeus' grandfather or great-grandfather or something.'

'Yes, I've heard that story more times than I'd like to recall, to be honest,' Cleo said, grinning. 'She's right though. And I think I knew the moment I saw Oliver, all those years ago.'

'I knew, the moment I saw Thaddeus,' Sophie said. 'Although I didn't know that I knew, if you see what I mean.'

'And I knew the moment I saw Toby Blackwood! You see. We've all experienced it. I told you. It's destiny.' Poppy marched towards the desktop computer and sat on the green leather, Captain's chair. 'Now why don't you grab a bottle of bubbly, Sophie? Or possibly two, and then we can do some serious surfing. Bloody hell! You don't even secure your computer with a password! Are you completely insane?'

'Since becoming friends with you, Poppy, that's a question I ask myself... A... Lot! But that's Thaddeus' computer, not mine. And the only things on there are stuff about boats, so unless you want to know how to sail one, build one, or do anything else in one, on one or with one, there's nothing for anyone to find. All the interesting stuff is, you'll be surprised to learn, under lock and key in a safe in our bedroom. I'll get the champers.'

24

'I am surprised. Okay. Ryan... Blackwood.'

Poppy typed in his name and felt an odd sensation in her stomach when a row of several images of the man appeared before her eyes, together with a long list of links.

'Wow!' Cleo said, leaning over Poppy's shoulder. 'George Clooney, eat your heart out. Sophie! Come and look at this.'

Sophie returned a moment later and dashed around the desk, leaning over Poppy's other shoulder. 'The bubbly's on its way. Let me see.'

'Well?' Cleo asked.

'I'm speechless. *That's* Ryan Blackwood? That's the guy you've been calling repulsive Ryan?'

Poppy glanced up at her and nodded. 'Yeah.' She noticed the look Sophie gave Cleo and quickly turned her head to see the same look on Cleo's face. 'What? Am I missing something?'

Cleo sighed. 'Glasses, if you ask me.'

'But he was pretty obnoxious to her,' Sophie said. 'And as Miff says, looks aren't everything. Plus, beauty's in the eye of the beholder.'

'Well this beholder thinks the eldest Blackwood has got the youngest beaten in the looks department,' Cleo said. 'And for once Poppy, you may have fallen for the *right* guy. If, after seeing Ryan, it's Toby you're still interested in, there may be hope for you yet.'

A knock on the door heralded the entrance of a waiter carrying glasses and three bottles of champagne on a tray. He placed the tray on the desk and without a word, popped the cork of one bottle and filled three glasses. He left as silently as he came.

'I thought you might be here for a while,' Sophie said. 'I told Thaddeus where we were if he needs us. I can't be long though. This is my party after all, so I must get back. Well,

Thaddeus' and mine. God, I love that man.'

'Oh don't get all gooey-eyed,' Poppy said, 'He's only in the other room, not miles away. Sometimes I think you two are joined at the hip.'

Cleo slapped her on the shoulder. 'When you love someone as much as Sophie loves Thaddeus, and I love Oliver, you miss them even if they're only in another room.'

'Really?' Poppy shook her head and clicked on the link for more images of Ryan Blackwood. She sipped champagne as page after page of photographs vied for attention.

There were photos of him playing tennis; dancing with a variety of gorgeous women; attending dinners and charity functions; skiing, sailing, getting into and out of sports cars, on and off yachts, climbing mountains. They just went on and on. Then to the obvious delight of her friends, a couple of photos of him staring directly at the camera, with a look in his eyes that would make any woman melt into his arms. Except Poppy.

'Bloody hell!' Cleo exclaimed.

'With bells on,' Sophie added.

Poppy groaned. 'Why aren't there any photos of him wearing a tatty old tracksuit? Or putting the rubbish out, wearing scruffy old pyjamas? Or...' Cleo's hand pressed into Poppy's shoulder.

'Even if there were, men like Ryan Blackwood would still look sensational.'

Sophie grabbed the mouse and continued scrolling. 'Are there any of him wearing... Oh, wow! There are.'

'No man has a right to look that good in bathing trunks,' Cleo said. 'Unless his name's Daniel Craig.'

'Thaddeus looks hot in trunks,' Sophie said. 'But he looks even hotter out of them.'

'So does Oliver,' Cleo said, with a smile.

Poppy snatched the mouse back. 'Ew! We're not here to look at pictures of some sodding playboy. We're here to do serious research.'

Cleo reached for the mouse. 'You speak for yourself. Sophie and I want to look at pictures.'

Poppy pulled it back from Cleo's hand. 'We'll look at pictures of Toby then. He's just as gorgeous and frankly, I've seen enough of Ryan Blackwood to last me a lifetime.'

She typed in Toby's name. There weren't half as many photos of him as there were of Ryan and yet more of Toby's photos seemed to have women in them. Blonde women, as Cleo helpfully pointed out.

'That makes me even more certain we're meant to be together,' Poppy said. 'I'm definitely his 'type' and he's obviously better at relationships than repulsive Ryan.'

'What makes you think that?' Sophie asked.

'Isn't it obvious? There're hardly any photos of Toby alone but there were loads of his brother, on his own. Toby's clearly better with people. And I can speak from experience.' She spotted Sophie's look but ignored it. 'Plus, Toby's not the sort of guy who wants his picture taken every five minutes, whereas repulsive Ryan must love the attention because there're so many photos of him. Anyway, I think we should stop looking at photos and start reading up on them.'

She clicked back to the search results for Ryan Blackwood and hit the first link: 'Blackwood does it again'.

'Shit!' Cleo said. 'It says the guy made a million pounds overnight.'

'What's so special about that?' Poppy said. 'Lottery winners do that all the time and Sophie did it twice. Once when Silas left her his estate and the second time when she found the Summerhill treasure.' She felt Cleo's finger dig into her back. 'Ow! What was that for?'

'For being almost as big a jerk as you think this Ryan guy is. You can't compare winning a million pounds on the lottery, or benefitting from a will, or even finding a long-lost family treasure with doing a property deal and making a million.'

'Cleo's right. And it says it's just one of many, similarly profitable deals. That's pretty impressive by anyone's standards. Have you read the next bit? It says he grew up in a tiny flat where he shared a bedroom, divided by a curtain, with his younger brother and sister.'

Poppy had read it. She was now reading the part after that where it stated that he "helped out" on his uncle's various building sites every afternoon after school and at weekends from the age of thirteen, after his own father died in a work-related accident. It went on to say that Ryan Blackwood learnt every job in the building trade, from bricklaying to plumbing, carpentry to plastering, stud partitioning to roofing, electrics to glazing and everything in between.

'He bought his first development property, via his uncle's company, when he was sixteen,' Cleo said, sounding impressed.

'I think I bought my first designer handbag at that age,' Poppy quipped.

Had she underestimated Ryan Blackwood? The guy was obviously determined. Was this going to be more of a challenge than she'd assumed?

Sophie read the next part out loud: "'Leaving school with little to show in the way of academic achievements but with a brain as sharp as a finely honed chisel and an eye for the next big thing, Ryan Blackwood made his first million at the tender age of nineteen. Details of his accumulated wealth are a closely guarded secret, but estimates are several hundred million pounds. He regularly appears on lists of the world's wealthiest men, including The Sunday Times Rich List but he keeps a very low profile for one of the UK's most eligible bachelors. Last year, younger brother Toby joined the Blackwood empire, having tried his hand at a variety of businesses before settling on property development. Ryan Blackwood has transformed a number of towns around the UK with his trademark – futuristic developments. Now with Toby on board, it's been said they're setting their sights firmly on the south east. One thing is for certain: If the Blackwood brothers come to your town, you can bet it's with an eye on the prize."'

'Well, that's the end of Goldebury Bay as we know it,' Poppy said.

'Look at the next bit,' Cleo said, pointing her finger at the screen. 'It says: '"Although both Blackwood brothers have been linked with several beautiful women over the years, including Hollywood A-listers, they remain single. Thirty-year-old Toby has been quoted as saying that he sees marriage in his future whilst older brother Ryan, thirty-nine, says that marriage is one contract in which he has no interest." So now we know. Ryan's thirty-nine.'

'I couldn't care less,' Poppy said. 'Who does he think he is? The arrogant bastard. From what I've seen of him, no woman in their right mind would even consider being his wife. I like what it said about Toby though. He sees marriage in his future. Well girls, if I have my way, he'll be walking down the aisle before repulsive Ryan makes another million.'

Cleo laughed. 'I'll drink to that. Although I think you'd better get to know the guy first.'

'What's there to know?' Poppy asked. 'I told you, it's destiny.'

'To destiny,' Sophie said, clinking glasses with Cleo and

Poppy. 'Here's to Mrs Poppy Blackwood.'

Poppy smiled. 'I like the sound of that. It has a certain ring to it.'

Cleo placed her arm around Poppy's shoulder. 'You do realise don't you, that if by some miracle you do marry Toby, repulsive Ryan will be your brother-in-law? And you'll have to be nice to your brother-in-law.'

'I can do that... If I have to.'

'Yeah right,' Sophie said. 'I think there's more chance of Ryan Blackwood getting hitched than you being nice to someone you don't like. And on that note, I think it's time I rejoined my party. Even I've had enough of Ryan Blackwood.'

Chapter Three

'Wonderful!' Poppy said, glancing towards the door of Betty's Pantry at around three o'clock the following afternoon. 'Don't look now but guess who's just about to walk in? Cleo! I said not to look.'

'Sorry.' Cleo stopped in mid-swivel on her chair in the curve of the bow window. 'But from the expression on your face and the sarcastic tone, I can only assume it's repulsive Ryan and I'm sorry but I've got to see him in the flesh. Don't worry. I won't make it obvious.'

'From what I hear,' Oliver said, 'You saw more than enough of the guy's flesh on the internet last night.'

Cleo grinned and leant across to kiss her boyfriend. 'There's no need to be jealous, darling. No man could ever compare to you in my eyes.' As Ryan opened the door and stepped onto the welcome mat, she turned and waved at Betty. 'Coo-ey, Betty! Poppy wants something sweet and sticky with her coffee. Do you have any Black... Forest Gateau?'

'I don't think I do, dear,' Betty called back, obviously, completely oblivious to the Black...wood reference. 'And I don't have any carrot cake either – which I know is now your favourite, isn't it, Poppy? But I do have chocolate fudge cake, coffee and walnut cake and some of those sticky finger buns. You love those. I'll bring over a selection and let you decide.'

Poppy's head dropped to her chest but when Cleo

swivelled round grinning, Poppy glowered at her. Even Oliver shook his head.

'Thanks a lot,' Poppy said, screwing up her eyes for added dramatic effect and trying hard not to look in Ryan's direction. 'You know that dress you've just bought? Well, I lied. Your bum does look big in it.'

'Now, now, girls,' Oliver mocked, twisting round in his seat beside Cleo and taking a sneaky peek towards the door. He quickly turned back. 'I think he's headed this way.'

Poppy's eyes flickered up and for the briefest of moments, met Ryan's. He looked both amused and annoyed at the same time – if that were possible.

He walked towards their table, nodded his head then walked right past and made his way to the table furthest from them.

Was that it? Not one word. The guy really was a jerk.

'So that's the famous Ryan Blackwood,' Oliver said in a low voice. 'I can't see what's so repulsive about him, Poppy. Although I suppose the guy could've said hello or something.'

'That's because you didn't have to spend fifteen, very long minutes in his company. Ooh! Here comes Toby.'

Poppy's heart thumped in her chest as Toby pushed open the door. Completely forgetting about Ryan, she waved enthusiastically at him and, judging by the expression on his face as he strode towards her table, he was similarly pleased to see her.

'Hello Poppy. It's lovely to see you again. How are you this morning? I hope—'

'Toby!' From the other side of the room Ryan Blackwood's commanding voice cut into the cheerful greetings. 'You're late.'

Toby blinked several times; anxious, blue eyes darted between Poppy and Ryan and back to Poppy.

'I *am* late,' he finally said to Poppy, as if that excused his brother's behaviour. 'It really is good to see you again.'

His expression changed from one of pleasure to a somewhat pained look as he turned to walk towards his brother, his gait a little less enthusiastic and his broad shoulders slightly hunched. Even his hair, which was the same colour as Ryan's and last night had seemed as lustrous, appeared a little dull and unkempt this morning. Or perhaps Poppy was imagining that. At least it was a sensible length, being cut to just below his ears, and it didn't have the kinks his brother's had.

'Call me,' she said.

Toby glanced back briefly and smiled. 'I will.'

For some reason though, Poppy wasn't at all sure that he would as she watched him join his brother.

'Did you get everything?' Ryan asked.

'Yes,' Toby said. 'I got it all. It's in my car.'

As Toby sat, Poppy glanced into the steely, cobalt eyes of Ryan Blackwood and quickly looked away.

'That man makes me so cross,' she whispered. 'How rude was that? Can't Toby even talk to me without that obnoxious git butting in?'

'I agree,' Oliver said. 'That was bloody rude.'

'I suppose you don't become a multi-millionaire by being nice,' Cleo said. 'Not that that's any excuse, of course. Manners cost nothing. Are you sure you really want to get involved with the Blackwoods? I wonder what the rest of the family's like. Didn't it say there's a sister? And what about their mother? I know it said the dad was dead. Could you imagine if the mother and sister are like Ryan, and Toby was the only nice one amongst them?'

Poppy shot a look towards the table where Toby and Ryan were now in deep conversation and shook her head. 'It doesn't bear thinking about. But surely they can't all be as bad as repulsive Ryan? I don't remember seeing anything about the mother. Perhaps I need to read up a bit more on the Blackwoods. Just in case.'

'I'd certainly want to know what I was getting myself into,' Cleo added. 'But I thought it was destiny. That's what you said last night. Having second thoughts, are we?'

'It's a pity you can't get a Wi-Fi signal in here,' Oliver said, before Poppy could tell Cleo to bugger off. 'But I have to say, Toby seems a bit of a dick. Why didn't he just tell Ryan to fuck off? I wouldn't let anyone speak to me like that, brother or not.'

'You don't *have* to say anything of the sort,' Poppy snapped. 'And we've all heard the way Ben talks to you and gets away with it but no one calls you a dick, and Ben's only your uncle.'

Betty shuffled over to the table, a two-tier cake stand in one hand and a tray with two coffees and a pile of tea plates, balanced in the other. 'Take your pick, Poppy. Sorry about the Black Forest Gateau dear, but there's not much call for that these days. As for the carrot cake, I can't seem to make enough of it. No sooner is one out of the oven and I've covered it in frosting than it's gone. I'd swear I've got rabbits eating them.' She winked, placed the plates on the table and, with a broad smile on her thin, bright pink lips, shuffled away with the tray of coffees towards the table where Ryan and Toby sat.

A few moments later, the mellifluous laugh Poppy had heard last night interrupted her decision-making and, as her hand hovered midway between a pink-iced, finger bun and a slab of chocolate fudge cake, she cast a glance in Ryan's direction.

He appeared to be listening intently to Betty but his eyes momentarily flickered towards Poppy and to her complete amazement, he smiled. And it was no ordinary smile. That smile, accompanied by the look in his eyes, could melt gold bars. She hastily returned her attention to the tiered cake stand and slid a slice of coffee and walnut cake onto one of the porcelain, rose-patterned plates.

'I think I'll have some of that,' Cleo said, grabbing a plate and a slice of cake. 'And don't you dare make any comments about the size of my arse.'

'What? Oh, I wasn't going to,' Poppy said, stabbing at her cake with her fork and fixing her gaze on Cleo.

Cleo frowned. 'What would you like, Oliver?'

'Apart from you, you mean?' Oliver wrapped his arm around Cleo's shoulders, kissing her on the cheek. 'I'll have a piece of chocolate fudge cake, please.'

As Cleo passed Oliver his cake, she nodded towards the street. 'Wow. Look at that limo.'

Oliver turned his head to look outside and Poppy glanced through the window. She expected to see one of those white, ostentatious, stretch limos which had become synonymous with the word 'limo' these days. Instead, a young woman was gracefully exiting a sleek, long wheelbase, black saloon, the door of which was being held open by a man wearing a simple but elegant grey suit.

The woman, whom Poppy noticed didn't even acknowledge the chauffeur's existence, wore a pale blue, floral skirt and a navy blue tailored, linen jacket and, together with designer high heels and matching navy blue handbag, exuded an air of refinement not commonly seen on the streets of Goldebury Bay.

The scraping of chair legs on the wooden floor briefly brought Poppy's attention back to the interior, as Toby sprang to his feet. He strode towards the door and flung it open, smiling brightly at the woman as she approached. The chauffeur appeared to be scanning the window as if looking for someone inside. Ryan, no doubt. The man nodded his head and then climbed back into the limo and drove off.

'Hello Toby!' The woman looked equally pleased to see him as she tossed a lock of mahogany-coloured hair over one shoulder and reached out for him with her other arm.

He stepped onto the pavement, swept the woman up in his arms and kissed her affectionately on the cheek.

Poppy couldn't believe her eyes. Who was this woman? A girlfriend? He'd told her he didn't have a girlfriend. But men have been known to lie about such things. From the colour of her hair, could this possibly be his sister? Were all the Blackwoods coming to Goldebury Bay?

Toby ushered the woman into the tearoom without so much as a glance at Poppy and led her, arm in arm towards Ryan, who, like his brother stood and kissed the woman on her cheek, but less affectionately. Unlike his brother, he clearly didn't feel the need to sweep her into his arms.

'You're early,' Ryan said, as Toby pulled out a chair for the woman. 'You're looking well. Did you have a good journey?'

'As well as can be expected under the circumstances,' the woman replied coolly. 'And yes, the journey was good, thanks. There was hardly any traffic once we'd left Gatwick. I was going to go to the house but I couldn't wait to see Toby. And you, of course. I could murder a cup of coffee. Thanks for the text by the way, Toby, telling me where you'd be. And thank heavens for satnav. I'm sure even Doug would've got lost without it. This place may be small but I've never seen so many winding streets.' She glanced around her with a less than enthusiastic smile. 'So this is Goldebury Bay.'

For a matter of seconds, a pair of large, cool blue eyes, very like Ryan Blackwood's, focused on Poppy, quickly surveying her before looking away.

Ryan's expression softened and he smiled. 'No Stephanie. This is Betty's Pantry. And this lovely lady coming over to take your order, is Betty.'

Stephanie gave him a brief smile. 'I see some things never change. You know what I meant. May I have a pot of coffee, please?'

'Coming right up,' Betty said, making a face at Poppy, Cleo and Oliver as she headed back towards the kitchen, as if to say: 'Did you see *her*?'

'So who do you think she is?' Cleo asked, leaning across the table towards Poppy.

Poppy forced her gaze back to her friends. 'No idea. Could be the sister. I hope Toby didn't lie and she's his girlfriend or something. God, I hope it is his sister. If it is, I hope she's more like Toby than Ryan although from what I've seen so far, I'm not holding out much hope on that score.'

'That's an awful lot of 'hopes',' Cleo said, with a smile.

'Well, you and Clara are always saying that one can never have enough hope.'

'I think she's the sister,' Oliver said. 'The resemblance is striking, and not just because of her hair. She's got the same, large blue eyes, and there's something about the way she walked in. She has an air of confidence about her, which Ryan clearly has, but she also seems nervous and unsure of herself, like Toby. He definitely seems unsure of himself if you ask me.'

'That's because Ryan bullies him,' Poppy said.

'How d'you know he bullies him?' Oliver queried. 'He just seemed a little impatient... and rude, that's all. He doesn't appear to be much happier now their sister's arrived, either. Assuming she is their sister, of course.'

Cleo leant in closer. 'Did you hear what she said? About going to "the house". House, not hotel. Did Toby say last

37

night that he'd rented a house somewhere? They don't come from around here, do they? Didn't he say they come from Dorset?'

Poppy shook her head. 'No. He said that he expected to be staying in Goldebury Bay for some time, but he didn't say where and I didn't get a chance to ask because repulsive Ryan summoned him. And he didn't say they came from Dorset, merely that Dorset was the last place he'd lived before coming here. Poole, I think. Sandbanks, to be precise.'

'I *wonder* where they're staying,' Cleo said quizzically.

Oliver took a final gulp of coffee. 'Does it really matter? All we need to know is what they're planning to do with the Goldebury Bay Yachting and Sailing Club and I don't suppose they're likely to tell us that until they're ready to.' He kissed Cleo and stood up. 'I'd better get to the restaurant. We're fully booked tonight. I'll take the bags, darling and I'll see you later. Try not cause trouble, Poppy.' He bent down, kissed Poppy on the cheek and grinned.

'I won't be long,' Cleo said. 'And don't worry, I'll make sure she behaves.'

'What! All I'm doing is eating coffee and walnut cake. How much trouble can I cause doing that?'

'Knowing you. A lot,' Oliver replied, and with a final smile for Cleo and a goodbye wave to Betty, he left the tearoom and headed towards Sutton's restaurant.

'I can't stay long,' Cleo said. 'I don't suppose you fancy doing an extra shift at the restaurant, do you? Or are you working at the pub today?'

Poppy shrugged. 'Ben gave me the day off. He said he thought I'd probably need it after the party last night, and he rather sarcastically added, "The One That Got Away can survive without your charm and friendly banter for one day, darling, I'm almost certain." One of these days I'm going to

38

punch him in the face… if someone else doesn't beat me to it.'

Cleo giggled. 'You know you love him as much as the rest of us. Besides, you give him a run for his money. So d'you fancy helping out then?'

Poppy glanced at Toby who was laughing with the woman she thought was his sister whilst Ryan looked on like some sort of ambivalent childminder, torn between joining in with the fun or keeping his distance.

'It doesn't look as if I've got anything better to do,' she said. 'I offered to help Sophie clear up after last night but she told me that Veronique's got it under control. I wish I had a firm of solicitors and the world's best P.A. at my beck and call.'

'Oliver and I could do with one of those. Especially now that Sophie's let us buy the freehold of Sutton's on such amazing terms. Oliver's got big plans to convert the upstairs into one large reception room and hire it out for parties and the like.' She leant forward and grabbed Poppy's hand. 'He even said that maybe we could hold our wedding reception there!'

'Bloody hell! When did he propose? You kept that quiet. Why didn't you tell me?'

'Hold your horses. He hasn't proposed. And that's the first time he's actually mentioned us getting married. To be honest, I was hoping he'd ask me when we celebrated our first 'moving in together' anniversary two weeks ago but no such luck.'

Poppy squeezed Cleo's hand. 'So much has been going on over the last few months, what with Sophie finding the treasure and, Thaddeus and her falling in love and moving in together. Then Thaddeus's dad being sentenced to four years in prison whilst that bitch Hermione only gets two, when everyone but that sodding jury and that stupid judge, knew she was the mastermind behind the whole smuggling operation. Perhaps Oliver hasn't felt the time was right. There's plenty of time for a wedding. You know you mean the world to him. You don't need a piece of paper to tell you that.'

Cleo smiled and shook her head. 'I know I don't. And I agree, the timing hasn't been right. Oliver and his dad – and me of course – have also been worried about his mum. I promised I wouldn't say anything but there was another little cancer scare at the beginning of July. No, don't worry, Mary's fine but we weren't sure for a while. She was really poorly but the tests were clear and she's been taking things easy for the last couple of months. Now she's fighting fit and raring to go again, thank God.'

'Why didn't you say something? You know I would've kept it secret.'

'Of course you would but you know Mary, she doesn't like a fuss and I promised her, Christopher and Oliver I wouldn't say a word. I feel a bit guilty actually. You remember that before Oliver and I got back together last year, he'd been saving to send his parents on safari once Mary was fully recovered.'

'Yes. And you organised that day out for her to the film set, to spend some time with real lions.'

Cleo nodded. 'Well, I think Oliver's sort of put it on hold since I moved in with him. I think he's torn between splashing out a fortune on his parents, and saving for our future. I keep telling him that I want him to arrange the safari and that we've got the rest of our lives to build a future together but you know Oliver. Always trying to do the best for everyone. So when we thought she may be sick again, it really threw him. He doesn't know what to do for the best.'

'Couldn't... couldn't you ask Sophie to lend you the

money?'

Cleo shook her head. 'No. Sophie's already done so much for all of us. I know she'd be more than happy to do it but it just wouldn't be right. Ben would help of course but as he helped pay for Mary's treatment, Oliver doesn't want to ask for more. Part of him wants to put the plans for the restaurant on hold but his mum would be furious if she thought he'd spent more money on her, instead of spending it on his business... or on me, come to that. She was very upset last Christmas when she discovered we'd spent so much on her and hardly anything on each other. So anyway, that would sort of take the edge off the whole thing.'

'That's one hell of a predicament,' Poppy said, casting a glance towards the table where Toby and the others were laughing and chatting as if they didn't have a care in the world. 'Let's get out of here. I'll come and help at the restaurant.' She got to her feet and linked her arm through Cleo's. 'I wish I could do more to help. I wish I could make a million pounds overnight. But as I don't even do the lottery, that's not likely to happen.'

Cleo smiled. 'I thought you were going to marry Toby Blackwood. Isn't that like making a million overnight?'

Poppy was tempted to glance over her shoulder as they waved a friendly goodbye to Betty and left, but knowing her luck, the entire Blackwood family would see her do it. And she wasn't having that.

Cleo had no such qualms.

'Was he looking?' Poppy asked, as she and Cleo headed towards Sutton's restaurant.

'Uh-huh. And he had the strangest expression on his face.'

'Strange? How? Good strange or bad strange? D'you think he's going to call me?'

'Why would he call you? And more to the point, why would you want him to? I thought you couldn't stand Ryan Blackwood.'

'I can't. Why're you going on about repulsive Ryan? I was talking about Toby.'

'Oh. Sorry. It was Ryan who was watching us walk out, not Toby. Toby was so busy talking to the woman, I don't think he realised we were leaving. But I'm sure she *is* his sister, so don't start worrying about that.'

'Bugger! Yes I'm sure she is too and I'm not worried. Well not about that. I wish he'd looked round though but I suppose you're right and because he had his back to us, he didn't see us, whereas that git Ryan was facing us.'

'Yes,' Cleo said. 'I'm sure that's exactly what it was. He'll call you, Poppy. I'm sure he will.'

Poppy wasn't as certain.

Chapter Four

A few minutes after Poppy and Cleo left, Ryan stood up. 'I've got to make a call. I won't be long.' As he made his way towards the door he heard his sister's voice:

'So Toby, have you met anyone?'

'As it happens, I have. Her name's Poppy and she's sitting... Oh, she's gone. She was at that table in the window just a few minutes ago. She was with some friends. You might've seen her when you came in. She's blonde, a very beautiful blonde.'

Ryan opened the door. He couldn't hear what else his brother said but then he didn't need to; he'd already heard more than enough. He pressed the speed dial on his phone and exhaled a long, slow breath as he waited for his call to be answered.

'Hello Ryan. How are things?'

'Hello Jules. I think we have a problem. Are you free for the next few weeks? If I send the car for you, can you come to Goldebury Bay?'

'Already? Is it serious?'

'I think so, yes. Yes it is.'

'Then of course I'll come. I can leave today.'

'That won't be necessary.' Ryan glanced back through the window and watched Toby and Stephanie chatting in an animated fashion. 'Stephanie's arrived and I'll be here for another two days before I have to leave. So Tuesday night, or Wednesday morning before I fly out, will be fine. Is that okay with you?'

'You know you don't have to ask. Even if it wasn't, I'd come.'

'Thanks. What would I do without you?'

'The same as you always do. Deal with it. You always have and sadly, you'll probably always have to. So is she like the others?'

Ryan didn't answer immediately. He stared at the chair which Poppy had so recently vacated and sighed.

'Yes. And no. She's certainly beautiful. Very beautiful. And blonde. And from the little I've found out about her so far, definitely not well off. But there's something different about her. Don't ask me what because I have absolutely no idea. Just trust me when I say, this one could really be trouble.'

'I trust you, Ryan. You know that. What I don't understand is how this could have happened so fast. I thought Toby only arrived there yesterday. Did he know this girl before?'

'No. He only met her last night. At a party, apparently.'

'Then… why are you so worried? Surely she can't have had time to get her claws into him yet?'

Ryan sucked in a breath and turned his back to the bow window. 'This woman doesn't need time. Five minutes and he'd be hers. Shit, five seconds would do it.'

'Language, Ryan.'

Ryan grinned into the phone. 'Sorry Jules. I was forgetting who I was speaking to for a moment.'

An affectionate and melodious laugh tinkled through the phone. 'I'm the one who's supposed to be forgetful, sweetheart, not you. And Stephanie? How's she? Any permanent damage?'

'Only time will tell but I don't think so. To be honest, she looks a hell of a lot better than I expected her to. And she's smiling and laughing with Toby, so that's something.

The last time I saw her she looked as if she was at death's door, and in floods of tears.'

'I shudder just to think about it. It could have been so much worse though.'

'I know. You and me both.'

'Ryan? I know I don't have to ask this but… she will be safe in Goldebury Bay, won't she?'

'I'll make damn sure she is. I'll make damn sure they both are. And I'll do anything and everything it takes. You know that, Jules.' Ryan heard the sigh of relief. 'I don't think we have anything to worry about, on that score. I wouldn't be going away if I did. But Doug'll be here. And it'll take more than some little piece of shit… excuse my language, to get past him. If you're worried, I can bring in extra security whilst I'm gone.'

'No, no. If you say it's fine, then I'm sure it is.'

'It is. But just to be on the safe side I'll get more help. Does that ease your concern?'

'It does. Thank you, sweetheart. So this girl… What did you say her name was?'

'I didn't. But it's Poppy. Poppy Taylor.'

'And you've met her?'

'Oh yes. I've met her.'

'And all that Doug has been able to find out about her so far, is that she's poor?'

'I don't know if she's poor, exactly, Jules. But she's definitely not rich. And it wasn't Doug who told me. He was with Stephanie, remember? Goldebury Bay is a small, seaside resort, full of people with nothing better to do than gossip. From what I've been able to glean so far, Poppy arrived here last year with her friend Cleo Merrifield, from Gibraltar. Cleo has family here. An aunt, I believe and also, history. Although apparently, the aunt was actually the girl's mother. Don't ask. There're some very strange people

45

here. Anyway, this Cleo's now living with her childhood sweetheart, Oliver Sutton, who owns a local restaurant. It seems Cleo and Poppy couldn't bear to be parted, so Poppy stayed here too. And this part you'll find interesting – she's a barmaid… and a waitress, and she used to work at the casino in Gibraltar.'

'No! Really. Well, I see what you mean, Ryan. I'm not sure whether to laugh or have a panic attack.'

'I thought you'd appreciate the irony,' he said.

'That girl is *definitely* going to be trouble, Ryan,' Jules said. 'Although… I'm rather looking forward to meeting her.'

'I had a feeling you'd say that. I can send the car today, if you like.'

'I'll start packing right away.'

Ryan slid the phone into his jacket pocket and headed back inside. He glanced briefly towards the empty table in the curve of the bow window and shook his head. He sighed deeply and rejoined his family.

He'd feel a lot happier with Jules around. She was always able to help him through any crisis in his life; to lift his spirits on the rare occasions when he doubted himself; to replace a frown with a smile; to wrap a supporting arm around his shoulders when a dire situation called for drastic action. But most of all, she believed in him. Trusted him. Loved him. And he knew she always would. No matter what he did. No matter what anyone else thought of him. And that meant more to him than any deal ever could. She was one in a million and he knew he'd never find another woman like her. Not that he'd even bothered to try.

Chapter Five

Toby stood on the York stone terrace of High House and admired the view. Even at this time of night he could see for miles, thanks to a clear sky and a glowing moon which shone like a spotlight directly onto Goldebury Bay. He now understood why his brother had rented, via the internet, this five-bedroomed Georgian property on a rolling, six-month tenancy.

Not only was it secluded, it came with the added bonus of high garden walls on three sides, broken only by an imposing fifteen-foot tall, wrought iron, double gate. On the fourth side, was a large terrace, below which was a sheer drop of possibly one hundred feet, plummeting directly to the rocks and the sea.

From where he stood on the west side of the terrace, he could take in, not only the sweeping curves of Goldebury Bay and the many coves leading towards Hastings and the west, but also the myriad lights still twinkling up at him from the homes of the residents of this tiny seaside resort. He felt like a rock star on a stage high above an audience, waving their mobile phones like candles in a darkened auditorium.

It occurred to him that one of those twinkling lights may be from Poppy's home and he scanned the scene before him, wondering which it was and what Poppy was doing inside. He could picture her face. Her perfect lips; her stunningly blue eyes, like none he had seen before; her peaches and cream complexion, lightly tanned from careful exposure to the summer sun, and no doubt, skilfully applied sunscreen, and her slim, graceful neck, leading down to a body nothing short of perfection.

He gripped the top of the stone balustrade in front of him; her image so vivid that he could smell her perfume; feel the touch of her hand; her warm breath emanating from those enticing lips as she spoke his name.

He had to see her again. No matter what Ryan thought or said. No matter what Ryan did. What right had Ryan to tell him whom he could and couldn't date? Okay, he'd made some mistakes in the past but so what? Hadn't everyone? Hadn't Ryan?

No. Perhaps not Ryan. Ryan was too careful to make mistakes. Ryan was too careful to do anything that might involve emotions or broken hearts. Had Ryan ever been in love? Truly in love? Toby doubted it. Ryan had always been in control. Ryan was in control of everything. Even his own feelings.

Toby wasn't like that. Toby took after their mother. She knew the meaning of the word *love*. She knew how to have fun. And despite what Ryan said there was more to life than work. There was more to life than money. There was love. And Toby would do anything for love.

Glancing over his shoulder to check that he was alone, he dialled Poppy's number. Would she still be up at eleven-thirty?

'Hello?'

He could hear the sleep in her voice.

'Poppy? It's Toby. Toby Blackwood. Did I wake you?'

'Toby! Toby, is that you? I was beginning to think you wouldn't call.'

The evident rustling of cotton sheets sent a surge of testosterone through him and unwittingly, he pictured Poppy in bed. In his bed. Wearing nothing but a smile and that intoxicating perfume of hers, the scent of which he hadn't been able to get out of his head. He leant against the balustrade, and feeling suddenly overcome with warmth, he adjusted the open neck of his shirt.

Finally, he was able to speak: 'I said I would. You knew I would. I haven't stopped thinking about you since last night. It's just that Ryan... That is... We've been so busy. Every time I've tried to dial your number, something's come up. I hope I'm not interrupting anything. I hope you're alone. Are you alone?'

'Yes Toby. I'm alone.'

Her voice held a seductive quality that sent Toby's emotions into overdrive.

'Do you like being alone?'

He heard the small intake of breath and held his own, waiting for her answer.

'Not particularly. Do you?'

He exhaled. 'Not at all,' he said. 'Would you... would you like me to come over?'

'Tonight?'

Had he been mistaken or was there a note of fear, not just surprise in that question?

'Well... You're alone, I'm alone and neither one of us like it. I just thought...'

Again the rustling of sheets but this time they conjured up a picture of the matron making his bed at the boarding school Ryan had sent him to, after Ryan had made his first million.

'I like you, Toby. I really like you and you don't know how tempted I am to say yes but... I've been working at Sutton's all afternoon and evening since leaving Betty's Pantry and I'm still tired from the party last night. To be honest I'm absolutely shattered. And if we do this... correction, when we do this, I'd like to know that I'd be able to stay awake.'

'I'm not sure whether I should be offended by that. I don't usually send people to sleep when I'm in bed with them.' He laughed but he wasn't sure that he was amused.

'No! No, I didn't mean that. I meant... Well, you know what I meant. I'd like to be able to give as good as I get. It's the standard I live by,' Poppy continued.

Her laugh sounded so sexy, so enticing that he was tempted to ignore her comment, book a cab as he couldn't take the limo without Ryan finding out, and do everything he could to make sure she stayed awake until the dawn chorus serenaded them both into a satisfied slumber. Her next words stopped him.

'Besides, I'm going to be up all night tomorrow. Did you know there's a lunar eclipse? It's the Harvest moon. That's a full moon but it's not just the Harvest moon, it's a Blood Moon because it's a full eclipse. Sorry, I'm so tired I'm not sure that made any sense. It's supposed to be visible from here and Sophie, Thaddeus, Cleo, Oliver and the rest of us are staying up all night at Summerhill to watch it. It starts just after one in the morning, is completely full around four and ends shortly after six. D'you fancy spending the night with me watching it? We won't be alone of course, so we won't be able to... do anything. But it should be fun and *very* romantic.'

Toby sighed and kicked a fragment of loose York stone with his foot. He peered into the increasing darkness as, one by one, the lights in Goldebury Bay went out, rather like his hopes for a night of passion between the sheets.

'It's not quite how I'd like to spend our first full night together, but being with you beneath the moon, any moon, definitely has its attractions. And you're right, it does sound very romantic. Why don't I take you out to dinner first? Then we can head up to Summerhill and join the others. Or better still, if it doesn't start until two in the morning, after dinner, why don't you and I find something else to do to pass the time?'

'I'd love that Toby. The thing is, we're sort of having a barbecue-cum-picnic thing in the evening. There'll be quite a few of us. Oliver's family will be there and so will Cleo's. Then there's Sophie's mum and her boyfriend Hugh, who're visiting from the Caymans plus Tony Hardman, Sophie's solicitor and his P.A., Veronique. Me of course. The Rev Paul Temple—'

'Okay, I get the picture. There'll be a lot of you,' Toby said, laughing. 'In that case, perhaps we could invite my family as well.'

'Your family? So the woman you were with today is your... sister?'

'Yes. My sister Stephanie. She's been... living abroad for the last few years.'

'Yes, of course. She's more than welcome. And, I suppose your brother too, although I'm sure he'll have more important things to do.'

'I'm not sure Ryan will come. He's leaving the country on Wednesday so staying up all night on Sunday might not seem like a good idea to him.'

'Leaving the country? For good?'

Toby chuckled. 'No such luck. Sorry, I didn't mean to say that. It was a joke. No, he's just away on business for a couple of weeks and then he'll be back.'

'Oh joy,' Poppy said, but she didn't sound very joyful to Toby's ears.

'Oh, and there's Jules. She's... sorry Poppy I've got to go. I'll call you tomorrow.' He shoved his phone into his trouser pocket seconds before Stephanie appeared. 'Oh, it's you.'

'Hello Toby. What're you doing out here?'

51

'Admiring the view. It's pretty spectacular by day but at night it's even better.'

Neither spoke for several seconds as the soft, swish-swoosh of waves lapped against the rocks below and the gentle breeze wafting in from the sea, rustled through the trees either side of the house.

'It's such a warm night for this late in September,' Stephanie remarked. 'I wonder if there'll be an Indian summer. I do hope so. Autumn's okay, but I hate British winters. I miss the heat already and I haven't even been here a day.' A wistful sigh escaped her. 'I miss him.'

Their eyes met in the darkness and Toby wrapped his arm around his sister.

'I know you do. But Ryan thinks this is for the best. And Ryan always thinks he's right.'

'He means well. I know that. But he's not like you and me. He doesn't understand. It's lovely to see Jules again though, isn't it?'

'Yes.' Toby felt Stephanie shiver. 'Are you cold?'

'No. Just tired. Very, very tired. I think I'll go to bed. Good night, Toby. Pleasant dreams.'

'And you.' He kissed her on the cheek and watched her walk back into the house. He then turned his gaze back down to Goldebury Bay and wondered whether Poppy was asleep, and where. He wished that he were with her.

Chapter Six

Poppy was running late. She'd overslept and it was now seven o'clock. She grabbed her handbag, slipped on her shoes and leather jacket and headed for the front door, her hair still wet from the shower. She'd slept badly after Toby's phone call, tossing and turning and wondering if she'd done the right thing.

Should she really have invited him and his family up to Summerhill? She knew Sophie and Thaddeus wouldn't mind and nor would any of the others but Ryan Blackwood was an obnoxious git and would more than likely put a dampener on the entire night.

But what could she do? She could hardly tell Toby he could bring his sister but not his brother. And who was this Jules person? A woman obviously. But who? Perhaps she was one of Ryan's women. Perhaps she was a friend. Perhaps Ryan would behave better with others around. Perhaps she should invite Timothy Richards as well, just to make the evening *really* special.

Oh hell. There was nothing she could do. She'd invited Toby and his family and she'd just have to keep her fingers crossed and see. If things got really bad and all else failed, she, Cleo and Sophie could shut themselves away somewhere with a few bottles of wine. It wouldn't change the situation but it would make her feel a bit happier for a short time and they could leave Thaddeus and Oliver to sort things out. At least Reverend Paul would be there to calm things down... for which Clara would no doubt thank her.

Dear Clara, Poppy was sure she'd understand.

Was she worrying for nothing? Ryan Blackwood didn't seem the kind of guy who would spend the night lying on a throw on the grass, looking up at the moon and stars, or even lounging on a reclining chair, as some of the others would be, watching the heavens. He was probably more interested in making his next million than in witnessing a celestial event unfold throughout the night. If he'd watch it at all, it would probably be the highlights on the news channel.

She raced out of the cottage – which Sophie had recently let her have on a 'peppercorn rent' – and pulled the door shut, remembering just a second too late, she'd left the keys on a hook in the hall. She turned and slammed both hands against the door in a futile attempt to stop it before the lock caught. The click of the catch held a somewhat mocking resonance and seemed to reverberate far louder than it probably did in reality.

She banged her palms repeatedly on the blackened oak door and immediately peered through the letterbox, although she had no idea why. No one else lived there. She studied the black iron flap, the word 'Letters' standing proud, as though some people may not know what the thing was for.

Could she reach the back of the Yale lock if she stuck her arm through the letterbox? They were not very far apart. Looking at the lock and the letterbox from here, it seemed possible. Her only other alternative was to call Sophie and ask her to bring the spare key. Sophie was bound to be up and if not, Thaddeus was an early riser; perhaps he would answer Sophie's phone. After five rings it went to voicemail.

'Hi Sophie, it's Poppy. I've locked myself out of the cottage. Will you call me when you get this message, please? I'm going to see if I can reach the lock and if I can I'll call you back. If not, is there any chance either you or Thaddeus could drop the spare down to me? Sorry. Call me. Love you.'

She rang Thaddeus' number but that too went to voicemail. She left a similar message, tossed the phone back in her bag and mock-thumped her forehead against the door. The keys to The One That Got Away were on that key ring and she had promised Ben that she'd get in early and do a stocktake before opening up. Already half an hour late, she had to do something.

Rolling up her sleeves, Poppy slid her left arm through the wide gap, the lock being on the right and therefore easier to reach with her left hand, but the outward opening flap of the letterbox didn't open quite as far as she'd thought. Her arm wouldn't go any further.

'Bugger.'

She slid her arm back and felt a sudden pull on her metal watch strap. What now? She yanked her arm but it didn't move. It had caught on something on the inside of the letterbox or the door.

'I don't believe this. Why do these things always happen to me?'

With the fingers of her right hand she reached inside, twisted her wrist and tried to free the catch on the strap but she couldn't get a firm hold and the tips of her fingers just brushed the tight clasp. The strap wouldn't budge and because it was caught, she couldn't twist it round. She tried again. Still nothing. This was ridiculous. She'd have to phone Cleo and ask Oliver for help.

She reached in her bag, and with one hand tapped the screen to call Cleo. That also went to voicemail as did Oliver's when she called him. This was getting beyond a joke. Where was everyone this morning? She had no choice

55

but to call Ben. What a prospect that was on a Sunday morning, especially as it was now seven-fifteen. She was about to press 'call' when she spotted someone jogging towards her in a black, hooded tracksuit. She waved frantically with her right hand. This was probably Cleo. She ran every morning and she had a black, hooded tracksuit. At last, Poppy was having some luck.

No. The rapidly approaching figure looked much too tall and far too broad to be Cleo. She may have put on a few pounds recently but her entire body couldn't look that big, even in a tracksuit. And the person in this black tracksuit was clearly a man. She could see that now.

'Excuse me!' She yelled. 'I wonder if you could…'

No way! It wasn't possible. The universe wouldn't be that unkind. But as he jogged closer she could see she was right. Ryan sodding Blackwood of all people. Why him? Why in God's name did it have to be him? She closed her eyes. She could tell from his footfall that he had covered the distance between them in a matter of seconds and she reopened her eyes, expecting to see that arrogant face right in front of her.

What the hell…? He was jogging right past. What on earth was this guy's problem?

'Oi! Blackwood! Can't you see I need some help?'

He continued for a few more steps, stopping suddenly some feet away. He let his head fall to his chest, raising it again as he turned, pulled the earbuds from his ears and sauntered back towards her.

'What seems to be the problem?'

'Apart from you, you mean? I'm stuck, that's the problem.'

'Do you make a habit of this?'

'We all have our little foibles. Yours is being a jerk, it appears.'

His mouth twitched into the tiniest of grins but his cool, appraising eyes travelled down the length of her T-shirt, jacket and jeans, finally returning upwards to her face.

'At least you're fully clothed this time. I suppose I should be grateful for that. But why, may I ask, do you have your hand stuck in someone's letterbox? Wait. Don't tell me. You know the owner.'

'Yes, I bloody do know the owner. And it's *my* letterbox. At least I rent it. The cottage, not the letterbox. Well both. That's irrelevant. Were you really going to ignore me? No wonder they say chivalry is dead. Clearly they've based that on you.'

'It seems you've learnt nothing from our encounter on Friday. You attract more bees with honey than you do with vinegar.'

'What *are* you going on about? What's this got to do with bees? Oh, I get it. You're telling me I need to be nice. Well for your information, I *am* nice. To most people. Don't raise your eyebrows at me! It's true. You don't know me. You know nothing about me. So don't be so quick to judge.'

'Unlike you, you mean? I know you have an uncanny ability to get yourself stuck in the most ridiculous places. Oh, for God's sake, I don't have time for this today. Let me see.'

As he hunkered down onto his haunches and peered into the letterbox, Poppy detected the same intoxicating aftershave, this time mixed with sweat and it sent her senses reeling.

'Your watch strap's caught.'

'Really? Tell me something I don't know.'

He glanced up and met her eyes, holding the look for what seemed like an eternity. It was probably little more than a couple of seconds. She was sure he was going to say something but he shook his head, pushed his hair and the hood half covering it, back from his face and resumed his efforts to free her, using his long fingers to feel around her wrist.

'Ow!'

'Sorry. It seems to be caught on a piece of metal which is wrapped around one of the screws holding the inside of the letterbox in place. I'm trying to push your hand forward like this and… There! I think I've done it.' He gently eased her hand out through the letterbox with his fingers.

Poppy snatched her hand away as quickly as she could and rubbed her wrist with her right hand.

'Thank you.'

'You're welcome. Perhaps you'd like to tell me where you're proposing to get yourself stuck next. It would probably save us both a lot of time.'

She sneered at him. 'How very amusing.'

'It wasn't meant to be. But you didn't answer my question. Why were you sticking your hand in your own letterbox?'

She lowered her eyes. 'I locked myself out. I've left the keys in the hall by mistake. I thought I might be able to reach the back of the Yale lock and get back in… but I couldn't.'

'Now it makes perfect sense.'

'Don't be sarcastic.'

'Actually, I wasn't. Do you need them?'

'No, but they get lonely if they're away from me for too long. Don't be a jerk. Of course I need them. Why would I be shoving my arm through my letterbox if I didn't need them?'

His lips twitched. 'With you, nothing would surprise me. I'm sure you'd have a variety of reasons. What I meant was, do you need them at this precise moment? Isn't there someone with a spare key? You said you rent the cottage… and the letterbox.' The twitch turned into a broad grin. 'Couldn't you call the landlord? Although I suppose it's a little early to be—'

'I did call her. She didn't answer her phone. I'm supposed to be at the pub early this morning and I'm already late. I work at The One That Got Away.'

'I know.'

'What? How do you know? Oh. I suppose Toby told you.'

He shook his head. 'He didn't. I must've heard it somewhere. Move over.'

'Don't you mean: 'Move over, please? Or weren't you taught good manners growing up?'

'No. But I was taught how to pick a lock. And before you make some facetious comment, my father wasn't a house-burglar, or any other sort of thief. He was in the building trade and picking locks comes in handier than you might think for a builder. So, would you like me to pick your lock and reunite you with your keys before they have a panic attack?'

'Oh! Um. Yes. Yes please.'

How on earth had he known almost word for word what she was intending to say about his father? Could he read minds as well as pick locks?

'Then move over… please.'

In less than a minute, the oak door swung open.

'How did you do that?'

Again that grin. 'I could tell you but—'

Poppy interrupted him with a loud tut. 'Oh, not that old chestnut: "I could tell you but I'd have to kill you."'

'Didn't anyone tell you it's rude to interrupt? Or weren't you taught any manners either? I was going to say: I could tell you but it's a trick of the trade. You'd have to come and

59

work for me.'

'I think I'd prefer the old chestnut option.'

He frowned. 'You'd prefer death to working for me? How delightful. Well... unless you're planning to stick your hand somewhere else or climb over any railings within the next ten minutes, I'll be on my way. I'll see you this evening.'

Poppy nearly choked. 'This evening?'

'Yes. Toby tells me we're all invited up to Summerhill for a barbecue-cum-picnic and to watch the lunar eclipse. Did you know that in several cultures, a Blood Moon, as they like to call it, is considered unlucky?'

'I'm beginning to understand why,' Poppy said, looking him directly in the eye. 'And did you know that others believe it to be a forerunner to the second coming? And a precursor to the end of days.'

'Basically, doom and gloom all round then. I'm looking forward to it.'

'Really? I wouldn't have thought it was your sort of thing.'

He grinned and his eyes sparkled in the early morning sunlight.

'To quote your words: "You don't know me. You know nothing about me. So don't be so quick to judge." Try not to get yourself stuck again. I've got a really busy day.'

He turned on his heel and jogged away without another word.

'You're the last person I'd call if I do.'

Chapter Seven

Despite Toby calling and offering to escort Poppy to Summerhill, she suggested they meet at the house. She wanted to get there early. Sophie didn't need any help of course; Veronique had organised the whole event, but Sutton's restaurant was providing the catering and it had become a kind of ritual now, that Oliver, Cleo and Poppy, would always be on hand – just in case.

Cleo and Poppy arrived at Summerhill shortly before six-thirty, Oliver having gone ahead, allowing plenty of time to ensure everything was ready for the barbecue-cum-picnic. The guests would start arriving at seven-thirty – just as the moon rose in the east. It would be dark about an hour after that and Sophie had arranged for the dance floor to remain from the party on Friday. The Golde Boys Rock Band were going to provide the music.

'Two parties in the space of a few days. Was this really wise, Sophie?' Cleo asked, as they joined her near the dance floor where she, Veronique and an electrician were checking the myriad fairy lights.

'Oh, hello you two. I'm beginning to wonder myself. I did suggest to Thaddeus that we should've had our party tonight and roll both events into one, but you know Thaddeus. He's such a romantic. He insisted that no celestial occurrence was going to upstage us.' She laughed. 'Not that I'm complaining, of course. And besides, who doesn't like a good party?'

'You're right,' Cleo said, with a smile. 'Plus it means

61

more business for Oliver and Sutton's restaurant so we're very happy. In fact, I think you should have more parties. At least one every month.'

'That's not a bad idea,' Sophie said. 'So Poppy, where's Toby? I got your message telling me you'd managed to get back into the cottage and that you had a feeling the entire Blackwood family might be coming tonight. I did call you back to say that was fine, but it went to voicemail.'

'Yeah, sorry about that. It's been one of those days. Um. Toby's coming later, and so is his sister, Stephanie. I... I don't know about Ryan, or some woman called Jules he may be bringing.'

'Ooh. Is that his girlfriend?' Cleo asked.

'No idea. D'you need any help Sophie? Or Veronique?'

'I think we're okay thanks,' Veronique said. 'You didn't see Tony inside, did you? He was supposed to have been here ages ago. He nipped into the office but he said he wouldn't be there long.'

'We didn't go inside,' Poppy said. 'We saw you two and came straight here. I'll go and look for him if you want.'

'No. Don't worry I suppose he'll get here when he gets here. He's probably on his way. I called and left a message.'

'Is there a problem with the lights?' Cleo asked.

'No,' Sophie said. 'Just a safety check, and we've added a few more around the dance floor.'

'There,' said Veronique. 'Okay, let's switch them on.' She waved to someone in the house and a few seconds later, the garden and Summer Hill Cliff were aglow with twinkling, coloured lights and solid bright shafts of light all around the cliff edges. 'Ta dah!'

'Wow! It gets better every time I see this,' Poppy said. She nudged Cleo. 'This is where you should have your wedding reception. This place is utterly magical.'

'Oliver's proposed?' Sophie and Veronique shrieked, in unison.

Cleo shook her head. 'No. Poppy and I were just discussing weddings the other day, that's all. I think he's worried about the expense, what with everything else going on. Oh! I didn't mean it to sound like that. Sorry. You've been so wonderful, Sophie, letting us buy the freehold of the building for a pittance, and everything.'

Sophie held up her hands. 'Cleo stop. Don't worry about it, please. I understand completely. Thaddeus is exactly the same. Constantly worrying about the expense of reopening Beaumont Boats. And we live together!' She linked her arm through Cleo's and they all began walking back towards the house. 'But, if you ever need anything, Cleo – and I do mean anything – you will tell me, won't you?'

Cleo squeezed Sophie's hand. 'Thanks Sophie. We're so lucky to have such good friends.'

'We're not going to have a group hug or anything, are we?' Poppy said. 'Because I don't think my street cred could cope.'

Cleo laughed. 'Since when've you had street cred?'

'Since I decided I would. I was talking to Julia and Hugh at the party on Friday. By the way, Sophie, your mum talks a lot of sense. It's all about having a positive attitude to life. Oh shit! Is that repulsive Ryan?'

'So much for the positive attitude,' Cleo said, with a grin.

'Okay, clever clogs. I'm positive that's repulsive Ryan. Is that better? What's he doing here so early? And where's Toby?'

'Oh,' Sophie said, looking a little flushed. 'That's what I meant to say earlier when you said he might be coming, but then we went off topic. Ryan bumped into Thaddeus this afternoon and he said that he wanted to discuss a

63

proposition with Thaddeus. And before you ask, I don't know all the details. All I know is, they were discussing boats, and you know what Thaddeus is like about boats. He suggested Ryan might like to come early and continue their discussion over a friendly drink.'

'You don't think he's planning on turning the old Goldebury Bay Yachting and Sailing Club back into some sort of upmarket sailing club for arrogant, ill-mannered jerks like him, do you?'

'It's possible, I suppose,' Sophie replied. 'Although he must know there's already a sailing club in Goldebury Bay. You'll have to ask Thaddeus. He's in the study with Oliver and Ben. Apparently, Ryan wanted to meet them too.'

Cleo looked surprised – almost as surprised as Poppy.

'Oliver didn't say anything to me about it.'

'I don't think he knew,' Sophie said. 'I think Thaddeus only told him when he arrived here. Ben was already here, because as you may or may not know, he's got a bit of a crush on our vintner.'

Poppy grinned. 'I wondered why Ben was in such a tizzy today. He must've tried on at least ten outfits this afternoon and asked for my opinion. I thought it was odd that he'd pay so much attention to his appearance just to come and watch the moon. That explains it.'

'He's not the only one,' Cleo said. 'How many outfits did you try on before we could come here this evening?'

Poppy tutted. 'Only a few.'

'A few hundred more like.'

'Well, as I don't have a few hundred outfits, we all know that's not true. I simply wanted to look nice for my first date with Toby. What's wrong with that?'

Cleo laughed. 'Nothing's wrong with that. You and Ben had the same concern about your appearance, that's all.'

'So this is a date?' Sophie queried. 'For you and Toby, I

mean. Why didn't he come with you then? Why did you tell him to come later?'

Poppy shrugged. 'I wanted to be here before the guests arrived in case there was anything you needed me to do. If I'd known repulsive Ryan was coming early, I'd have told Toby to come too. I'm going in via the kitchen. I don't want to have to speak to that man again today.'

Ryan was standing with his back to them, about twenty feet away, at the open, double doors of the front entrance. Poppy grabbed Cleo with the intention of veering off to the side of the house and leaving Sophie and Veronique to welcome him. She didn't care if he saw her and she had no intention of acknowledging him if he did. After all, hadn't he tried to jog right past her this morning and ignore her? Well, two can play at that game.

'Hello Poppy!' Ryan called out, suddenly turning to face them. 'How very nice to see that you haven't got yourself stuck somewhere. Although I suppose the night is young. Aren't you going to say hello and introduce me to your friends?'

Poppy hesitated for one second before forcing a huge, fake smile and meeting his mocking eyes.

'No. I'm going to take a leaf out of your book and try to ignore you.'

She could see Sophie's horrified expression, but more importantly, she saw the smile on Ryan's arrogant face falter for just a second. Well worth the small upset it caused Sophie.

Sophie hastened towards Ryan and, with a laugh in her voice that must have sounded fake even to her, said: 'Oh Poppy, you're always joking. Hello, you must be Ryan. I'm Sophie Summerhill, Thaddeus' girlfriend and this is Cleo Merrifield, Oliver's girlfriend, and this is our friend, Veronique.'

'How delightful to meet you all,' he said, looking genuinely pleased to do so and behaving as if Poppy's words hadn't had the slightest effect.

'Please go in,' Sophie added. 'Thaddeus is in the study with Oliver and Ben Sutton. I understand you wanted to meet them. You can't miss it. It's the third door on the left-hand side of the hall. Can I get you a drink? Although Thaddeus will have some in the study. Actually, let me show you the way.' She glowered at Poppy as Ryan turned towards the doorway.

No longer needing to use the side entrance, Poppy followed the others and Ryan stepped aside to let them pass. He didn't say a word as she wafted through the doorway and neither did he look in her direction as Sophie led him through the Great Hall.

'You shouldn't have said that,' Cleo scolded when Sophie and Ryan were out of earshot. 'Just because he's a jerk, that doesn't mean you have to be one too. You're forgetting he's Sophie and Thaddeus' guest, and by the sounds of it, possibly a future business partner. I don't think Sophie was very happy.'

Poppy sighed. 'I know. That man just brings out the worst in me. I wouldn't have said that if Toby had been with him. I'll apologise to Sophie but don't even consider asking me to apologise to him because he's been far ruder to me. He can't even say hello without being sarcastic.'

'A bit like someone else we know,' Cleo quipped.

Poppy grinned and placed an arm around Cleo's waist. 'You mean Ben, of course. Um, I hate to say this, and please don't take it the wrong way, but I think you're right. You have put on weight. Oh my God! You're not—'

'Don't say it!' Cleo said, looking seriously concerned. She looked around before pulling Poppy to one side. 'Where did Veronique go?'

66

Poppy stared at Cleo's tummy. 'I think she went towards the kitchen. Yes. Yes she did. You're not, are you?'

'I'm not sure,' Cleo said in a low voice. 'I thought it was because I've been eating so much this summer, especially chocolate brownies. I haven't missed a period and I'm on the pill, so I don't see how I can be, but... well, I felt really sick this morning when I woke up and that's one of the signs, isn't it? Plus, I've been feeling very emotional lately, and that's another sign, isn't it?'

'Don't ask me. How would I know? You need to speak to Clara. Or Julia. They've had kids so they'll know. Oh God, Cleo! Wouldn't it be incredible if you were? You do want kids, don't you? You've always wanted kids.'

'Shush! Someone might hear you. Yes, I've always wanted kids and yes it would be incredible. Better than incredible. But it's really bad timing. Mary's better now, as I told you, but Oliver still wants to organise that safari thing for her. Then there's Sutton's and his plans for that. And... well, we haven't even discussed having a family. I know he wants kids. I think it's just something we haven't had a chance to talk about, or even think about really, what with everything that's been going on.'

Poppy gently poked at Cleo's tummy. 'If you want my opinion, not that anyone ever does, I would say the sooner you and Oliver discuss babies, the better. You need to go and see the doctor. Or why don't you do one of those home tests? They're pretty accurate these days, or so I've heard.'

Cleo glanced around again and then rifled in her handbag, pulling out a small white bag bearing the Goldebury Bay Pharmacy logo.

'I bought it on my way to pick you up. I was going to talk to you about it earlier but you were in such a state about your date with Toby tonight and what to wear, so I didn't. The girl in the chemists said I don't have to wait until the morning to take this one. I can take it any time of day... or night.'

'Oh Cleo! Why didn't you tell me to shut up? This is more important than what I should wear on a date.' She grabbed Cleo's hand and led her towards the stairs. 'There's no time like the present. Unless you want Oliver to be with you when you do this?'

Cleo shook her head. 'No. If it's a false alarm, I'd rather Oliver didn't know. He's got enough on his mind right now and if what Sophie said about Ryan wanting to meet him, is true, he may very soon have a lot more. The last thing he needs is his paranoid girlfriend giving him baby scares.'

'And if it's not a false alarm?'

They stared into each other's eyes and, without another word ran as fast as they could up the stairs to the large family-sized bathroom on the first floor.

Chapter Eight

'Where've you two been?' Sophie snapped, as Poppy and Cleo pushed the kitchen door open with a flourish. 'I've been looking for you for the last fifteen minutes. And why those strange expressions? What've you been up to?'

'Nothing!' Poppy said, her arm linked through Cleo's. 'We were… just discussing the vagaries of life, that's all. I'm really sorry about being rude to repulsive Ryan earlier, Sophie. This is your house, he's your guest, and I had no right to do that in front of you.'

'That's okay,' Sophie replied, waving an arm in the air in a dismissive gesture. 'But I do wish you'd stop calling him repulsive Ryan. Someone may hear you. *He* may hear you. And I've no idea what's going on, but I took some snacks into the study just now and the four of them are already huddled around the desk looking very business-like. And they've only been in there for five minutes! Well… a bit longer than five minutes but you know what I mean.'

Poppy nodded. 'I promise I won't call him repulsive Ryan again. I wonder what they're talking about. Any chance we could listen at the door?'

Sophie tutted. 'No Poppy, we can't.' She grabbed a pile of plates, loaded them onto a tray and picked it up. 'But you could make yourself useful and bring the rest of the plates, the cutlery, and those napkins, outside. We've just checked the weather forecast and it's going to be a dry and very warm, night. Even though it did look like rain earlier.

Most of the stuff's outside already and this is the last of it.'

Poppy and Cleo exchanged glances.

'Where is it?' Cleo whispered as Sophie headed towards the side door.

'It's safely wrapped in tissue inside the paper bag and hidden in my handbag. Don't worry. I still think we could throw it in the bin and no one would ever see it but I understand how concerned you are – note that I didn't say paranoid, even though I think you're a nutter – so I'll take it home with me and dispose of it in one of the public bins nearby.'

Cleo grinned. 'I know you think I'm mad, but Silas is always going through the rubbish and that cat has a truly astonishing knack for finding things. Just imagine it. We're all sitting under the stars, with the fairy lights twinkling and Silas trots out with that thing stuck in his mouth.'

Poppy burst out laughing at the image.

'And what if Thaddeus should see it?' Cleo continued. 'Then he'd start thinking it was Sophie's. And I can't risk Oliver finding it at home. Cleover's always searching for scraps. Anyone would think we didn't feed that crazy dog. She's discovered how to jump onto the recycling bin and open the lid of the rubbish bin next to it. She dived in head first the other day and Oliver had to get her out. It would be just my luck she'd find it and she'd take it straight to Oliver. Then I'd have some explaining to do.'

'Okay.' Poppy still couldn't stop laughing. 'Don't worry I'll get rid of it but remember, this is the one and only time I'm ever going to carry around a stick with your pee on it in my handbag, however well wrapped up it may be.'

'Are you two coming or not?' Sophie called from the other side of the open, kitchen door.

'Coming,' Cleo said, giving Poppy a final smile.

Carrying loaded trays, they followed Sophie down the

garden path towards the tables and chairs forming a long row near the dance floor. It was beginning to get dark and the full moon over Summer Hill Cliff cast a wide, shimmering white trail like a bride's veil, spread out behind her down the aisle.

'Poppy!'

Poppy turned to see Toby waving from the doorway of the house. Unlike Ryan, who had been wearing jeans, a V-necked T-shirt and a bespoke, tailored jacket, Toby wore a charcoal-grey suit, very like the one Ryan had worn the night she met him, and a pale pink shirt. He'd clearly made an effort to look good tonight, so why did he seem overdressed somehow?

'Toby! You're here.'

She dumped the tray on the table and hurried towards him but stopped in her tracks a few feet away. Stephanie, immaculate from head to toe in a figure-hugging, fawn dress and Bolero jacket, with matching shoes and bag, linked her arm through his in a decidedly possessive gesture. A moment later, an elderly, aristocratic-looking woman, wearing a silver-grey trouser suit identical in colour to her coiffed hair, stood to the other side of him, also linking her arm through his. It was as if they were sending Poppy a message.

'Let me introduce you to my sister,' Toby was saying. 'Stephanie, this is Poppy. Poppy, Stephanie.'

Poppy met Stephanie's cool, blue eyes and smiled. 'It's lovely to meet you Stephanie.'

'Likewise,' Stephanie replied in a less than friendly manner.

Toby didn't seem to notice. 'And this is Jules,' he was saying, smiling at the elegant woman on his right. 'Jules, meet Poppy.'

Poppy smiled, not expecting a reciprocal gesture, but to

71

her surprise, Jules reached out an aged hand. Was she expecting Poppy to take it and curtsy, or kiss it and bow?

'I'm very pleased to meet you, Poppy,' Jules said, with seemingly genuine enthusiasm. 'I've heard so much about you. I'm sure you and I will be firm friends. And you're even lovelier than I'd been led to believe. I can definitely see the attraction. Come and tell me all about yourself.'

Poppy looked from Jules to Toby, to Stephanie and back again.

'Er. I'm not sure there's much to tell. And it really depends on what you've heard so far.'

Jules smiled. 'Yes,' she said. 'I suppose it does.'

Poppy had never been so glad to see Tony Hardman, and as she spotted him from the corner of her eye, she yelled his name and waved as though he were her dearest friend,

'I'm so sorry, Jules,' Poppy said. 'But there's Tony and I really need to speak to him about... something very important. Please excuse me. I don't mean to be rude, but it really can't wait. I'm sure I'll see you later. I'll send a waiter over with drinks, but feel free to either go into the sitting room or take a seat out here. Sorry Toby. Excuse me Stephanie.'

With a smile and a beckoning hand for a nearby waiter, Poppy left them to it and trotted towards Tony.

'Hello Poppy,' Tony said. 'What can I do for you?'

'Be my shield. See that woman over there in the grey trouser suit?' She nodded towards Jules.

'She looks very swish,' Tony said. 'Who is she?'

'She's called Jules but other than that I have no idea. Toby brought her. You remember Toby from the party on Friday? I think she's something to do with his brother. I thought she was his girlfriend or something.'

Tony shot her a look. 'How old's Toby's brother?'

'Thirty-nine.'

Tony's eyebrows almost went over his head. 'Thirty-nine! Good heavens. The man's obviously into cougars. Perhaps he's after her money. She looks terribly well off. But then the brother is very well off from what I've heard so perhaps she has another appeal.'

Poppy laughed and shook her head. 'I don't think she's his girlfriend now. I said I thought she was, before I saw her. From the looks of it, and the way she held on to Toby, she's either the mother, an aunt, or possibly their grandmother. Of course, you may be right. The guy may very well be into women at least twice his age. Anyway, whoever she is, she wants to interrogate me. And you know how I feel about that.'

Tony grinned and patted her hand. 'I'll tell her I'm your solicitor and I must be present at all times.'

'I can't afford you,' Poppy said.

'This one's on me. Now have you seen Veronique? I'm late and she's going to kill me.'

'She was headed towards the kitchen about ten minutes ago. I'll come with you. I know this is none of my business, Tony. But are you and Veronique an item now? She really is fabulous and so organised.'

'You're right, Poppy. It is none of your business.' He smiled and kissed her hand. 'But yes, I can say without fear of contradiction, we are.'

'So I really am the only one without a boyfriend then.'

They entered the house via the front door and went into the kitchen. Having checked the coast was clear, Poppy nipped back out through the side door. She had intended to join the others but curiosity got the better of her and instead of turning right, she turned left towards the back of the house and the study.

She could hear voices and laughter. The window of the study must be open. She made her way towards it and stood a little to the right, leaning back against the wall of the house.

'I could tell you some stories about Poppy, darling, which would positively make your hair curl. She's a bit of a handful but we love her.'

They were talking about her! That was Ben's voice. Bloody hell, he really could tell some stories about her and they weren't necessarily stories she would like anyone to hear. Why were they talking about her? Was this something to do with Ryan trying to stop her seeing Toby? Was he asking questions about her? She had put a stop to this. She didn't want that man to know anything about her. She was happy to tell Toby everything about herself. But not Ryan Blackwood.

'Meow!' That didn't sound a bit like Silas. She tried again. 'Meow, meow, meow!'

'What the hell…?' Thaddeus said, sticking his head out of the open window.

Poppy immediately put her finger to her lips to stop him saying her name. She drew her other finger slowly across her throat, pointed to herself and at Thaddeus and made a shape with her hand like a glove puppet to indicate it talking. Surely that message was clear enough? She mouthed it just in case. 'Stop talking about me or you're dead.'

Thaddeus shrugged and shook his head. He nodded and pointed with one finger towards the side of the house. He then 'walked' two fingers through the air and turned his back on her.

'I think it's time we joined the others,' he said. 'They must be wondering where we've got to and I'm starving. Let's go and eat.' He glanced back out, smiled at Poppy and slammed the window shut.

Poppy headed towards the front of the house. She could

always count on Thaddeus. Why couldn't she meet someone like him? Well, someone like him who would love her in return, of course.

'So this is where you've got to,' Toby said, bumping into her as she turned the corner at the front of Summerhill.

'Toby! Um. I was just... looking for Silas, Sophie's cat. I was sure I heard him meow. Have you got a drink? Oh, I see you have. Where's Stephanie? And Jules? Who is she by the way?'

Toby smiled. 'You look sensational tonight, Poppy. But then I expect you always do. Would you like to dance? The band's just started playing.'

'I'd love to. But tell me, who's Jules?' she asked again.

He took her hand and led her towards the dance floor. 'She's our grandmother. Between you and me, I think she's here to chaperone us. Stephanie and me, that is. Ryan's flying out on Wednesday morning for two weeks and it seems he doesn't trust us to be alone. I wasn't expecting Jules. Mind you, I wasn't expecting Stephanie either. Ryan only told me on Friday night that she'd be arriving on Saturday. But let's not talk about them. Let's talk about us.'

He pulled her to him in a close embrace and Poppy smiled up into the bluest, sexiest eyes she'd ever seen. Until the image of a darker, cooler pair of eyes popped into her head. Why on earth was she thinking about *him*? And at a time like this? What was wrong with her?

And then she saw him. He was walking towards the dance floor. He stopped at the edge and casually leant against one of the upright, corner beams which were there to support a cover in case of rain. He looked directly at her and as Toby spun her round, Ryan's cool gaze seemed to follow her. Finally, he turned and walked away.

Forget Ryan Blackwood. Toby was here now and she was in his arms. That's exactly where she wanted to be. She was happy. They were having fun. And she couldn't wait until it was time to watch the eclipse. She'd grab one of the throws Sophie had provided, find a secluded spot and spend the night with Toby. Perhaps not quite in the way they could've spent last night but at least they'd be together and she could find out more about him.

'I'm hungry,' she said. 'Are you hungry? I think it's all this dancing. Dancing always makes me hungry.'

Toby smiled down at her. 'Let's get something to eat then. And afterwards, let's find a quiet spot where I can get to know you much, much better.'

As Toby led her from the dance floor, she spotted Ryan sitting on a throw on the ground with Sophie and Thaddeus, Julia and Hugh and Veronique and Tony. Jules was in a chair next to Ryan. Clara Pollard, Paul Temple, Christopher and Mary Sutton and GJ and Miff completed the group. And now Ben, Cleo and Oliver were headed in that direction.

'Toby,' she said. 'As much as I want to be alone with you, couldn't we just get some food and join the others for a while? They're lovely people and it looks as though they're having fun.'

'Of course we can. If that's what you'd rather do.' He glanced around him. 'I don't see Stephanie though. I wonder where she is. Why don't you get some food and join the others and I'll go and look for her. I'll be back in a bit to join you.'

'Oh. Okay.'

She watched him walk away before joining the others and sitting on the ground between Sophie and Cleo with Ryan at right angles to her.

'I meant to get something to eat before I sat down,' she said. 'I don't know what the matter is with me these days.'

'Stay there. I'll get it,' Thaddeus said. 'I suppose it goes without saying that you want some chocolate brownies.'

'You know me,' she said, with a laugh.

Ryan was giving her an odd look and she met his eyes, hoping that her stare was cool and uninterested.

'You really do have a sweet tooth, don't you?' Ryan said.

'It's the only thing sweet about me. Is that what you were going to say?'

He held her look.

'No. I have a feeling you can be incredibly sweet when you want to be. And a lot more, besides.'

'Have you seen Stephanie, Ryan?' Jules asked, before Poppy could respond to that strange comment.

He suddenly looked concerned. 'No. Not for some time.' He got to his feet.

'Toby's gone to look for her.'

Ryan glanced down at Poppy. 'When?'

'A couple of minutes ago. There's no need to worry. Sophie had lights positioned all around the edge of the cliff for the party on Friday to make sure that no one fell over.'

Ryan glared at her. 'That's not funny.'

Poppy glared back. 'It wasn't meant to be. What *is* your problem? This is Goldebury Bay, for God's sake. Nothing...' She was about to say that nothing bad happened in Goldebury Bay but that wasn't true, of course. 'I'm sure nothing'll happen to her and Toby will find her very soon.'

'Perhaps. Excuse me.'

'I'll help you look for her,' Oliver said.

'May I be of assistance?' Reverend Paul offered.

Poppy glanced from one person to another as one by one all the men leapt to their feet, even GJ. Although he didn't leap; Oliver had to help him up.

'What's going on?' Poppy said. A hand on her shoulder

made her jump. It was Thaddeus. Without a word, he handed her a plate of food and joined the others. Poppy glanced around. 'I don't believe this. It's like something out of the movies. Do we really need a search party?'

'A Blood Moon's always a bad omen, Poppy,' Miff said. 'Better to be safe than sorry.'

'She did only arrive here yesterday,' Cleo said, getting to her feet. 'She may've wandered off and got lost.'

'Not you too? She's got a phone, hasn't she? If she's lost, she'll call. And she's a grown woman, not a twelve-year-old. Oh bloody hell.' Poppy put her plate on the throw, stood up and followed Cleo and the others, only to turn back to grab a chocolate brownie. 'Sustenance, Miff. In case it's a long search. Oi! Wait for me.'

This was ridiculous. Instead of eating, drinking, dancing and generally having fun, everyone was now searching for sodding Stephanie Blackwood. She'd throw the bloody woman over the cliff herself if she found her. Where had she seen her last? Wasn't it over near the ninety steps down to the cove?

Poppy glanced in that direction. The others appeared to be covering everywhere else, so she'd go there. But there was no way she was running down all those steps and back up again. Not for anyone.

She reached the top of the steps and peered down. The sea resembled a lake tonight, almost silver in the light from the moon, giving the impression that one could skate to the horizon, and so calm that the incoming tide merely whispered on the sand. It was beautiful. Breathtakingly so.

Something caught her eye. Was that a figure on the shore? Two figures? One staring out to sea, the other walking towards the first. Was one of them Stephanie? She couldn't quite make them out but it looked as if one of them was a woman.

'Anything?'

Ryan's concerned voice made her heart pound as she spun round to face him.

'Bloody hell! You scared the life out of me. Where did you come from?'

'The house. There's no sign of her. I didn't intend to frighten you. Have you seen anything?'

'Why are you making such a fuss? She's a grown up. Can't she go for a walk on her own if she wants to? I don't understand why you need a search party.'

He looked her directly in the eye. 'You're right. You don't understand. Have you seen her or not?'

Was that fear in those usually cool, blue eyes? Or irritation because he was having to put himself out to do something for someone else?

Poppy tutted. 'As a matter of fact, I think I have. Down there.'

He came and stood beside her, peering in the direction her finger was pointing.

Did he always have to smell so good? Did he have to stand so close? Did he have to look so—?

'Stephanie?' His voice nearly deafened her. 'Stephanie, is that you?'

Poppy couldn't see if either figure heard him – although they'd have to be deaf not to – but the one walking, stopped for a second before continuing.

Without as much as a glance in her direction, he said: 'Find Toby. Tell him to come to the cove.' Then he was running down the illuminated steps as if Stephanie's life depended on it.

'Don't you mean: "Please"? Oh what's the point? The guy's a jerk.'

She watched him for several seconds before heading back towards the house. Ryan Blackwood definitely had a

79

problem but she'd find Toby and give him the message anyway. Just in case.

Chapter Nine

'Well it's been a pretty eventful night so far,' Poppy said, lying on a throw and staring up at the moon which had just begun to turn red. 'But not in the way I was hoping. What d'you think that Stephanie business was all about?'

'Haven't got a clue,' Cleo replied, her head resting against Poppy's shoulder. 'What did Toby say?'

'Before repulsive Ryan sent him and Stephanie home like naughty children, you mean?'

'He didn't actually send them, Poppy. I told you. When they came back from the cove, Stephanie said she didn't feel well and Toby offered to take her home.'

'Yes. And Jules went with them because she was tired. Yeah, right. They all went home except Ryan. Why did he stay?'

'Why don't you ask him? Did you see the size of that guy who came with the chauffeur to pick them up? He was about fifteen feet tall and just as wide. He looked like a bouncer or something. And the chauffeur's not exactly small.'

'No, I missed that. Toby didn't even say good night.'

'He did. Via Sophie.'

'Did I hear my name?' Sophie came and sat on the throw, handing Poppy three champagne glasses. 'Hold these whilst I pour.' Poppy sat up and Sophie popped the cork and poured the wine. 'Thaddeus, Oliver, Ben and Ryan are just coming but I told them to bring their own drinks. So, have I missed anything?'

'Nope,' Poppy said. 'I thought this lunar eclipse thing would be way more exciting than it is. It's very pretty but very slow. I'm tempted to go home to bed and watch the highlights on the news tomorrow.'

'Heathen,' Cleo said, sitting up, taking a glass of champagne and knocking it back in several large gulps. 'God, you don't know how glad I am to still be able to drink this stuff. May I have another?'

Sophie raised perfectly arched brows. 'Thirsty?'

Cleo grinned. 'You have no idea.'

'She thought she was pregnant,' Poppy explained. 'But it turns out she's just getting fat.'

'What!' Sophie exclaimed. 'When? How?'

'Really? You need us to explain how?'

Sophie tutted. 'Don't be facetious, Poppy. You know what I meant.'

'Don't say anything to Thaddeus,' Cleo said. 'Or to Oliver for that matter. I haven't told him. I felt sick this morning and what with the weight gain...' She shrugged. 'I just wanted to be sure, so I bought a test. It was negative.'

'Oh,' Sophie said. 'How do you feel about that?'

Cleo raised her glass of champagne in a toast. 'How do you think I feel? Here's to not being pregnant.'

'I'd love to have a kid,' Sophie said.

'So would I. But not at the moment. And as silly as this sounds, I'd like to be married. Or at least engaged, first. Not for moral reasons or anything like that. I want to experience the thrill of Oliver proposing. And then walking down the aisle. Perhaps it's just me but I think those things sort of pale into the background once you've had a child.'

'I get that,' Sophie said. 'You put your child's needs before your own. And getting engaged and married should be all about you. Well, you and your other half.'

'Exactly,' Cleo said.

Poppy sighed. 'The way my love life is going. I'll never have an "other half" to think about.'

'You will, Poppy,' Cleo replied. 'The right man for you is out there somewhere.'

'Hmm. The right man for me is currently at home with his sister. Thanks to repulsive Ryan.'

'Speaking of whom…' Sophie said. 'And you promised not to call him that.'

'It's all happening tonight.' Thaddeus was walking briskly towards them with Ryan by his side. 'The alarm's gone off at Ben's gallery. Don't worry, nothing serious. They think it's a fault with the new wiring but he's gone to check. Clara's hurt her ankle. Don't panic Cleo, she's fine but Paul's taken her home. What else? I think that's it… for now.'

'Bloody hell!' Poppy exclaimed. 'Perhaps Miff was right about a Blood Moon being a bad omen or whatever.' She glared at Ryan. 'And it certainly hasn't done me any favours.'

'Where's Oliver?' Cleo asked. 'Ben didn't drag him off with him, did he?'

Thaddeus shook his head. 'No he's… he's in the house with the others. Julia and Hugh and Veronique and Tony. He'll be out soon, I think. Move over Poppy and let Ryan sit down.'

'I'm fine,' Ryan said. 'Don't worry about me.'

'Don't you need to go home and check on Stephanie?' Poppy asked. 'After all, you did have us all running around looking for her. You seemed really worried. Aren't you worried now?'

'No. Toby's with her. And Jules. She doesn't need me.'

'But you're the eldest. Surely it would've been better if you'd gone, instead of Toby?'

He regarded her with knowing eyes. 'Some people

83

might think that but they'd be wrong. Stephanie would rather be with Toby.'

'That I can believe.' From the corner of her eye Poppy saw the look Sophie was giving her and hastily added: 'They seem very close. I don't suppose there's much difference between them age-wise.'

'There isn't,' he said. 'Stephanie's thirty-two. Toby's only thirty, but I expect you knew that.'

The arrogant bastard. He was baiting her. "Toby's only thirty". How dare he? He might as well have added: 'So he's too young for you.' Well, she didn't care what he thought.

'I'm bored,' she said. 'Is it okay if I make some coffee, Sophie?'

'Yes, of course. You know where everything is. Help yourself.'

'Anyone else want coffee?' Poppy asked, getting up.

'I'd love some,' Ryan said, and the look he gave her was clearly a challenge.

She smiled. 'Anyone else?'

There were no other takers so Poppy made her way towards the house. She half expected Ryan to follow but when she glanced back, he had taken her place on the throw. God, he made her mad. First he sends her 'boyfriend' home then he sends her to get him coffee. Who did the man think he was? He could get his own coffee. She'd make herself some and go and talk to Julia and Hugh and Veronique and Tony.

Shoving the kitchen door open with some force, she came face-to-face with Oliver, who looked as if he'd seen a ghost.

'What's up with you? You look like you've been caught stealing the family jewels. You're not are you?'

'Cleo's not with you, is she?'

84

Poppy looked all around and opened and closed the door. 'Not as far as I can see. Unless she's invisible.'

'Why does everything have to be a bloody joke with you? You could've just said no.'

'Okay, calm down. It was obvious she wasn't with me. I wouldn't have let the door shut in her face, would I? What's wrong?'

Oliver wiped the back of his hand across his forehead. 'I can't tie this fucking bow, that's what's wrong. And now there's a knot in the middle of it.' He waved what looked like a piece of red silk in the air. 'But don't you dare say a thing. This was meant to be a surprise. I've been planning this for days. Only now I don't know what to do and I can't even tie a simple bow. I thought it would be romantic. Red's the colour of passion, right? How would I know it's called a Blood Moon? Well okay, perhaps I've heard it called that in the past. But I didn't think that was bad. I didn't know it was a bad omen. I had this whole speech planned. About how my passion had turned the moon red and... Oh shit. That sounded so much better in my head.' He flopped onto a chair, propped his arms on the table and dropped his head in his hands.

'Are you saying what I think you are? Are you... proposing? Oh, Oliver. I didn't know you cared.' Poppy clasped her hands together and placed them in front of her heart.

Oliver turned his face towards her and gave her a feeble grin. 'I don't, you silly mare. And at this point in time, I don't think I can go through with it. She'll be upset, won't she? If I propose when there's some portent of doom in the heavens.'

'Oliver!' Poppy walked across the room and put an arm around his shoulder. 'Cleo won't give a damn about portents of doom, or anything else for that matter once you get down on one knee. You are going to get down on one knee, aren't you?'

'I'd planned to. Are you sure?'

'Absolutely. Cleo loves you, Oliver. And nothing, and I do mean nothing, would make her happier than if you propose to her tonight. Now what's this bow you can't tie?'

'A bow tie,' he said, holding the red, silk tie in the air. 'I tried to tie it but it got knotted so I came in here to get some scissors or something sharp to free the knot. I'm getting dressed up for the occasion.'

Poppy laughed. 'So I see. Don't give me that pathetic grin. You'll look gorgeous. How did you get it into a knot? Oliver, you can't tie this and then put it on. It's not elasticated.'

'I'm not that stupid. I had it on but somehow one end got knotted.'

'Give it to me. I'll do it.'

'Thanks Poppy. I was originally planning to wait until the full eclipse but that's not for another hour or so and I'm worried that Cleo might be too tired by then. I talked to Thaddeus and he thinks I should do it before and then Cleo and I can watch the eclipse together as an engaged couple... or fall asleep together, which is the more likely scenario.'

'She'll be too excited to sleep. But she may want to do something else, if you get my meaning.' Poppy winked, picking at the knot.

'I'll be too tired to do that. And too bloody stressed. I'm sure she'll say yes. But what if she says no?'

'You silly sod. She's not going to say no. There. All done. Now put your jacket on and let me do up this tie.'

He slid the black tuxedo jacket across his broad shoulders and Poppy tied the tie.

'Do I look okay?'

'You know what, Oliver? You look better than okay. You look absolutely perfect. Er. Just one thing. You do have a ring, don't you?'

'Of course I have a ring. You remember when Sophie opened the chest containing the Summerhill treasure and Cleo saw that ring?'

'The one with the huge ruby surrounded by diamonds? It fell out and landed at her feet, didn't it?'

'That's the one. Well Sophie, let's say, sold it to me for a very, very good price.' He pulled the ring out from his pocket and held it up in front of Poppy.

'Oliver!' Poppy gasped. 'It's beautiful. Especially since you've obviously had it cleaned. This will outshine the moon. Hey! Why don't you do a practice run with me? And let's face it, the way things are going, it'll be the only time anyone will ever propose to me.'

Oliver looked a little doubtful. 'Well... It's not bad luck or anything, is it?'

'Not as far as I know.'

'Right. Okay. I'll get down on one knee like this and then I'll—'

'I don't think we need a running commentary, Oliver. Just say what you're going to say to Cleo.'

He held up the ring and took her left hand in his. At that moment the kitchen door swung open and Ryan loomed in the doorway, a look of bewilderment on his face.

'Forgive me, but I thought you lived with Cleo,' he said, a deep furrow forming between his brows.

Oliver leapt to his feet and the ring flew out of his hand.

'Now look what you've done,' Poppy snapped. 'He does live with Cleo. He was practising, that's all. Not that it's any of your business. Did you see where it went, Oliver?'

Oliver shook his head and searched with frantic eyes.

'I came in for that coffee,' Ryan said.

87

'Really? No one cares. Why don't you make yourself useful and help us look for the ring?'

Ryan shook his head, walked over to a wicker basket containing bread and offered it to Poppy.

'Are you completely mad? I don't want bread! I want to find Cleo's ring.'

He sighed, put his hand in the basket and pulled out the ring, holding it in front of her between his forefinger and thumb. 'But you may want this. And no, this doesn't mean we're engaged.'

Poppy stared at it, as did Oliver.

'Don't give it to me,' she said. 'I don't want it. Give it to Oliver.'

Ryan's lips twitched. 'I'm afraid he's not my type,' he said, before walking over to Oliver, who seemed unable to move, and handing him the ring. 'Yours, I believe.'

'Shit!' Oliver said. 'Thank God you saw where it went. I would never have thought of looking there. I think I'd better go and propose before anything else happens. I'm beginning to think Miff was right. '

'Um. I know you're excited, Oliver but I think that's your phone. At least, I hope it's your phone.' Poppy nodded towards Oliver's vibrating trouser pocket.

Oliver glanced down, threw Poppy an exasperated look and answered his phone.

'So,' Ryan said, leaning back against the worktop and shoving his hands into the pockets of his jeans. 'What does a man have to do to get a cup of coffee around here?'

'Make it himself,' Poppy said, with an exaggerated smile.

Ryan studied her face for a moment before smiling back. 'I can do that.'

'You won't believe this,' Oliver said, stuffing his phone back into his pocket and yanking his bow tie undone. 'That was Ben. It wasn't faulty wiring of the alarm that set it off; the power seems to have gone off to the gallery, the pub and possibly my restaurant, amongst others. Ben says that entire part of the promenade's in darkness, including the streetlights. I've got to go and check the freezers. I've got backup generators but I've got to go and check.'

'Oh, Oliver, no,' Poppy said. 'What about the proposal?'

Oliver shrugged. 'Even I can take a hint. Everything's gone wrong tonight. I'm not going to tempt fate further by proposing. This is the rest of our lives we're talking about. Cleo's and mine. I want it to be right. It can wait. I can wait. I'd better quickly get changed, go and tell her and then head to the restaurant. I don't want her to see me dressed up like a dog's dinner.'

'Is there anything I can do?' Poppy asked.

'It's none of my business,' Ryan said. 'But if Poppy will show me where they are, I can sort out the generators.'

Poppy wasn't sure she liked the idea of her and Ryan being alone together in the cellar of the restaurant, especially as it would be dark if the generators hadn't kicked in. But if it would help Oliver and Cleo, she'd do it.

Oliver shook his head. 'Thanks Ryan, and you, Poppy but I'd rather go myself. There may be other problems.' He trudged towards the door and disappeared into the hall.

'I didn't really believe any of that Blood Moon being a bad omen stuff but now I'm not so sure.' Poppy said. 'Poor Oliver. He said he'd been planning this for weeks. And poor Cleo. She'd be devastated if she knew.'

'You're not thinking of telling her, are you?'

'Of course I'm not. Oliver wants it to be a surprise. I just know... well, I just know how happy she would've been.'

'So she'd definitely have said yes?'

'Of course she would.'

Ryan shrugged. 'A man never knows. Not for sure. Not

until he actually asks.'

Poppy studied his face. 'That almost sounds as if you're speaking from experience. Did you propose to someone and she turned you down? Or... have you recently proposed? Are you engaged?'

He shook his head. 'No. Not me. But why do you look so surprised? Is that such an improbable notion?'

'Yes. It said that you... I mean, I think Toby mentioned that marriage didn't interest you.'

'Did he?' His gaze was fixed on her. 'Now that surprises me.'

'It... might not've been Toby. I might've heard it from someone else.'

'Perhaps.'

'Is it... Is it true?'

'Does it matter?'

She cleared her throat. Was it getting warm in here? Or was it her imagination? Why did he have to look at her like that?

'Not to me,' she said.

'Then why did you ask?'

'Um... Just making conversation. But I think I'll make some coffee instead. D'you still want some?'

'Yes. And I'll even say please.'

Chapter Ten

'I can't believe it's the first of October and I haven't heard a word from Toby,' Poppy said, hunched over Clara's oak dining room table. 'Repulsive Ryan was supposed to have left yesterday, so it can't even be because that jerk is stopping Toby from calling me.'

'Ryan's gone?' Clara asked, passing Poppy a large slice of carrot cake.

'As far as I know, yes.'

'Give the man a chance,' Cleo said, pouring tea for the three of them. 'It's only been a couple of days. I'm sure he'll call.'

'But I'm running out of time. It'll be Christmas before we know it and there's no way in hell I'm going to be alone this Christmas.'

'You won't be alone,' Cleo said. 'You've got us. You'll never be alone.'

'Really? I love you all, you know that, but it's not the same as having a man of my own to cuddle up with, is it? I can picture it now. It's snowing, we're all at Sophie's, there's a massive tree surrounded by presents, Silas is curled up on the rug next to Cleover – yes, even they get on together. There're carol singers outside with flickering lanterns in their hands, the smell of mince pies baking in the oven, the clink of sherry glasses. You and Oliver, Sophie and Thaddeus, Clara and Paul, Julia and Hugh,

Veronique and Tony... Need I go on? You're all cuddled up in pairs on every available chair. And then there's me. Sitting on my own on the floor, roasting chestnuts on the fire for want of anything better to do with my hands.'

Cleo laughed. 'I can't see you roasting chestnuts, somehow. And since when have any of us, other than GJ and Miff and possibly Mary and Christopher, ever drunk sherry?'

'And aren't you forgetting someone?' Clara said. 'Ben doesn't have anyone either. So there'll be you and him.'

'Thanks very much. I think that's just made things worse.'

'You could always call him,' Clara suggested.

'I hope you don't mean Ben.'

Clara grinned. 'Of course I didn't and you know it. I meant Toby. You could call him.'

'And say what exactly? "Hello Toby, it's Poppy. Why haven't you called me, you pillock?" Or words to that effect.'

'No. You could ask him out for a drink. Or better still, you could call and say you wondered how his sister is. That way it wouldn't sound as if you're desperate and it would make him think you're a kind and caring person.'

'I *am* a kind and caring person. Most of the time.'

Clara reached out and squeezed Poppy's hand. 'I know you are, dear. But Toby may not. There's no harm in showing other people that beneath that sharp-tongued, fun-loving exterior, there's a heart of gold.'

Poppy grinned. 'Well, I wouldn't go that far. I'm not sure my heart's made of gold. But I'm not going to call Toby. He should call me.'

'On the subject of gold,' Cleo said, her eyes glowing with excitement and her cheeks flushed. 'I think Oliver may be about to propose.'

Poppy choked on her tea.

'Oh Cleo! That's wonderful,' Clara said.

'What makes you think that?' Poppy queried when she'd stopped coughing. 'Has he said anything? You thought you were pregnant the other day and look how wrong you were about that.'

Now Clara choked. 'You thought you were pregnant! When? How?'

Poppy tutted. 'Not another one who doesn't know how? I know Paul's a vicar but—'

'Stop right there, Poppy,' Clara said, laughter in her eyes. 'You know very well what I meant. So Cleo, have you been to the doctor? Was it negative?'

Cleo shook her head. 'I did one of those home pregnancy tests the other day because I thought there was a chance I might be. There's been so much going on lately and I do sometimes forget to take my pill first thing in the morning. But anyway, I'm not.' She shrugged. 'Which is a good thing. It really is.'

Clara leant over and hugged her daughter. 'There's plenty of time, darling.'

'I know there is,' Cleo said. 'I'm glad it was negative. Honestly I am. It's too soon to be starting a family.'

Poppy suddenly realised that her best friend was lying, possibly even to herself.

'You're not saying that's why you think Oliver may be about to propose, are you?' Clara asked, looking doubtful.

Cleo shook her head. 'No. Oliver doesn't know about it. I didn't want to give him anything else to worry about – unless it was positive, of course. And it wasn't.'

'I understand,' Clara said. 'But at least his mum's fine now, so that's one less thing on his mind. I'm having lunch with Mary on Saturday so it'll be interesting to see if she knows anything about a proposal.'

'You think he'll tell his mum before he asks Cleo?'

'No, Poppy, I don't.' Clara said, smiling. 'But Mary can read her son's mind at times, I swear she can. I'll let you know if she says anything, Cleo. Unless you'd rather it were a surprise.'

Cleo appeared to consider the question for a moment.

'Er. Isn't that your phone, Poppy?' Clara said, nodding towards Poppy's ringing handbag.

Poppy grabbed it and pulled out her phone. She recognised the number from his previous call and she smiled at the others.

'Hello. Oh hi, Toby. This is a lovely surprise. How are you?'

'Hello Poppy. I'm fine thanks. And much better for hearing your voice again. I was wondering if you'd like to have dinner this Saturday.'

She was tempted to make a facetious remark along the lines of her liking to have dinner most days but this wasn't the time for sarcasm.

'I'd love to.' She gave a thumbs up sign to Cleo and Clara who were watching her intently.

'That's great. We'll pick you up at eight. Is that okay? '

He'd said: "We". Did that mean he'd be using the chauffeur? Was he picking her up in the limo? Something told her to clarify.

'We?'

'Oh,' Toby said. 'Um… Je te verrai samedi, mon amour.'

'What? Did you just say something in French?'

'Yes, I said, 'I'll see you Saturday, my love.' After you said, "Oui".'

'I didn't say, "Oui". I said, "we" as in more than one person.'

'I thought you were being sexy by speaking French.

Don't you speak French?'

What was he going on about? He'd said that as if he thought everyone spoke French.

'Non. And that's the limit of my French. Why would I need to speak French to be sexy? I can be sexy in English. In fact, I can be sexy using no words at all... just... body language.' She placed her hand over the speaker so that Toby couldn't hear and shook her head at Cleo and Clara who were giving her very odd looks. 'I really know how to pick them.'

'That sounded pretty damn sexy to me,' Toby was saying. 'Now I really can't wait until Saturday.'

'Nor can I, Toby. But you didn't answer my question. You said 'we' – and don't start the whole French thing again, please. Um. When you said Ryan wanted Jules to chaperone you, that was a joke, wasn't it? She's not coming with us, is she?'

'I'll save the French for Saturday then,' he said. 'And no, it wasn't a joke. Ryan has brought her here to keep an eye on us and report back to him, I'm sure of that. But don't worry, Jules won't be coming to dinner. It'll just be you, me, Stephanie and her new friend, whose name I can't remember for the life of me.'

Surely she couldn't have heard that correctly.

'Did you just say that Stephanie and a friend are coming with us?'

'Yes. You remember when she wandered off the other night? Well, she met someone on the beach. They only exchanged a few words because Ryan charged in, as he does, and by the time I got there, he was gone. But she saw him again yesterday and they had coffee together. Now, we're going on a double date. Won't that be fun?'

Poppy flopped down on the chair. 'Oh Oui. Lots and lots of fun.'

'I knew you'd think so. See you Saturday.'

Poppy tossed her phone on the table. 'I think you're right, Cleo. I do have crap taste in men. We're going on a date with his sister and some guy she's just met. Won't that be nice?'

Cleo smiled sympathetically. 'Actually, it is nice. It means Toby's a decent guy, that he cares about his sister and also, that he wants you and her to get to know one another. There's nothing wrong with that.'

'I agree,' Clara said. 'It means he's kind and considerate. It also shows that family's important to him. And that's an added bonus.'

'I suppose you're both right.'

'We are,' Cleo said, decisively. 'Stephanie's very lucky to have a brother like Toby.'

'Yeah. I don't suppose repulsive Ryan would even think about taking his sister on one of his dates,' Poppy said.

For some reason, that didn't make her feel any happier.

Chapter Eleven

Poppy walked into the restaurant and froze. She couldn't believe her eyes. The evening had already got off to a bad start and now this. Perhaps she should just call it quits and go home.

From the moment she had asked the chauffeur his name – which he'd told her with a smile, was Doug – Stephanie had scowled at her. And she'd been scowling ever since.

'Don't get too friendly with him,' Stephanie had told her when Doug closed the limo door and made his way round to the driver's seat. 'He's Ryan's man. Everything we say and do gets reported back.'

Not even Poppy could believe Ryan was that oppressive... although he had gone overboard when Stephanie had wandered off during the evening of the Blood Moon.

'Really? Well, let's give him something to report then,' Poppy said, with a wink and what she hoped was a friendly grin.

'I'd rather not,' Stephanie replied coolly. 'And nor would Toby. You've got a lot to learn about this family.'

'Stephanie's right,' Toby confirmed. 'It's probably best not to rock the boat for the time being. You look lovely by the way.'

'Thanks.'

Poppy hadn't been able to think of anything else to say, so she'd said nothing further, and nor had Toby or Stephanie. For the entire five-minute journey from her cottage to Sutton's restaurant, all three of them had merely stared at the passing scenery.

And now this.

Timothy sodding Richards was Stephanie's new friend. Could this evening get any worse?

At least he didn't look any happier about the situation than Poppy but he quickly adopted a smile as he stood up to greet them.

'Hello Poppy,' he said. 'I wasn't expecting to see you tonight.'

'Same here,' Poppy replied.

'Do you two know each other?' Stephanie sounded even less friendly than she'd been in the limo.

'It's such a small place,' Toby said. 'I wouldn't be surprised if everyone knows everyone else in Goldebury Bay.'

'And if the other night was anything to go by,' Stephanie said, 'most of them are related.'

Poppy was very tempted to stick out her foot so that Stephanie would trip over it as she strode towards the table. Timothy was beginning to look like a nice guy in comparison to Stephanie Blackwood. This was going to be a long night. A very long night.

'What would you like to drink, Poppy?' Toby asked as they joined Timothy.

'White wine, please. A barrel of it.'

Toby grinned. 'One barrel of white wine coming up. And you, Stephanie?'

'I prefer red,' she said, sliding into the padded bench seat opposite Timothy.

'We'll have both,' Toby said. 'Hello, Timothy. I'm Toby, Stephanie's younger brother. I'm very pleased to meet you. I just missed you the other night in the cove. What would you like to drink?'

'Likewise and I'm fine at the moment, thanks.' He picked up a glass containing ice and a clear liquid and took a gulp. 'I've started without you. I was early.'

Poppy had to decide which was the lesser of two evils. Sitting beside Stephanie or next to Timothy. She picked the devil she knew and Timothy budged up slightly to give her more room, grinning as he did so.

'Well, this is cosy,' he said.

'That's not quite the word I'd have used to describe it,' replied Poppy.

A waiter called Dave, whom Poppy knew of course, promptly came and took the drinks order, returning moments later with a bottle each of red and white wine. Toby, like his sister, was drinking red, which meant that Poppy would have a bottle to herself, unless of course Timothy wanted white wine with his meal. She really hoped he wouldn't. She had a feeling she'd need the entire bottle to get her through this date.

'Stephanie tells me you've written a book, Timothy,' Toby said. 'And that several publishers are bidding on it.'

'Yeah. I'm pretty certain it's going to be a bestseller. It's got everything – drugs, piracy, smuggling, love, lust and betrayal. Not to mention witchcraft, mystery and murder. There's even a search for a long-lost treasure. And it's all based on fact.'

'Fiction more like,' Poppy said.

Timothy looked directly at her and smiled. 'I was going to tell you this the other day when we had coffee but as you were having so much fun at my expense, I didn't. You may be interested to know that I've now changed the names, to protect the… not so innocent and turned it into a novel rather than keeping it as a biography. I've even altered the setting. The story now unfolds in a place called 'Black Beach Cove'. It was my agent's idea. I'm not sure about it.'

99

Poppy couldn't believe it. 'You've changed the names? When did you do that? You should've told me. I might've been nicer.'

He shrugged and took a large gulp of his drink. 'I didn't want to spoil your fun. Besides, I was quite enjoying our little banter.'

'So... there's nothing to directly link the book to Thaddeus or his family, or Sophie. Or anyone else in Goldebury Bay?'

He shook his head. 'Nothing. Don't get me wrong, I'm no saint. I didn't do it for the Beaumonts and the Summerhills, or anyone else for that matter. I did it because Sophie's lawyer, that Tony Hardman guy, had a quiet word with me. To paraphrase, he mentioned the libel laws in this country and how off-putting it can be to publishers if they hear whispers of possible libel actions waiting in the wings. I was tempted to ignore that, but when he started talking about injunctions and such, together with the possibility of long delays, I decided it was easier to turn the thing into a novel. And I'm rather glad I did, as it happens because I've had far more interest since. My agent even thinks she can sell the film rights. I can almost see Johnny Depp playing Barnabas Beaumont, can't you?'

'No. I can't see Johnny Depp wanting anything to do with your book. But I am glad you've changed it. I suppose I should say thanks but I'm not going to.'

He smiled. 'I wouldn't expect you to. Some people will still know, Poppy. They'll guess it's about the Beaumonts and the trials. And Sophie's recent find is being talked about everywhere. Once she decides which museum to sell the majority of the treasure to, it'll be an even bigger story.'

'I'm sure this is all very interesting,' Stephanie said. 'But I think it's you two who should be on a date. It appears we're in the way, Toby.'

'I'm so sorry, Stephanie,' Timothy said, looking genuinely apologetic.

'I wouldn't go on a date with him if he were the last man on earth,' Poppy said, realising too late that her comment didn't reflect well on Stephanie's taste in men.

Toby frowned, glancing at Stephanie before focusing his attention on Poppy. 'Well, this is awkward. Does this mean that you two don't really get along? I wish I'd known. I didn't even think to ask. I'm not quite sure what we should do now.'

Was it too late for her to salvage this date?

'We don't hate each other,' she said. 'We even had coffee together the other day. I'm sure we can manage an evening in one another's company without coming to blows. Can't we Timothy?'

'Of course we can,' Timothy said, looking almost as anxious as Poppy.

'As delightful as that sounds,' Stephanie said. 'I was hoping to have a pleasant evening out, not be in the centre of some petty squabble.'

Poppy really didn't like Toby's relatives. Stephanie was as bad as Ryan.

'It's not a "petty squabble",' Poppy said. 'And I think we were all hoping to have a pleasant evening out. We still can. I haven't got a problem. Have you, Timothy?'

Timothy shook his head. 'None whatsoever. Let's start again, shall we?'

Stephanie and Toby clearly weren't convinced. Poppy looked around the packed restaurant. There was one empty table although it did have a reserved sign on it.

'There may be another alternative,' she said. 'Hold on and I'll be back in a minute.'

She knew Oliver was in the restaurant tonight but the kitchen was like Piccadilly Circus. The staff were toing and froing with a variety of food from fridges to sinks to worktops to hobs to ovens and finally, to plates. In the midst of all the hustle and bustle Oliver stood, calmly twirling fine strands of gooey, melted sugar around the handle of a wooden spoon whilst giving orders to his team.

Poppy made a loud groaning sound and Oliver glanced up.

'Oh, it's you,' he said, continuing to make the caramel sugar curls which would sit atop his delicate, chocolate lace cup desserts without the need to watch what he was doing. 'How's the date going?'

'Badly. To put it mildly. How d'you do that without looking? I burn myself with the hot sugar syrup unless I concentrate completely.'

He smiled. 'Years of practice. Why's the date going so badly? Cleo told me that it's a double date with his sister. Who's the other guy? Assuming it is a guy.'

'It's a guy. I suppose you could call him that. It's Timothy Richards.'

'Shit!' Oliver dropped a globule of hot sugar syrup on his hand.

'Sorry,' Poppy said. 'That's exactly what I do. It hurts, doesn't it?'

Oliver nodded and rinsed his hand under a tap whilst Poppy took over the process. She scooped up a spoonful of the hot syrup and holding the wooden spoon in the other hand, let the rich, brown liquid which resembled molten glass, trickle down onto the wooden handle which she twisted to make the curls.

Oliver poured himself a glass of water. 'When did she meet him? Oh wait, come to think of it, Ryan told us that she was talking to someone in the cove the other night when he got down to her. He asked us afterwards if we knew a writer called Timothy Richards. So the guy asked her out that night? Wow. Was it love at first sight or something?'

'More a matter of two evil spirits recognising one of their own, in my opinion. Here, you'd better do this or I'll end up burning myself. So what did you say to Ryan about him? And whilst we're on the subject, I keep meaning to ask why you were all talking about me in Thaddeus' study. And more to the point, what you were saying.'

Oliver grinned. 'We told him the truth about Timothy. That the guy used to be a reporter and was good at his job – which basically meant he's a shit – and that he'd written a book based loosely on several past and present residents of Goldebury Bay. As for talking about you, I honestly don't remember, other than Ryan asking if you were single and saying that he thought there was a very strong possibility that his brother would be asking you out. So why's the date going badly? Apart from the fact you're sharing it with Timothy Richards and you clearly don't like the sister.'

'Let's put it this way. A frozen chicken has a warmer personality than Stephanie. And Timothy and I started... debating shall we say, the merits of his book, much to her annoyance. That's why I'm here. Ooh, but I must tell you this first. Timothy's changed his book to a novel. It no longer claims to be biographical. Isn't that great?'

'Shit. What made him do that?'

Poppy smiled. 'Tony Hardman – and the thought of losing money. Anyway, the restaurant's packed, apart from one table and that's marked 'reserved'. Is there any chance you're just saving that in case any of the family come in? I know you sometimes do that.'

Oliver shook his head. 'I wasn't, not tonight. We were fully booked. But you're lucky. Someone cancelled about ten minutes ago. I just haven't told the staff to remove the sign. Why?'

'Can I have it? I want to suggest we split up. Stephanie and Timothy can stay where they are and Toby and I'll have the reserved table. Is that okay?'

Oliver shrugged. 'It's fine by me.' He glanced up and grinned. 'But I'm not sure how your co-daters will take it.'

'Frankly Oliver, I don't give a damn how they take it. Thanks a lot.' She turned to leave but stopped and glanced back. 'By the way, Cleo told Clara and me the other day that she thinks you may be about to propose. And before you say anything, I haven't said a word. But you are still going to, aren't you?'

'Of course I am. But what made her think that I was?'

'No idea. Except when I saw you in the kitchen that night you looked like you were about to explode with a mixture of excitement and fear. Perhaps you've been acting a little strangely and she's picked up on that. I just thought I'd mention it. Thanks for the table. Any chance you could put some arsenic in Stephanie's food?'

'Thanks for the heads up. But no, to the arsenic.'

Poppy tutted. 'And you call yourself a friend.'

Chapter Twelve

To Poppy's surprise, Stephanie, Timothy and Toby were more than happy to go along with her suggestion. Stephanie even smiled when Poppy said that she and Toby would move to the other table.

'I think that's an excellent idea,' Stephanie said. 'That way we can all enjoy ourselves.'

'I'll see you later,' Toby said, winking at his sister. 'Have fun, you two. But don't forget the car's coming for us at eleven.'

'How could I forget?' Stephanie said.

'We're leaving at eleven?' Poppy queried as she and Toby changed tables. 'You've certainly planned ahead.'

Toby sat opposite her, suddenly looking a little deflated. 'I'll order more wine. We'll let Stephanie and Timothy keep those. As for planning ahead, it wasn't my choice. Ryan called this morning. He wants me to join him in Dubai. They're sending the jet. I've got to be at the airport by twelve-thirty at the latest.'

'Ryan's got a private jet? And he's making you go to Dubai? Tonight?' Poppy couldn't believe it.

Toby nodded. 'Technically, tomorrow but yes, he's insisting I go. The jet belongs to one of Ryan's companies and he shares it with his co-director, so it's not exactly his. I'm really sorry, Poppy. It's good though. He wanted me to go this afternoon but I told him I had a date with you and I couldn't go until tomorrow.' Toby shrugged. 'He said we'd compromise. I could go on the date but I'd have to leave straight after.'

'Who the hell does that man think he is? Sorry. I know he's your brother, but honestly! You're not fifteen years old. Couldn't you have said that you'd leave at seven or something?'

'I tried. But Dubai's three hours ahead and the flight'll take around six and a half hours. He wants me there for a meeting in the morning, so I've got to go tonight.'

'But it's Sunday tomorrow.'

Again, Toby shrugged. 'That doesn't bother Ryan. Every day of the week's the same to him. It's business as usual. I think the only day he ever takes off is Christmas Day and even then he'll be on the phone or checking messages. Nothing matters to him except making money.'

'How awful. But... that's not strictly true, is it? You and Stephanie seem to matter to him. She said in the limo that he gets Doug to report back your every move, and I thought he was going to have a heart attack on Sunday when she wandered off.'

Another shrug. Toby's limited body language was beginning to irritate her.

'Stephanie's made some choices Ryan didn't agree with. He's determined she won't repeat them. I suppose he has her best interest at heart – and mine too for that matter – but the problem with Ryan is, he always thinks he knows what's best for us, whether we agree or not. Mum left when Stephanie and I were very young. Dad died not long after, so Ryan sort of took on the role of parent. We moved in with Jules but Ryan made all the decisions even then.'

'I'm so sorry, Toby. How old were you?'

Yet another shrug but under the circumstances, Poppy forgave this one.

'I was two when Mum left, which made Stephanie four and Ryan, eleven. Dad died about eighteen months after. He was a builder and he fell off a scaffold.'

106

'Oh God, Toby. I'm really, really sorry. That's dreadful.'

'Life's like that sometimes. The worst part was Dad didn't have any life insurance. He and his brother Joe jointly owned the building firm and in those days, it was just the two of them. There was a bit of money in the bank, and our Uncle Joe helped out, but things were pretty dire. Jules worked in a pub and had no money to speak of. She got extra work as a waitress and later, as a croupier, to help make ends meet. We still struggled though. Then Ryan made his first big deal and the Blackwoods haven't looked back since. Not that I knew much about the ins and outs back then of course because I was young, but I was well aware that we were poor and Jules likes to remind us, from time to time.'

'Are you ready to order?' Dave, their waiter, asked.

'Sorry Dave. No. Give us a moment,' Poppy said.

He smiled. 'No problem, Poppy. Call me when you're ready.'

'I've been doing too much talking,' Toby said. 'And we'd better get a move on I suppose. I've got to leave in less than three hours.' He scanned the menu, closed it and stared directly at Poppy. 'I know what I want.'

She got the distinct impression that he wasn't just talking about food and his next words confirmed it.

'You could always come with me. To Dubai I mean. We're staying at the Burj Al Arab Hotel, which I bet you've heard of. It's pretty special. We'll be in meetings most of the time, knowing Ryan, but my nights will be free.' He reached across the table and took her hand in his. 'And it wouldn't cost you a penny. I'll even make sure you've got money to spend whilst I'm working. There're some fabulous shops. In fact, you don't even have to pack. We'll buy everything you need when we get there. What d'you say Poppy? Will you come?'

Chapter Thirteen

'Just think,' Poppy said. 'I could be sunning myself by a pool right now, wearing an expensive, new bikini and drinking an almost equally expensive cocktail, shaded from the scorching midday sun by a parasol. Instead, it's nine a.m., I'm wearing a plastic apron and I'm gutting fish, having got soaked on my way to the restaurant this morning. I'm beginning to think I made a huge mistake by saying no to Toby.'

Cleo laughed. 'And you could've been having sex every night for the past week. Did you forget about that part?'

'I've been thinking about nothing but that *part*... and the rest of him of course, ever since he asked me.'

Cleo grinned and looked Poppy directly in the eye. 'Why didn't you go? You said you were crazy about the guy. Plus, you don't want to be alone for Christmas. After two weeks of sex in the sun, you would've established a pretty good relationship... or not, depending on how good the sex was and how well the two of you got on.'

'Yeah, and I was seriously tempted, believe me. If only to see the expression on repulsive Ryan's face when I stepped out of the private jet with his brother. But I couldn't go. This place is so busy and then there's the pub. I couldn't just tell you and Oliver, along with Ben that I was hopping on a plane and had no idea when I'd be back.'

'Oh Poppy! That's not the only reason you didn't go, is it? Because if it is, you're a bigger fool than I think you are.' Cleo elbowed Poppy in the ribs. 'And as you know, I already think you're an idiot.' She smiled. 'Seriously though, none of us would want to stand in the way of you having fun.'

'I know. When he called me yesterday to say he'd be out there for another week, he asked if I'd like to change my mind. He said I could still go if I wanted to. All I had to do was say the word. Apparently, Stephanie and Jules are going out there tomorrow and Ryan's sending the jet for them.'

'Well then, go! You deserve to have some fun. You deserve to have some sex.'

'I totally agree. But it's too high a price to pay.'

'What is? It wouldn't cost you a thing. He said so. Besides, after so long without it, I'd have thought you'd be offering to pay him.'

'Oh, I would. But it's a six-and-a-half-hour flight and I'm not spending six and a half hours on a jet with just Stephanie, Jules, a pilot and one other crew member, no matter how much free sex is waiting for me at the other end.'

Cleo shook her head. 'If you want my opinion – and you're getting it anyway, so don't bother to comment – it sounds to me that you're not as crazy about Toby as you say you are.'

'I am. What I'm not crazy about is the baggage that comes with him. You get on so well with Oliver's family, and Thaddeus' lot are lovely – with the exception of his dad and one cousin, of course – so Sophie won't have any problems with them but I've got the prospect of Stephanie, Jules and repulsive Ryan in my future if Toby and I have a relationship, and that thought's enough to make me join a convent. I honestly don't think I can bring myself to like any of them.'

'Even after the things Toby told you about Ryan

virtually bringing him and Stephanie up with Jules' help? Doesn't that put Ryan in a different light? And you haven't said more than a few words to Jules, so you don't really know what she's like. Don't you think you'd get on? Especially as you have so much in common.'

'What? Both of us being barmaids, waitresses and having worked in casinos, you mean? I'm not sure that guarantees we're alike. All that says is that neither of us had any idea what we wanted to be and we both ended up doing jobs just to pay the bills.'

'Is that really how you feel? I thought you liked working here and in Ben's pub.'

'I do. But it's hardly rocket science, is it? Sometimes I just feel that there's more to life than this. Especially when I have to gut fish instead of lounging by a pool. Sorry. Forget it. I'm just in one of those moods.'

'Hmm. I'll make us some coffee and get you a chocolate brownie. Perhaps that'll cheer you up.' Cleo grabbed two large mugs and walked to the semi-automatic coffee machine. 'D'you think Stephanie has offered to take Timothy to Dubai?'

'I don't think so. I bumped into him yesterday in Betty's Pantry and he didn't say anything about jetting off to warmer climes. He did tell me something interesting though. Stephanie's married. Well, she's actually separated now. And it's not her first time. She's been married twice before.'

'You're kidding. She's younger than us.'

'Only by a year. But I know what you mean. Married three times by the age of thirty-two. And it sounds as if this one will also end in divorce.'

'If she's going out on dates with someone else, I should think so.' Cleo giggled as she placed a pile of deliciously gooey-looking chocolate brownies on a plate and slid it across the worktop towards Poppy. 'I can now understand why Ryan was so worried when she wandered off. He probably thought she'd gone to look for husband number four.'

Poppy laughed, washed her hands and carried the plate over to a table. 'And she found Timothy Richards. I almost feel sorry for the guy.' She sat and flopped back against the padded backrest. 'I know he wrote some awful stuff about Thaddeus' family during the trials but he doesn't seem quite so bad now, somehow. Especially since he's changed his book to a novel and removed all references to the Beaumonts and Summerhills.'

'True. He has redeemed himself slightly in all our eyes because of that.' Cleo brought the coffee over and sat opposite. 'You're not... interested in him, are you? Romantically, I mean.'

'God no. Although... he is very good looking and he does make me laugh. In a good way. Sometimes I laugh with him now, not just at him. And I suppose I could do a lot worse.'

'Stop right there,' Cleo said, her mug hovering just an inch or so from her lips. 'No matter how much the guy may have changed his ways, I don't think Thaddeus would ever accept him. Especially not after he made Jeremiah's affair public knowledge. Thaddeus's mum felt so humiliated, so Thaddeus told Oliver that she wouldn't even come back to meet Sophie or attend their moving in together party. Of course, Mercedes has got her new baby girl, so I don't suppose his mum wanted to leave her either. But even so.'

'I know. Thaddeus said he's hoping they'll all come back for Christmas. But as for me and Timothy, I don't think of him in that way at all. I still think Toby's the man for me. I've just got to get used to the fact that he comes with the rest of the Blackwoods. Although Stephanie's not

112

a Blackwood now. I can't believe she's had three husbands. I wonder what they were like and why the marriages failed.'

'I wonder why Toby didn't mention she'd been married three times. He told you about their parents, and growing up. He even told you that Ryan tries to stop them from making what he sees as mistakes. You'd have thought he would've said: "and Stephanie's already made three huge ones" or something like that.'

'You're right. That is odd. But perhaps she doesn't want people to know. She and Toby seem very close. He might've felt it wasn't his place to tell me.'

'And yet she told Timothy on their first date.'

'That's true.' Poppy took a refreshing gulp of coffee and picked up a chocolate brownie. 'You know, there's something very odd about that woman. I've got the strangest feeling that she's going to be trouble in ways we can't even imagine yet.'

Cleo raised her brows. 'Miff said the same thing on the night of the Blood Moon. Well, she said something along the lines of not seeing a weever fish buried in the sand until it stings you. I can't remember the exact words now. But the thing is, we all know weever fish are poisonous. Miff really didn't like Stephanie.'

'I don't think any of us liked Stephanie.'

Chapter Fourteen

It did nothing but rain every single day for the following week and by the end of it, Poppy would have willingly endured a six-and-a-half-hour flight with Stephanie and Jules just to see the sun. She didn't even care about the sex part anymore. Even the thought of being in Toby's arms paled in comparison to what it would feel like to have warm rays of sunlight caress her bare skin.

Leaning her elbows on the bar of The One That Got Away, she stared out the front window at the curtain of rain. It was like Niagara Falls out there. Not that she knew what Niagara Falls was like, never having been there but she had seen them on TV and with High Definition and Surround Sound that was virtually the same as having experienced the real thing, or so many people believed these days.

She stood upright and looked around for something to do but as she'd already spent the last hour doing everything that needed to be done, she knew that was a waste of time. The pub was emptier than an old saloon in a ghost town today and she wouldn't be at all surprised if she opened the door and a ball of tumbleweed rolled in. Okay, it was Sunday and teeming down outside but it was now midday. The pub had been open since eleven and other than two weekend visitors she hadn't seen a soul.

She'd known the couple, dressed in matching raincoats and odd-looking hats, weren't locals partly because she knew virtually everyone in Goldebury Bay now, at least by sight if not by name, and partly because they had said: "We 'ave ze warm bi-erre, non?"

She'd been tempted to reply: 'Non,' just to see what they said, but that had reminded her of that ridiculous conversation she'd had with Toby, and that she could have been basking in the sun instead of serving a couple of Frenchies. So she'd kept her sarcasm to herself and poured them the coldest beer she could find, on this, the wettest, coldest day of the year so far.

She let out a long sigh. Surely someone in Goldebury Bay fancied a decent pint and a packet of crisps. Someone. Anyone. She smiled and shook her head. God. She'd even be pleased to see Stephanie Blackwood-not-Blackwood-whatever-her-name-was, right now.

And that reminded her yet again of the sun she wasn't getting... and the sex. She glanced up at the row of large, circular metal lights hanging over the bar and, tipping her head back, she closed her eyes and leant against the timbered wall behind her. A girl could dream.

She could feel the warmth of the sun on her face, hear the gentle splish-splash of the azure waters lapping at the sides of the pool, smell the coconut oil of her suntan lotion and taste the cocktail she was about to drink... Wait. Was that rain she could hear? And a door—

'Are you meditating or did you have a late night?'

Her eyes shot open and so did her mouth. Ryan Blackwood was standing in the doorway and he looked so bright against the backdrop of the dismal weather, with the pub lights glinting in his red-brown hair, that he could have been an angel or something. The only disappointment was that he appeared to be alone as the door swung shut behind him with a resounding clonk.

'What the...?'

He raised his eyebrows and a smile crept across his lips.

115

'It's lovely to see you too, Poppy.'

'Humph! What could possibly have given you the idea that I'm pleased to see you?'

He grinned. 'My mistake.' Walking towards the bar, he glanced around. 'Tell me, has there been some sort of plague epidemic in Goldebury Bay which is keeping everyone in their homes? Or was it something you said? This place is quieter than a morgue.'

'Perhaps they all heard you might be popping in. What do you want?'

He shook his head and laughed. That same melodic sound she'd heard just a few times before.

'I see you haven't changed, Poppy. Remind me when Toby opens his hotel that I must employ you to train the staff in the art of customer service.'

'Toby's opening a hotel! Where? When?'

Again the raised eyebrows – a little more pronounced this time.

'Hasn't he told you? I am surprised. It's usually... but never mind that. Yes. Although he has to get it built first. As to where. It's a place dear to our hearts – yours and mine that is – the derelict Goldebury Bay Yachting and Sailing Club. When? God alone knows.'

'That place isn't dear to my heart. I suppose you were being sarcastic.'

'Actually, I wasn't. May I have a pint of beer... please? One of the local brews. I don't mind which. You decide.'

'Me? Hmm. If I'd known you were coming, I'd have ordered in some Deadly Nightshade but as I had no idea that such a treat lay in store, it'll have to be a pint of Goldebury Bay Gold, I suppose.'

She pulled a pint from the barrel and thumped it on the bar in front of him, sending little droplets of golden liquid up into the air, a couple of which landed on his hand as he held out a ten-pound note.

'Thanks,' he said, shaking his hand. He took a long drink from the glass before giving her an odd look. 'You have no idea how much I've missed this.'

'Yeah. I don't suppose the beer in Dubai tastes as good as real British ale.'

'I wasn't talking about the beer.'

She met his eyes. 'Oh?'

He grinned. 'I was referring to the British weather. It's so damned hot in Dubai.'

She turned away, retrieved a clean cloth from a small cupboard behind her and wiped the remaining spots of beer from the aged oak bar.

'Yeah, right. It must've been hell. Lounging by the pool, soaking up the sun. I'd swap this for Dubai any day of the week.'

'And yet you didn't.'

'What?'

'Swap. You had the opportunity and yet you didn't take it. Why was that?'

She didn't like the look he was giving her. She didn't like the question either.

'I can't afford to jet off to Dubai on a whim.'

'It wouldn't have cost you a penny.'

'Or even a United Arab Emirates dirham. Don't look so surprised. I Googled the currency.'

'In case you changed your mind?'

'No. Simply because I like to know these things.'

'Well. Then strictly speaking, a fils would be the nearest equivalent to a penny... but from the expression on your face, you don't want me to tell you that.'

'The man's a genius.'

'So I've been told. So why didn't you?'

'What? Hop on your private jet and let you whisk me

away. I mean, let Toby whisk me away.'

He blinked. 'Either option. Why didn't you come? I'm sure most women would've jumped at the chance.'

'It has probably escaped your notice but we women are not a herd of camels, or even a train or caravan of them, before you correct me. We're not all the same.'

'Herd is also correct. For camels, not women, before you snap my head off. And I have noticed. At least, I'm noticing now. But you still haven't answered my question and I'm getting the impression you don't want to. Why is that?'

'God! You're worse than an eight-year-old with your constant questions. I didn't go because I have a job. Two jobs, to be precise. And I don't like letting people down. Especially not when those people are my friends. On top of that, I like to pay my own way. Or as much as I can afford. And I can't afford Dubai. Not even one little 'fils' of it. Okay? Happy now?'

'More than you might expect. So... are you the kind of girl who insists on paying for her half when someone takes her out to dinner?'

'No. That's different.'

'How?'

'What is it with you? Don't you have anything better to do than interrogate me?'

He grinned. 'Not at this precise moment, no. Although I can think of several things I'd rather be doing, given the chance. And unlike you it seems, I'd take that chance if it were offered and I'd worry about the consequences later.'

'Bully for you. I can be spontaneous too, you know. I take chances all the time.'

'That's good to know. So why is a man paying for dinner different from a man... whisking you away to foreign climes?'

'Oh bloody hell! I don't know, okay? It just is.'

He smiled. 'One final question. If a man asked to take you to dinner in…Paris, let's say, would you be happy to go and not worry about paying your way?'

Poppy held his look. 'That would depend on which man was asking.'

'Let's say… Toby.'

'I'd still have to make sure it didn't clash with my work rota but yes… if Toby asked me I'd go and I wouldn't worry about it.'

First a smile, followed by a frown. 'So you'd go to Paris but not Dubai. I'm not following the logic of your argument.'

'I don't have an argument. I'm simply telling you what I'd do. Paris isn't far away. I could get back fairly easily from there. Dubai is on another continent. Paris would only be for dinner. Dubai would have been for a week – or two weeks, as it turned out.'

The frown deepened. 'So are you saying there's a limit on what you're willing to let a man spend on you? And how much time you're willing to give in return?'

'I'm not sure I like what you're insinuating. But actually, yes. Yes, there is. I'll admit it may not make sense to you but it does to me. And I only do what feels right to me. Toby's rich. To him, taking me to dinner in Paris is probably the equivalent of a guy from Goldebury Bay taking me to… oh I don't know. The Dead Llamas, Horse or Hamster.'

Ryan nearly spilt the glass of beer he was lifting to his lips.

'Taking you where?'

'Um. It's our favourite curry restaurant. It has a mixture of Tibetan, Nepalese and Indian dishes and its real name is The Dalai Lama's House of Heaven. It's owned by a Polish

119

couple who moved here from Warsaw, oddly enough. I just call it that because…' She shrugged. 'Well, because I do.'

The expression on his face was something between a broad smile and someone trying not to burst out laughing. He placed his glass on the bar and shook his head.

'Okay. So what you're actually saying is that you won't let a man spend more on you than he can really afford and that you need to know you're able to get yourself home from wherever that man takes you, should you feel the need.'

'All I'm saying is, if Toby asked me to go to dinner with him in Paris, I'd go… Probably. Er… where is he by the way?'

'Paris. Strange as that may seem.'

'What's he doing in Paris?'

Ryan glanced at his watch. 'Having lunch, I'd imagine.'

'You know what I meant. When… when's he coming back? He said he'd be back today.'

The door of the pub burst open and several of the locals piled in and headed to the bar, calling out friendly greetings to Poppy.

'It appears you have customers,' Ryan said. 'I'll see you soon, Poppy.'

He left his half-finished beer on the bar and marched towards the door before she could say another word.

Chapter Fifteen

Sophie passed Poppy a large glass of red wine before filling the other glasses on the coffee table, which was actually, the now empty, treasure chest, adapted for its current use by the addition of a piece of heavy-duty glass. They all agreed it was the tackiest coffee table imaginable, but they loved it. It reminded them all of how strange, yet wonderful, life can be sometimes.

'So what did Toby say when you called him?' Sophie asked.

'He said that he's as disappointed as I am and that he thought he was coming back today but Stephanie wanted to do some shopping in Paris – as you do – and Ryan wouldn't let her go unless Toby went with her.'

Cleo shook her head. 'Why couldn't Jules have gone? Or more to the point, Ryan, as he's the one laying down the law.'

'That's exactly what I said. Apparently Jules *has* gone but she says she's too old to wander around the shops all day so Ryan insisted Toby had to go too. Ryan, of course, has more important things to do. That's what Toby said, anyway.'

'That's ridiculous,' Clara said. 'Stephanie's a grown woman. Surely she can shop on her own. Unless what Ryan really meant was that he's afraid to let her loose with a credit card and wanted someone to watch the bank balance.'

'I think that's what he's so busy doing,' Poppy said. 'I

thought he cared about his family but all he really cares about is money.'

'I think I just heard the front door, Sophie,' Oliver said.

Sophie smiled. 'Excellent. That'll be Thaddeus and that means we can eat at last. Once I've nagged him about being gone so long, that is.' She winked and headed towards the sitting room door which was closed to keep in the warmth from the fire roaring in the grate.

'So Ryan dropped them off in Paris then came back here alone,' Oliver continued. 'I wonder why. He could've counted his money just as easily in Paris.'

'Why would anyone want to be in Paris when they could be in Goldebury Bay?' Clara suggested.

'Really? You are joking, right?'

'No Poppy, I'm not.'

'I agree with Clara,' Paul said. 'There's no place quite like home.'

'I'd take Paris any day,' Poppy said, as the others stared towards the door. 'And if I had a private jet, I'd be there right now. It's rained here every day for a week.'

'It was raining in Paris when I left.'

Poppy twisted round and glowered at Ryan.

'What're you doing here?'

Sophie scowled at her. 'Ryan's joining us for dinner, everyone. Poppy, would you come and help me in the kitchen, please? Right now, if you don't mind.'

'Fine.'

Poppy stomped towards the door, glared at Ryan's smiling face as she passed and followed Sophie to the kitchen.

'I know you don't like him, Poppy but Thaddeus has invited him to dinner, so I really hope you'll be polite, even if you can't be nice.'

Poppy folded her arms across her chest and slumped

122

against the worktop.

'I'll try. But why is it that everywhere I go that man appears? I'm sick of seeing him.'

'I can't answer that. But I can tell you that Thaddeus likes him and whatever you may think, that's good enough for me.' She wrapped an arm around Poppy's shoulder and hugged her. 'I know you'd rather it was Toby and I'm sorry he's in Paris but at least you've spoken to him. Did he say when they'll be coming back?'

'He's not sure. He said he'll call me. He thinks they'll probably be back by next weekend.'

'Wow! That's a lot of shopping. No wonder Ryan's worried about the credit card.' Sophie winked and kissed Poppy on the cheek. 'So are we good?'

'Yeah. I'll try to be polite, but nice is too much to ask. I'm sorry, Sophie but there it is.'

'I'll take polite. Now find another glass for Ryan, plaster on a smile and let's do this.'

Poppy got a glass down from the shelf and followed Sophie back into the sitting room where Ryan was sitting in the chair that Poppy had vacated.

'Sorry,' he said. 'I'm in your seat.'

'Stay there,' Poppy said, giving him her sweetest smile. She handed him the empty glass and walked to the chair farthest away.

Sophie filled his glass with wine whilst everyone else exchanged silent glances.

'You were talking about Paris as I came in,' Ryan said, taking a mouthful of wine. 'Curiously enough my brother, sister and grandmother are there at the moment.' He met Poppy's look and held it.

Was he challenging her? Big mistake.

'That's what I was telling them. Toby didn't seem that keen to be there when I spoke to him this afternoon. But then shopping isn't really a man's thing, is it?'

He smiled. 'Isn't it? Toby usually enjoys it. In fact, all my family enjoy spending money. Myself included.'

'Then I'm surprised you didn't stay in Paris with your family. There's nothing in Goldebury Bay to spend your money on.'

'I'd have to disagree. I can think of at least one thing I'd happily spend it on.'

'What's that?' Oliver asked.

It was a second or two before Ryan dragged his eyes away from Poppy and answered Oliver.

'The Goldebury Bay Yachting and Sailing Club, for one.'

'Can you tell us what you have planned?' Paul asked, wrapping one arm around Clara. 'Many of us have a keen interest in what happens to the place.'

'Me for one,' Sophie said. 'Especially as it's effectively just to the left of Summer Hill Cliff.'

Ryan nodded. 'I understand your concern. As soon as we have one or two substantive plans we'll be showing them to the residents of Goldebury Bay and asking for their input. I believe it's important to work with a community rather than present them with a fait accompli.'

'How considerate,' Poppy said.

Ryan shot her a look before continuing: 'The idea at the moment is for a four-storey... boatel.'

'A what?' Sophie queried.

'A boatel. It's like a motel but for boat owners.'

'Isn't that called a marina?' Poppy asked, not bothering to mask her sarcasm.

'I can appreciate your scepticism and yes, I'd agree. But this is aimed at people who would rather spend their days on the water and their nights on dry land, preferably in a comfortable bed, where every convenience is just the push of a button away.'

Sophie frowned. 'Four storeys, did you say? So that means two storeys taller than the present building. Or are you working on different dimensions? What sort of square footage do you anticipate?'

'These are all points under consideration at the moment, I'm afraid, so I can't give you any definitive answers. I can however assure you that we'll discuss it with you and Thaddeus, together with the others of course, before going forward with any proposals.'

'Is that your usual company spiel?' Poppy said.

'Yes, Poppy, it is. But it's not a spiel. It's something I happen to believe in. As I said at the start, I prefer to work with people, not against them.'

'On that note,' Thaddeus said. 'I think it's time we ate. I'm starving.'

Ryan stood up and faced Sophie. 'I give you my word, Sophie. And all of you, of course that nothing will happen to the site without full disclosure, discussion and if necessary, compromise. Please believe that.'

'I do Ryan,' Sophie said. 'And thank you. That means a lot.'

Ryan held back as the others headed towards the dining room, with Poppy being the last. He reached out and took hold of her arm, just as she was about to pass.

'Do you really have feelings for Toby?'

'What kind of question is that? And please, will you let go of my arm?'

'I'm sorry.' He released her but blocked her path between two chairs. 'I need an answer.'

'It's none of your business.'

'I'm making it my business.'

'Well, I'm not interested in what you're doing. You have absolutely no control over me. You may instil fear or whatever in Toby and Stephanie but it doesn't work on me. Now please get out of my way.'

He seemed both hurt and surprised. 'I wouldn't like to think I instilled fear in anyone, well, with the possible exception of one or two people, but certainly not Toby or Stephanie. Not the sort of fear you're alluding to in any event. And definitely not you. I'm not asking this for me. I'm asking for Toby.'

'I don't understand.'

'For once, can't you just answer a simple question with the honest truth? Do you have feelings for Toby? Genuine feelings?'

Poppy tilted her chin up and looked him in the eye. 'Yes. I believe I do.'

Something momentarily flashed in his eyes and then it was gone.

'Thank you. Then may I give you a piece of advice? But first let me say this. I don't think Toby's the man for you, or that you're the woman for him. No, please. Let me finish. He's young and sometimes foolish, but his heart is in the right place. I won't see him hurt. You may laugh at me, spar with me, make fun of me, as much as you like. But don't try that with Toby. You may find the idea of the boatel amusing. I'm not convinced of it myself, although I wouldn't say that in front of the others. But it's Toby's idea and this is Toby's project, so poke fun at me as much as you like but don't criticise the boatel in front of Toby. Please. And if you're hoping for any sort of future with him, don't let him hear you criticise it to anyone else. One final thing – I'd rather not see you get hurt either. So be very careful what you wish for.'

He stood aside and held out his hand to indicate that she was free to pass.

What could she say to that? She couldn't think of

anything. Better to walk away. Why was that so difficult?

'Are you two coming?' Thaddeus asked, popping his head around the door.

'Yes, Thaddeus! Wait for me.'

Why did her legs feel so strange? Why was it difficult not to look back? This was stupid. They were only going into the next room. And Ryan was coming too... Wasn't he?

Chapter Sixteen

'I don't understand why I feel so nervous,' Poppy said, sitting on the rug in front of the wood-burning stove in her cottage. 'It's not even our first date. We've already been out to dinner – although that was a bit of a disaster, I'll admit.'

She leant back and studied the deep red polish she had been painting on her toe nails.

'Sorry, I didn't hear a word of that,' Cleo said, carrying two large glasses of red wine and placing them on a small side table next to Poppy's two-seater sofa. 'Oliver texted me whilst I was in the kitchen pouring the wine. What did you say?'

Poppy tutted, grabbed one of the glasses and took three large gulps.

'I said that I'm really nervous and I don't know why.'

'Well, it has been three weeks since you last saw him and you have only been on one date. Although I suppose if you count the evening of the Blood Moon, two dates. And then there was that strange business with Ryan at Sophie's last Sunday.'

'Yeah. I'm still not sure if he meant that as a friendly piece of advice or a threat.'

'I don't think he meant it as a threat, Poppy. A mild warning, if that, but I don't believe he was suggesting that he'd cause you any harm or anything. Do you honestly feel that he might've meant it in that way?'

Poppy shook her head. 'I don't know. It was such a

strange thing to say. I keep going over and over it in my head but I just can't remember what he said, word for word. He was so serious and he looked concerned. Then when we went into dinner, he was sweetness and light to everyone and barely gave me a second glance.'

'I'm not sure I'd agree with that,' Cleo said. 'The part about him barely giving you a second glance, that is. Every time I looked in his direction, he seemed to be looking at you.'

'You must've been imagining it. What I found really odd was that he seemed more than happy to talk about his business, how he got started, his uncle – even his dad's death to a certain extent but when we mentioned his mum, all he said was that he hadn't seen her in years because she hadn't wanted to keep in touch. Don't you think that's weird?'

'A little, yes. But having had a rather strange 'mother figure' myself for many years, I don't think that reflects badly on him, necessarily. The bit I found curious was why he made some jokey remark on the three or four times Sophie or I asked him about all the women he's been photographed with, and smoothly changed the subject.'

'Yeah. And when Paul asked him if there was anyone special in his life at the moment, what did he say? Something like: "I thought for one brief moment there might be but let's just say that I doubt I'll be requiring your services in that regard." I mean, that's weird, don't you think?'

Cleo nodded. 'Yep. It's almost as if he met someone once, thought about getting serious, changed his mind and decided he wouldn't do that again. It's like he's closed himself up as far as falling in love's concerned. And the guy's only thirty-nine.'

'Oh well. That's his problem. I'm so pleased that Toby's

back. He called me every day from Paris. But I've told you that already. And he says he's brought me something back.'

'You've told me that too. What you haven't told me is whether tonight's the night you break your sex drought.'

'God, I bloody hope so. I've changed the sheets, put clean towels in the bathroom and bought some of those posh little soaps for the shower. I even dusted everywhere and tidied my wardrobe and all my drawers, just in case he checks them out.'

'Why on earth would he do that?'

'Well, I would if I went to his place. Didn't you check Oliver's out?'

Cleo sniggered. 'Not his wardrobes and drawers, no. Just his body but then I already knew how perfect that was so I didn't waste any time. I just jumped straight in. Or perhaps that should be on.'

Poppy drew her knees up to her chest and hugged them, balancing her glass in one hand.

'I hope he's romantic. I thought I'd probably pounce on him after such a long time without sex but I'd like it to be slow, you know? To take our time undressing one another, touching and kissing and… well, all that stuff.'

She grinned across at Cleo who was curled up on the sofa.

'Don't stop on my account.'

'I'm not. But if I talk about it anymore I probably will pounce on him… the minute I open the door.'

'What time's he coming? And I mean to pick you up, before you make any dirty jokes.'

Poppy grinned again. 'At eight. He seems to have a thing about eight.'

'Then you'd better get a move on. It's seven-fifty now.'

'Bugger! But I've only got to put my dress on and brush my hair. Everything else is fine. My make-up looks okay,

130

doesn't it?'

'You look gorgeous, Poppy. Toby Blackwood doesn't stand a chance. Ryan may not be requiring the Reverend's services, but his brother may be, and sooner than he thinks.'

'Oh my God! Was that the doorbell?'

Cleo swung her feet off the sofa. 'He obviously can't wait to see you. You go and get dressed. I'll get the door.'

Cleo put her glass on the table and walked into the hall. Poppy yanked open the wooden door beside the fireplace in the sitting room and dashed up the steep, curved stairs to the tiny hall above which led to her bedroom and the bathroom.

Despite Cleo's confirmation that her make-up looked fine, she ran into the bathroom and checked it anyway and then raced into her bedroom and wriggled into her figure-hugging red dress.

'Poppy! It's... you'd better get down here. Fast,' Cleo yelled.

That sounded odd. Why hadn't Cleo said it was Toby? And why the sudden rush? He was ten minutes early, after all.

Perhaps it wasn't Toby?

Had something happened to him?

Oh God! Had he had an accident or something?

Without bothering to check her dress, she ran down the stairs in her stockinged feet and raced towards the hall.

Cleo was smiling. Why was she smiling? Where was Toby? What was going on? Why was the front door closed?

'It's for you,' Cleo said, stepping aside and pulling open the front door.

Poppy couldn't believe her eyes. A pristine, white carriage, drawn by four superb white horses adorned with glistening headpieces, waited in the road in front of her cottage. Two liveried footmen stood beside it and an immaculate coachman held the horses' reins from his seat high above the front of the carriage. The road and the pavement leading up to her door which were still wet from yet another day of rain, were strewn with white rose petals.

She had stepped into her very own fairy tale.

But where was her handsome prince?

Another footman appeared from beside her door and bowed.

'Your carriage awaits,' he announced.

Poppy glanced at Cleo and they both smiled.

'I'll see you later,' Poppy said.

Cleo pulled her back by her arm.

'You may want to put on some shoes before you take that step. And a coat. And an umbrella might be wise. That is an open-topped carriage, after all. Why would he arrange for an open-topped carriage at the end of October?' Cleo shook her head.

Poppy laughed. 'Don't be a grouch. I think he's trying to be romantic. I was dressed as Cinderella the night we met. But you're right about the shoes. And perhaps even the coat. And I suppose the umbrella wouldn't take up any room.'

'I'll get them,' Cleo said. 'Stay there.'

'Oi mate,' someone called out from a car behind the carriage. 'You gonna be long? Bit late for a wedding, init?'

One of the footmen approached the driver, pulled out something that looked like money and handed it to the man. Whatever it was, it seemed to do the trick. The man switched off his ignition and waited patiently.

Cleo returned with the things Poppy needed. 'Have a magical evening,' she said.

Poppy slipped on her shoes and coat. 'I will. Thanks, Cleo. Ooh! Can I give you a lift back to your place?'

Cleo shook her head. 'No thanks. Oliver's coming to

pick me up any minute. In fact, I think I see his Land Rover now, so the sooner you get into your carriage and go to the Palace or wherever, the sooner I'll be home in the warm. I'll slam the door behind me when I leave.'

The footman beside her held out his arm for Poppy to rest her hand on and after walking over the blanket of rose petals, she was helped into the carriage where a cosy, white throw was placed across her legs. With a final glance at Cleo and a smile and a wave, Poppy sat back and the coachman flicked the reins. They headed off to... She had no idea where.

Chapter Seventeen

'Did you see that, Oliver?' Cleo asked when she got into the car after collecting her things from Poppy's and closing the front door.

'I couldn't really miss it, could I? Was Toby sitting in the carriage? I didn't see him, only the footman with Poppy.'

'He didn't come with it.'

Oliver gave her an odd look. 'That's a bit strange, isn't it? Surely if you're taking someone on a date, you pick her up yourself. You don't get your lackeys to do it, however well turned out they may be.' He started the engine and headed towards home.

'I think he's trying to be romantic. Poppy was wearing a Cinderella costume the night she met him. I assume he's either arranging for her to go to his house, where there'll no doubt be an orchestra playing so that they can dance together. Or the carriage will take her to somewhere exceedingly posh, and there'll be an orchestra and dancing there. Either way, they'll no doubt have a ball, in more ways than one.'

'It must've cost a fortune. But I suppose to him, it's nothing.'

'It's bloody ridiculous,' Cleo said. 'It's October and it's been raining every day, including today. That's an open carriage. If it chucks it down like it did earlier, Poppy is more than likely going to get pneumonia. If he must throw money around like that, you'd have thought he would've paid for a bloody roof.'

'I'll remember to get a roof if I ever do something like that for you, my darling.'

'If you waste your money on something like that, you'll be needing a roof... to sleep under because I'll kick you out of the house. Even though it's actually your house.'

'It's *our* house, Cleo.'

'It's your name on the deeds.'

Oliver pulled up at a set of traffic lights and turned to face her.

'Does that bother you? If you want me to change it, I'm happy to. You know that everything I own is yours.'

Cleo shook her head and smiled. 'No, of course it doesn't. I didn't mean it like that. I'm in a funny mood, that's all. It doesn't bother me one little bit. Honestly, it doesn't.'

He smiled back and drove on.

A few seconds later, he said: 'So... do you think what Toby did was romantic then? Even if it was impractical.'

'I suppose it was. In a way. But it was too over the top. I mean, who's going to have to clean up all those rose petals? The road-sweeper, that's who. Littering's an offence even in a tiny place like Goldebury Bay. In fact more so in a place like this because it's too small to have litter flying around everywhere.'

'You really didn't think it was a good idea, did you?'

She shook her head. 'To be honest, no I didn't. And as much as Poppy was smiling, if I know her – and I do – she thought it was a bit too much as well. Besides, first he asks her to go to Dubai with him, all-expenses paid. Then he flits off to Paris with his sister. Then he does this. Doesn't the man do anything that doesn't involve spending a fortune?'

'That's not entirely fair, Cleo. He didn't seem to want to

go to Dubai. Ryan made him and he only went to Paris because Ryan insisted on it, apparently. Plus, let's not forget that he took Poppy to our restaurant for their first date. He could've whisked her off somewhere really expensive but he didn't.'

'I suppose so. I don't know. It's just that... well... Poppy said that Ryan told her the Goldebury Bay Yachting and Sailing Club development is actually Toby's project, not his.'

'When did he tell her that?'

'Last Sunday night. But don't say anything because I'm not sure he wants anyone to know. And that's weird, if you ask me. But not as weird as the fact that Toby doesn't seem to be making much of an effort to get to know people here. Ryan went to see Thaddeus and he asked to meet you and Ben. Why wasn't Toby there? I thought it was Ryan's deal and Toby was just helping out. I thought Ryan wanted to retain control of everything but when he said that stuff to Poppy about it being Toby's project, well, it got me thinking. If it's Toby's project then why isn't it Toby running around introducing himself to everyone? And why does it seem as if Ryan has to make him do anything work-related?'

Oliver pulled up outside their cottage and swung round to face Cleo.

'There's something I need to tell you, Cleo and I don't want you to get cross. You keep secrets from me – like the one you've just told me – if Poppy or Sophie or anyone asks you to, right?'

'Yes. But I have to if they ask me to and I usually end up telling you anyway. Like I just did.'

'I know you do. And it's the same with me. If Thaddeus or Ben ask me to keep something between me and them.'

'I know. That's fine with me too.'

'Ryan told us something that evening of the Blood Moon. Several things, actually. One was that this development was Toby's but that he – Ryan that is – would be fronting it until it was finalised, for reasons he said he'd rather not go into except to say that Toby wasn't quite such a workaholic as him. He said he'd be fully involved and that he had a few ideas which he'd like to discuss with us. One was about the possibility of Thaddeus building boats specifically for the project, and two others were that he'd like a pub and a restaurant inside and would Ben and I be interested in having smaller versions of our businesses in the boatel.'

'Wow! And would you?'

Oliver shrugged. 'It's early days yet and he made it clear that things may not go as planned but yes, I think so. I told him that I'd need to discuss it with you, and Thaddeus said the same about Sophie.'

'But he didn't ask us. How typical. Poppy's right about him then. He is an arrogant jerk.'

'I don't think he is. He actually said that he realised he should've been discussing it with you and Sophie, too, and possibly even Poppy – although I don't know why he thought Poppy has any say in our businesses. Anyway, he said he'd like us to keep it under wraps for the time being and he'd sit down with all of us nearer the time if that was okay with us.'

'And you said yes.'

'Yes. Well nothing definite was discussed and I was going to tell you but then it went out of my head because I had other, more important things on my mind. Another thing he told us that night was about Stephanie.'

'What about her?'

'Again, he asked us to keep it to ourselves but he said he felt we should know that his sister was getting out of a

137

difficult marriage with a rather unpleasant guy and that she was struggling to deal with it. He thought there may be repercussions but he believed he had everything buttoned up. He'd appreciate it if we'd let him know if we noticed anything unusual – or anyone.'

'What! That sounds almost sinister. What did he mean by "anything unusual"? And he does realise this is a seaside resort, doesn't he? We do have visitors here, even at this time of year. Does he want you to tell him every time a tourist pops up in Goldebury Bay? What are you? Some kind of bodyguards?'

Oliver shook his head. 'No. He has bodyguards for her. Don't look like that. Lots of rich people have them. And by the sounds of it, the Blackwoods are very, very rich. Anyway, he said that he was sure he was being overly dramatic and that there probably wasn't anything at all to worry about but if anyone started asking questions about his family, would we tell him.'

'And you kept this from me? Thank you very much!' Cleo shoved open the car door and jumped out, slamming the door behind her.

'Cleo! Darling. Please don't be mad.'

'I'm not. Not really. But why didn't you tell me?'

'I... I forgot about it. I didn't take it seriously. He didn't seem that worried and I don't see what the problem is or why it concerns us.'

'And when Stephanie wandered off and we all went searching for her, you didn't take it seriously then?'

'I told you. I had other things on my mind. She was fine so that was that.'

'Other things on your mind. Huh! What on earth could be more important than telling your girlfriend that Stephanie's husband may be dangerous or something and that he might turn up here and try to drag her back to him...

or worse? Because that's what he was saying, you know.'

'Was he? Okay, yes. I suppose he was but... well, he said it was under control so I left it at that. I couldn't start worrying about that as well.'

'Oh God! It's not your mum again is it? There hasn't been another cancer scare and you're keeping this one from me?'

'No, darling! Mum's fine.'

Cleo breathed a sigh of relief. 'Then what was so bloody important that made all that slip your mind? What else did Ryan say?'

'Nothing. Let's go inside.'

He wrapped his arm around her waist but she shoved him away.

'Oliver! I can tell you're keeping something from me. What is it? Tell me, Oliver or I'll... I'll spend the night at Mum's. You've been acting really weird ever since the Blackwoods arrived. What the hell is going on?'

He reached out for her. 'Nothing, Cleo. I swear to you. It's got nothing to do with the Blackwoods.'

'Then what has it got to do with? I mean it, Oliver. I thought you were going to propose but it's been weeks now and you haven't, so I was clearly wrong about that. Along with everything else I've been wrong about lately. Oh God!' Cleo stared at him with a horrified expression on her face. 'You're not... You haven't... Are you dumping me, Oliver? Have you met someone else?'

Oliver was even more horrified. 'No! Of course not. Why would you even think that? I love you, Cleo. I love you with all my heart. With every fibre of my being. You should know that. And for your information you were right. I was going to propose. On that very night, in fact. I had it all planned out but I couldn't tie that stupid bow tie and then I lost the ring whilst practising and then Ryan found it and then I got the call about the power and—'

'You were going to propose?' Cleo stopped him in full flow. 'Honestly? You were?'

His expression softened. 'Yes, Cleo. I was. And you knew it.'

'I thought you might be. But now you've changed your mind? Why? Have I done something wrong? Has something happened to give you doubts? Have—'

'Stop!' He stepped closer and gently pulled her into his arms. 'I haven't changed my mind. I was just waiting for the right moment, that's all. After the whole Blood Moon debacle, I wanted to make it perfect. There's another full moon this coming Tuesday. It's called a Hunter's Moon and it's bright white – or at least I hope it is. I had a 'red is the colour of passion' speech planned the first time. This time I've been racking my brains to think of something to go with white. All I can think of is that it's a symbol of a white wedding and that sounds really pathetic, even to me. And now I'm wondering if I should try to do something more romantic. Not quite as over the top as what Toby did tonight because you didn't like that, but something special… only with a roof. But now it won't even be a surprise.'

He looked down into her eyes.

'Oh Oliver. That doesn't sound pathetic. That sounds wonderful. To me, at least.' She smiled. 'But you don't need to wait for "the right time" to ask me and I don't care about it being a surprise. I love you, Oliver. With all my heart and soul. You don't have to propose under a full moon and I definitely don't want you to hire a carriage and four white horses. Anytime, anywhere would be the right time. I want to marry you more than anything in this entire world.'

He held her away from him and beamed at her, his eyes

140

so full of love that anyone walking past would see it. He got down on one knee and took her hand in his.

'Then how about now? Cleo Merrifield, I adore you. I want to spend the rest of my life with you. And after that, I want to spend eternity with you. You're the air I breathe. The sun on my face. The wings that give me flight. You're everything to me. You already make me the happiest man alive just by being with me. Will you make me feel like a god by saying you'll be my wife. Will you marry me, Cleo? Please, please, marry me.'

Cleo burst into tears.

'Oh yes, Oliver!' she sobbed. 'Yes, yes, yes. I'll marry you.'

She flung herself into his arms and he almost over balanced. He managed to steady himself and he held her slightly from him as they stared into each other's eyes.

'Oh shit!' he said. 'The ring's inside the house. I forgot the sodding ring. I knew I'd screw this up no matter what. I—'

'Oliver! Darling, darling, Oliver. We can get the ring in a moment. And you didn't screw it up. It was perfect. Now please shut up and kiss me.'

Oliver grinned. 'We've only been engaged for five seconds and you're giving me orders already.'

He tightened his arms around her and kissed her deeply.

'Yes,' Cleo said when he finally loosened his hold. 'And the next order is: take me inside and make passionate love with me all night long.'

'I'm happy to take orders like that any day of the week,' he replied, sweeping her up in his arms and carrying her inside.

Chapter Eighteen

Poppy yawned and rubbed her eyes as Clara swung open the heavy oak door of Hope Cottage.

'Good morning, Clara,' she said. 'Although six a.m. on a Sunday isn't morning in my book and there's nothing good about it from what I can see. Which isn't much. I seriously hope you've got coffee.'

Clara smiled, linked her arm through Poppy's and led her into the hall.

'It is a good morning, sweetheart. A very good morning indeed. And I've got something far, far better than coffee. I've got champagne. Lots and lots of it.'

Poppy stared at her. 'Has the Reverend proposed? Congratulations, Clara!'

'Not guilty!' Paul called out from the sitting room. 'But it's not a bad idea.'

Clara and Poppy exchanged excited looks.

'Thank you, sweetheart,' Clara whispered, looking like Christmas had come early, for her at least.

'Okay, so it's not you and Paul... Cleo!' Poppy saw the ring the minute she and Clara stepped into the sitting room. 'Bloody hell! Congratulations! I'm surprised you can lift your hand with that on it.' She covered her eyes with both hands. 'I'm being blinded by its radiance from here. Let me see.'

She hurried to Cleo and they hugged, making weird little 'squeeing' noises for several seconds.

'When did he do it? How did he do it? Why isn't he

here? Tell me everything.'

Cleo laughed and Clara handed her and Poppy a glass of champagne.

'First, let's have a toast,' Clara said, raising hers. 'To my darling daughter, Cleo and her wonderful fiancé, Oliver. May you have an abundance of joy, peace and love in your lives and may you never shed a tear unless it's a tear of happiness. Here's to a wonderful future together.'

'To Cleo and Oliver,' Paul said.

'I'll drink to that,' Poppy said.

Cleo smiled and hugged her. 'You'll drink to anything. Thanks Mum and Paul. I'm going to phone Dad and Melanie in a minute and tell them, but I wanted you and Poppy to be the first to know. And I've called Sophie too and asked her and Thaddeus to call in, if that's okay?'

'Of course it's okay, sweetheart. It's more than okay. You can call Leo and Melanie from here if you like.'

Cleo nodded. 'Thanks, Mum. So Poppy, what happened last night? Oh God! I didn't... interrupt anything, did I? Was he there when I texted you? You could've brought him with you.'

Poppy flopped into a chair and shook her head.

'No to all of that. He didn't stay the night. He didn't even come in. He just dropped me off in that bloody silly carriage, kissed me goodnight – which was actually really nice – and then told me he'd call me.'

Cleo dropped onto the arm of the chair. 'You're kidding?'

'I wish. And it had all been going so well up to that point. We had an entire restaurant to ourselves and... But we're not here to discuss my total lack of any sort of sex life, we're here to celebrate your engagement. Are you going to have a party? Have you set the date? Can I be your bridesmaid? And you'd better say yes to that last one or you're dead.' Poppy beamed at her and knocked back her entire glass of champagne.

Clara poured Poppy another and filled the rest of the glasses. 'There's the doorbell. That'll be Sophie and Thaddeus.'

'I'll get it,' Paul said, striding towards the hall.

'This had better be good,' Thaddeus said moments later, looking almost as tired as Poppy had when he came into the sitting room.

Cleo waved her hand in the air.

'Shit! So the silly bugger's done it at last. Congratulations, Cleo.'

'Thanks, Thaddeus but please don't call my fiancé "a silly bugger",' she said, laughing.

'Congratulations!' Sophie screamed, making Thaddeus tip his head away from her and stick a finger in his ear, although he was smiling at the time. 'Let me see the ring. Oh Cleo, it's gorgeous.'

'It should be, Sophie. It's from the Summerhill treasure. Are you… are you sure you wanted to sell it to Oliver? And for such a ridiculously low price? It's worth several thousand more than the pittance he gave you for it.'

'Will you stop,' Sophie commanded, with a smile. 'That ring was meant for you. The second you saw it, your eyes lit up. It even fell out of the chest and landed at your feet. I said you could have it then and there but you wouldn't take it. So when Thaddeus told me that he thought Oliver was going to be proposing to you, I offered him the ring. I didn't want anything for it but he insisted I must take something.'

'I'm so glad you said that, Sophie because when he gave it to me this morning, I couldn't believe my eyes. It was like a second proposal all over again.'

'What? Wait a minute,' Poppy said. 'Are you saying he

144

didn't have the ring with him when he proposed? When did he propose then? And where, exactly?'

'It was last night, after we left your place. We... we were having a tiny little disagreement about not always telling one another things that our friends tell us – that's you lot by the way. And... it just happened. He got down on one knee outside the cottage – our cottage – and he said the most wonderful things, which I'll tell you later because I don't want Thaddeus or Paul groaning as I'm saying it. But because it wasn't planned, he didn't have the ring. It was inside.'

'Why didn't he just go in and get it?' Poppy asked.

Cleo grinned. 'Because once he'd asked me and I'd said yes, a ring was actually the last thing on my mind, surprising as that may seem.'

'But surely... oh, I see,' Poppy said, letting out a wistful sigh. 'At least someone was having sex last night.'

'Does that mean you weren't, Poppy?' Sophie asked. 'Didn't your date with Toby go well?'

Thaddeus and Paul groaned and grinned. 'May we leave you girls to it?' Thaddeus suggested. 'I think Paul and I would rather talk about something else.'

'Yes, yes. You can go,' Cleo said.

'Congratulations again, Cleo.' Thaddeus came and hugged her, kissed her on the cheek and smiled. He turned to kiss Sophie. 'I suppose I should get you one of those. Would you give me a good price too?' He winked.

'What's mine is yours, my darling,' Sophie said. 'Just take your pick. Oh my God! Are you serious, Thaddeus?'

He kissed her on the lips. 'You'll have to wait and see, won't you? Come on Paul, let's leave them to it and go to Betty's Pantry.'

'Right behind you,' Paul said, stopping only to kiss Clara.

'Well,' Poppy said, knocking back a second glass of champagne. 'It looks like everyone's getting engaged except me – and Clara, if you so much as mention Ben, I'll hit you over the head with that bloody bottle.'

Chapter Nineteen

Poppy stepped over the threshold of her cottage and checked she had her keys before slamming the front door shut behind her. For the first time in days it wasn't raining and she sucked in a lungful of fresh, crisp, early morning, autumn air. Despite the fact that she hadn't seen Toby since last Saturday, she would be seeing him tomorrow so all seemed right again with the world. Glancing down the road, she spotted a figure she recognised, even from behind.

'Oi, Blackwood!' she yelled.

Ryan stopped, seemed to hesitate for one second as he had the last time they'd met like this and finally turned to face her. This time though, he remained where he was.

Poppy jumped down the steps and strolled the twenty feet or so towards him.

'I haven't seen you for nearly two weeks,' she said. 'Been whisking people away on your private jet, have you?'

He raised his brows. 'I'm surprised you've noticed my absence, especially since Toby's been back for almost a week. Did you enjoy your carriage outing, by the way?'

Poppy frowned. 'I only noticed you weren't around because things have been so pleasant lately. As for that *wonderful* evening, how do you know about that? Have you had your little spies watching us?'

He grinned. 'Ah, sweet Poppy. You say the nicest things. I'm glad you had such a *wonderful* evening but I'm sorry to disappoint you. Firstly my spies as you call them, aren't "little" and secondly, they haven't been watching you. As to how I know about it, let's just say, I saw the invoice.'

'My God! You even go through Toby's papers. You really are unbelievable.'

Ryan stiffened. 'Believe what you will. It makes no difference to me now.'

'Well,' Poppy said, leaning closer. 'As you're always saying how busy you are, let me save you some time. It's Halloween tomorrow – but I see you're already wearing your costume, so you know that. That *is* a mask you're wearing, isn't it?' She smirked but other than Ryan's eyes narrowing for a split second, he ignored her sarcasm, so she continued: 'Toby and I, together with several of my friends, are going to Summerhill for supper and Halloween games. No need to get your spies to tag along. I'm happy to give you a blow by blow account over breakfast in Betty's Pantry on Sunday. Which is where Toby and I will be going... when we get out of my bed, that is. Oh wait, you'd better make that lunch.'

Was the man ill? He'd suddenly gone almost deathly pale and as his smooth-shaven skin was still tanned from the Dubai sun that was no mean feat.

He took a noticeable deep breath and held her look.

'You sound very confident. But I take it, from the importance you seem to be placing on Saturday, and the fact that you have no such "blow by blow" account to give me from the night of the carriage ride, this will be the first night you spend together. As my mother used to say, on the rare occasions she bothered to talk to us at all: "Don't count your chickens before they hatch."'

What did he just say about his mother? But more to the point, was he saying that Toby wouldn't spend the night?

'Are you suggesting that he won't want to spend the

night with me? That he doesn't find me attractive. That he… that he's not interested in me in that way? Well you're wrong. He told me he wanted nothing more than to spend the night with me. Not that it's any of your business.'

'And yet you're offering to tell me all about it over breakfast. Sorry… lunch. As to him wanting to spend the night with you, of course he does. Any man would. But the question is, will he? He may want to but does he want to enough? Only he can answer that. Now if you'll excuse me, as you said yourself, I'm a very busy man, and as much as I would love to discuss who will and will not be sharing your bed… and for how long, I've got to be on the jet in a couple of hours. Enjoy Halloween, Poppy.'

He turned away but she stopped him.

'Blackwood!'

'What now?'

She stepped closer and looked him in the eye.

'You're not thinking of taking Toby with you, are you?'

He grinned. 'I wasn't. But it's not a bad idea. In fact, I could send him instead and I could take his place. How does that sound? Then you and I could have breakfast in Betty's Pantry. Or lunch. Or better still, we could order in. Not that we'd have time to eat.'

'Ew! You have *got* to be kidding.' She shivered for dramatic effect and watched as his grin disappeared. 'Why are you so determined to try to stop us having a relationship? Me and Toby, that is. Is it about money? Because Toby has it and I don't. D'you think I'm after his money? Is that what's worrying you? Because if it is, I can tell you now it's not about the money. It's about him. I'd want him even if he were poor. In fact, it might be better if he were then he wouldn't be able to afford to hire carriages and… oh bugger. Forget I said that bit.'

His lips twitched ever so slightly. 'Personally, an open

149

carriage in late October wouldn't have been my first choice but Toby is nothing if not romantic. And yes, it is about the money in a way. But not entirely. I know you won't believe this but I do have your interests at heart, not just Toby's. I told you at dinner nearly two weeks ago that Toby's not the man for you and that you're not the woman for him. I stand by that. But it's not up to me. It's up to you and it's up to Toby. As for it being better if Toby were poor… as I think I also said that night, be very careful what you wish for.'

'You've done it again! Is that some sort of threat? I think Toby and I could have a future together, if you would just leave us alone. And… and if you want me to sign something right now, right this minute saying that whatever happens between Toby and me, I will never try to take, or claim, even one penny from him, I'll happily do so.'

'Well, that's a novelty. I would definitely have asked you to sign a prenuptial agreement if your relationship did go anywhere, but a pre-sex contract might not be a bad idea.'

'And now you're making fun of me. You think it's too soon for me to be thinking about a future with Toby, don't you? You don't believe in love at first sight. You think I'm just some stupid, penniless, blonde barmaid-cum-waitress who sees a rich guy and tries to get her claws in him. Well if that's the case, surely I would've tried to get my claws in you, not Toby? You seem to be the one in control of the private jet, and probably everything else. Or are you saying that I knew I had absolutely no chance of getting my hands on you, so Toby's the next best thing. Is that what you're saying?'

He tipped his head to the side and looked deep into her eyes, so much so that Poppy fiddled with the buckle on her handbag and focused her eyes on that.

'You're the one who seems to be doing most of the

150

talking, Poppy. I just came out for a run. And I really must go but I will say this. I'm not making fun of you. I do believe in love at first sight. You're far from stupid and I no longer think you're trying to get your claws into Toby. I think you do believe you have feelings for him. As to you "knowing" you had absolutely no chance of getting your hands on me, I don't know what made you think that but it's irrelevant, isn't it? Because it isn't me you want to get your hands on, is it?'

Poppy raised her eyes to his and for one brief moment she wasn't completely sure.

Chapter Twenty

'What's up with you?' Cleo asked Poppy. 'You've been in a really odd mood since you got to work yesterday. I thought you'd cheer up once you were here with Toby tonight but if anything, you seem to be worse.'

'What?'

'I rest my case,' Cleo said. 'What *is* up with you?'

'Nothing.'

Cleo sat beside her on the sofa. 'This isn't about me being engaged, is it? Nothing's going to change between you and me, you know that, don't you? I told you that when I moved in with Oliver and I was right. I'm telling you the same thing now.'

Poppy shook her head. 'I know it won't. It's not about that. I'm really happy for you both.'

'Then what is it? And if you say it's nothing, I'll punch you.'

Cleo held up her fist in front of Poppy's face and Poppy laughed.

'It's... Oh! It's Ryan Blackwood.'

'You're in a mood because of...' Cleo glanced behind her, following Poppy's line of sight. 'I see. You mean he's here. Didn't you know? Sophie and Thaddeus invited him.'

'He told me he was going away yesterday.'

Cleo nodded. 'He did but only to Paris. He got back this afternoon. I'm glad he's made an effort and dressed up.'

'I don't think he has. A blood-sucking vampire is his true personality. Oh God. He's coming over here.'

'Hello Ryan,' Cleo said. 'That's a pretty impressive outfit. If vampires looked like you, I don't think any woman would mind being bitten.'

'You speak for yourself,' Poppy mumbled.

'Hello Cleo,' Ryan said, with a broad smile. 'It's good to see you again. You make a rather stunning witch. You could cast a spell on me anytime. Congratulations by the way. Oliver told me the happy news. And I think he was looking for you.'

'Thank you. I'd better go and find him then. See you later. Have fun.'

Poppy leapt up to follow Cleo but Ryan stood in her way.

'And Poppy. Always a delight. You decided not to dress up, I see. Which is no doubt exactly what you said about me.'

How could he possibly have known that? Did he know her so well that he could anticipate what she would say? Damn the man.

'Oh sorry,' she said. 'Were you talking to me? I thought you were having a conversation with the snakes in my hair. You speak their language, after all.'

Sod it! Why did he have to have such a wonderful laugh?

'I only wish I had Medusa's powers,' she added. 'Turning you to stone seems very appealing right now. Then the rest of you would match your heart. Excuse me.'

She flounced past him into the hall, the plastic snakes on her head jiggling and writhing as she walked and the sound of Ryan Blackwood's infectious laugh ringing in her ears – although he didn't seem to be laughing now.

'There you are,' Toby said, handing her a Bloody Mary. 'I thought there were only going to be a few friends here tonight like on that lunar eclipse, red moon thing. The place

153

is almost as packed as it was for their moving in together party.'

'I know. I think Sophie wants to have a party every month. There's another one next week for Guy Fawkes Night although it's going to be next Saturday, not on the actual day. I expect most of the residents of Goldebury Bay will be popping in to that one, so it'll be even more crowded. The local council have a spectacular fireworks display and Sophie's donated money to it so it'll be even better than usual. It'd be the perfect opportunity for you to meet everyone.'

'I thought I had.'

'I mean the locals, not just our circle of friends and relatives.'

'Why would I need to meet the locals?' He frowned and took her arm.

He led her towards the open, double front doors of the house where a canopy had been constructed to make a walkway between Summerhill and a newly erected marquee.

'Don't you want to meet them? I thought your intention was to discuss your proposed development with everyone before finalising any plans.'

'Who told you that?'

'Ryan. Where're we going?'

'To the dance floor in the marquee. When did he say that?'

'Um. A few weeks ago.'

'Well, don't believe everything he tells you. He told me he wouldn't be coming here tonight and yet he's here.'

Poppy stopped and made Toby stop too. 'Is something wrong, Toby? You don't seem yourself tonight.'

'Sorry. I've got a lot on my mind, that's all. I shouldn't bring my work home from the office though, should I?' He smiled down at her. 'You look so beautiful tonight Poppy, even with those plastic snakes on your head.' He bent his head closer. 'And on the subject of snakes... why don't we sneak away from here for an hour or so. No one will notice in this throng and I've got a snake of my own that wants to come out and play.'

Did he just say that? Did he really use the word snake as a metaphor for his dick? Is this what dating a thirty-year-old was going to be like? Snakes and open-topped carriages on cold, wet nights.

She'd imagined being curled up with him in front of her wood-burning stove, talking about the things they both loved doing: him telling her about his life, his work, his interests; her telling him about her travels through Europe; all the other places she hoped to see; her love of the simple life; her friends; getting excited about spending Christmas together; drinking wine; eating mince pies; sharing long, slow kisses with the taste of the wine and the fruit still fresh on their lips, followed by slow, gentle love-making leading to the most incredibly passionate sex.

'I can't, Toby. I promised Oliver and Cleo I'd stay 'til the end in case they need me. Oliver's doing the catering. I'm really sorry.'

He clearly wasn't happy if the expression on his face was anything to go by.

'Fine. Let's just dance then. But you don't know what you're missing.'

He almost dragged her onto the dance floor.

'Actually, Toby. I think I'm just beginning to realise.'

Chapter Twenty-One

Poppy needed time to think. She wanted ten minutes alone. Just ten minutes. But everywhere she looked, there were crowds of people. There were even a couple of people with Thaddeus in the study. She could go upstairs to one of the bedrooms; Sophie and Thaddeus wouldn't mind but what she really needed was fresh air. That would clear her head.

She eased her way through the crowded kitchen, checking with Oliver that he didn't need any help but as all he was doing was checking that everything was under control, he told her he was sure he had it covered.

Opening the door from the kitchen to the side of the house, she turned left and followed the paved path leading to the rear. The moon was on the wane but having been full just four nights ago, it illuminated her way like a massive spotlight. Added to this were the rows of glass jars, filled with flickering tea lights along both sides of the length of the York stone slabs, so much like a runway that Ryan Blackwood could land his private jet here.

She shook that image from her head but as she neared the corner of the house she heard a rustling sound behind her and turned, knowing exactly who was there.

'Are you bloody well following me?'

'Yes,' Ryan said.

She could see the mischievous smile from here. At least he'd been honest. She had to give him that.

'Why? Toby's not with me.'

'So I see.'

'Then why are you following me?'

'Because I gave my spies the night off.'

'How very amusing. What do you want?'

'I saw an opportunity and I decided to take it.'

'What sort of opportunity?'

She hoped she didn't sound as nervous as she suddenly felt. There wasn't another person in sight and he was slowly, silently, closing the distance between them, the long black cloak he was wearing, flapping like the silken wing of a bat – and sounding similarly menacing to her ears.

They were completely alone. Even if she screamed, no one would hear her above the music, laughter and cacophony of voices which seemed so far away at this precise moment. He could murder her if he wanted to.

Now she was being ridiculous. Not even Ryan Blackwood would stoop to that.

She backed away just to be sure. She needed to keep some distance between them.

'You look nervous, Poppy. Are you nervous?'

'Should I be?'

'I think that depends on one's perspective.'

'What's that supposed to mean?'

'It means I'm going to do something that I should've done on the night we first met.'

'What? Call the police?'

Ryan burst out laughing.

'No Poppy. I don't need anyone's help for this.'

She didn't like the way he was looking at her. She didn't like what he was implying. She didn't like the fact that goose pimples were prickling her flesh. Or the way her heart was pounding in her chest, her breath coming in short, sharp gasps. And she definitely didn't like the thrill of excitement bubbling up inside her.

157

'I'll scream,' she said, as he finally closed the distance between them.

'Another time, I hope you will. But not tonight. Tonight I'm just going to show you that I'm not made of stone.'

She opened her mouth but all that came out as he reached out his arm and pulled her to him was the word: 'Ryan'.

Chapter Twenty-Two

'Ryan Blackwood kissed you!' Cleo said, and from the inflection in her voice, she wasn't sure if that was a good thing, or a bad.

Poppy, Cleo and Sophie were huddled together in a quiet corner of the sitting room where Poppy had found her friends after searching frantically for them... at the same time as she had searched for someone else.

But there was now no sign of Ryan Blackwood. Like the vampire he'd been dressed as, it seemed he'd vanished into the night.

'Then what happened?' Sophie asked. She sounded as if she had decided it was a good thing.

Poppy's cheeks burned as she remembered exactly what had happened. Every last detail of it.

'He just stopped and walked away.'

Cleo and Sophie exchanged astonished looks.

'What? Just like that. Without a word,' Cleo said.

Poppy nodded. She couldn't bring herself to speak.

'I don't understand,' Sophie said.

'Join the club,' Poppy managed.

'What did you say?'

'I... I was too... shocked to say anything.'

Cleo sighed. 'What was it like? I bet he's a good kisser, isn't he? And did he just kiss you or did he try it on? Where were his hands?'

'Cleo!' Sophie laughed. 'But yeah. Did he? And was it a passionate kiss? He looks the sort of guy who'd throw you on the bed, rip your clothes off and make mad, passionate love to you all night. What? Don't look at me like that. He does. I'm just saying.'

Poppy shook her head. 'Well, he didn't. And I'd have kneed him in the balls if he'd tried it.'

That was a lie and she knew it but there was no way she was admitting that to her friends. Not after everything she'd said about him.

And she definitely wasn't going to tell them that, after pulling her to him, his hand slid slowly down her arm, in a lover's caress, until his fingers entwined hers. Or that his other arm had eased her closer and closer to him so that her body was so tightly pressed against his she didn't know where hers ended and his began. Or that his kiss was so soft, so gentle and yet somehow so all-consuming that she felt as if her very soul was leaving her body and entering his.

'But you let him kiss you,' Cleo pointed out.

Poppy cleared her throat. 'Only because I didn't have time to think. It… it all happened so fast.'

Another lie.

'So it was just a quick kiss then?' Sophie asked. 'But was it good? I mean, would you like him to do it again?'

And again and again. But she wasn't going to tell them that, either. Or that when he'd suddenly pulled away, just as she could feel the passion building in his kiss, she'd been so mesmerised that it had taken her at least five seconds to open her eyes. Or that she could still feel his arms around her even when she saw him disappear into a crowd of revellers heading her way.

'You're being very coy about it,' Cleo said. 'I'm beginning to think you rather like Ryan Blackwood but you're too pig-headed to admit it. Probably even to yourself.'

160

'I don't like Ryan Blackwood, I can assure you of that!'
That was true, at least.

'So…' Sophie hesitated. 'You're still going to take Toby home and have sex with him then? Is that the plan? And you're going to pretend that Ryan didn't kiss you? Or are you going to tell Toby what his brother did?'

'What I don't understand,' Cleo intruded before Poppy had a chance to reply, 'is why Ryan did it. I mean, you've made it abundantly clear that you don't like him and although Oliver says he thinks the guy likes you, I can't see it, myself. He's always being sarcastic to you and he's never once given you a compliment or anything, well, not in a nice way, in any event.'

Sophie nodded. 'That's true. And why kiss you tonight? I mean let's face it, you've looked better.'

'Thanks!' Poppy said.

Sophie laughed. 'I didn't mean it like that. I meant you looked stunning on the night he met you and you looked really good on that night of the Blood Moon but he didn't try to kiss you then. Or did he? You said you were alone with him in the kitchen for a while that night. Did anything happen then? Have you been keeping more secrets from us?'

Poppy shook her head. After Oliver had proposed, she'd told Cleo and Sophie the story of how she'd helped Oliver with his tie that night and how Ryan had found the ring after Oliver lost it, and that when Oliver left and she made coffee, Ryan had actually said the word "please", without being reminded to do so – probably for the first time in his life.

'No. I told you, I made coffee and a few minutes later, your mum came in with Hugh, Veronique and Tony.'

'Okay,' Sophie said. 'And that night he joined us for dinner, you looked lovely then. But that was the night he

161

gave you that speech about not wanting to see his brother get hurt. Although he did ask if you had feelings for Toby, didn't he? And he also said he didn't think Toby was the man for you, or that you were the woman for Toby. Perhaps that was his roundabout way of saying that he fancied you himself.'

'Yeah,' Cleo said. 'And seeing you tonight with plastic snakes in your hair, he was unable to restrain himself any longer.' A burst of laughter escaped her. 'I'm sorry but I just don't see that somehow.'

Poppy lowered her eyes. 'I think… I think it may have something to do with Toby but I'm not sure. To tell you the truth, I'm not really sure about anything anymore. Let's get a drink.'

'Now that, I agree with wholeheartedly,' Cleo said.

Chapter Twenty-Three

'There's something I need to tell you,' Toby said, an hour or so later.

Poppy had been trying to avoid him. She'd also been searching for Ryan.

'Oh, okay. Um. Have you seen your brother?'

Toby frowned. 'Yeah. He left over an hour ago. Parties aren't really his scene. He finds them boring.'

'Is… is that what he said?'

Toby shrugged. 'No. He just said he hoped he'd see me later.'

'So… he's coming back?'

'I don't think so, no. I think he meant he hoped to see me at home later.'

'Oh, did he?'

Did that mean that Ryan Blackwood thought his kiss had been so good that Poppy would no longer want his younger brother? That she'd send Toby home tonight and not take him back to her bed. The arrogant bastard!

But did that mean there was a possibility that Ryan wanted her for himself?

'And that's what I need to talk to you about,' Toby continued. 'Can we go somewhere quiet?'

She let him lead her towards the door, her mind in a whirl. Then she stopped.

'Toby, if you're saying that you want to go somewhere and have sex, then I'm really sorry but the answer's no. I… I've got a bit of a headache. I think I need to get a good night's sleep.'

'I don't want to have sex.' He shrugged. 'Well, that's not true. I do. The point is, I can't.'

'What? What d'you mean by "can't"? Can't physically or can't emotionally?'

He gave her an odd look. 'If you're suggesting there's something wrong with my equipment, forget it. That bad boy has never let me down for a day in my life. And he's not going to start now. I could cure that headache in five seconds flat but you certainly wouldn't get any sleep. The reason I can't is because Ryan won't let me.'

Poppy wasn't sure whether she should be pleased or furious. What did he mean by Ryan wouldn't let him? Toby wasn't a fifteen-year-old. His brother couldn't tell him whom he could and couldn't go to bed with.

'Are you saying that Ryan has told you that you can't have sex with me? That he came right out and said it? When? When did he say that? Tonight?'

Toby shook his head. 'No. He said it when I was in Dubai.'

'Dubai? But that was weeks ago. Oh! Is that why I haven't seen you very much and more to the point, why you didn't want to come in after our date last Saturday? I thought it was strange after you'd gone to all the trouble and expense of the rose petals, the carriage, booking an entire restaurant just for us, the quartet. If anything says, "I want to have sex tonight," that did. But all you did was kiss me and go home. Sorry, I'm trying to get my head around this. Ryan actually told you that you couldn't have sex with me? You're thirty years old, Toby. He can't tell you what to do!'

'Strictly speaking, he didn't say I couldn't. In fact, he said I could have sex with you whenever, wherever and as often as I wanted. But I could do it without his money.'

'What!' This wasn't making any sense. No sense at all. 'I don't understand, Toby. What're you saying? And what's his money got to do with it?'

'I'm saying...' Toby said, looking around to make sure no one was listening, 'I'm telling you that Ryan wants me to marry the daughter of a friend of his – his co-director in one of his companies, actually. That's why he wanted me to go to Dubai. She was staying with friends there. She was in Paris, too. That's where the family live.'

'What?'

Toby nodded. 'He's really serious this time. It makes complete sense to him. I suppose he thinks it's sort of pooling our resources. He thinks she's the perfect woman for me.'

'What?' Poppy said again. She couldn't believe what he was saying. 'This isn't the eighteenth century, Toby. Older brothers can't force their younger brothers to marry people they don't want to! Why don't you just tell him to sod off? I can't believe the man. I thought... well, I don't know what I thought. First I thought he was just an arrogant jerk. Then I thought – stupidly it seems – he was a decent guy. Now I realise the tyrannical bastard thinks he can buy and sell anything and anyone just because he's got money. God, I hate that man!'

'He's my brother, Poppy.'

'I'm sorry, Toby, I know he is. And it says so much about you that you still care about him even though he's... he's trying to manipulate you. No, worse than that. He's trying to control your life. And not just your life. The lives of anyone who happens to cross his path. I'd like to ring his bloody neck. Sorry. But I would.'

'I feel the same way sometimes. And so does Stephanie.'

Now Poppy understood why Stephanie was so unhappy.

So unfriendly. Had Ryan Blackwood forced – or at the very least, manipulated her into unhappy marriages just to suit his purposes? This was incredible. This was no better than… than slavery or… or selling people for the sex trade. This made Jeremiah and Hermione's smuggling and Barnabus and Sophia's piracy pale in comparison.

But hold on.

She'd just told Toby this wasn't the eighteenth century. Stephanie and Toby weren't gullible people searching for a better life and Ryan didn't have them under lock and key. They could just say no. They could simply walk away.

'But you don't have to do it, Toby. Not if you don't want to. Nor does Stephanie. He can't force either of you to marry someone you don't want to. And he can't tell you who you can and can't have sex with either.'

'That's easy for you to say. You don't know Ryan. He'd do anything to get what he wants. Absolutely anything.'

Now she really did have a headache. Was that why Ryan had kissed her? Is that what he meant when he'd said he was going to do something he should've done the night he'd met her? He should've led her on to keep her away from Toby. Made her think there was a possibility he was interested in her. How far would he be prepared to go to keep Toby and her apart? To make sure that Toby complied with his wishes and didn't fall for her? The man really was a complete and utter bastard.

He'd certainly made a mistake if he thought he could control *her*.

'Toby. Come home with me and stay the night. We'll show Ryan bloody Blackwood that he can't tell either of us what to do.'

166

Chapter Twenty-Four

Poppy frowned over her coffee as she sat in the curve of the bow window in Betty's Pantry. Even the rain seemed to be reprimanding her this morning as it lashed ferociously against the glass.

'I love you, Poppy,' Thaddeus said. 'You know that, but sometimes you're such a bloody idiot I want to grab you by the throat and shake some sense into that crazy head of yours.'

'Why?' Poppy whimpered like a lonely puppy. 'What've *I* done wrong? If you want to grab anyone by the throat, it should be that bastard, Ryan Blackwood. And you should strangle him while you're at it.'

'Nope,' Oliver said. 'I'd have to go along with Thaddeus on this. You're an idiot, Poppy.'

Cleo tutted. 'I don't think calling her names is going to help the situation, is it? We all know she's an idiot at times. Even she knows she's an idiot sometimes. The point is, where do we go from here?'

'I don't think we should do anything,' Sophie said. 'Yes, Poppy may have behaved like an idiot but no real damage has been done, has it? We should wait and see what happens.'

'Will everyone please stop calling me an idiot! I'm not an idiot. Well okay, sometimes I am, but Toby told me, so it's not just me saying it. It's him. And if anyone should know what Ryan Blackwood's really like, then surely it's his brother?'

'But we've only got Toby's word for it,' Sophie said. 'I know you think he's your destiny, Poppy, but I'm sorry to say that I'd take Ryan's word over Toby's any day of the week.'

The others all nodded in agreement.

'Why? What has Toby ever done to make you doubt his word? And what has Ryan done to make you believe his?'

'Well, for one,' Thaddeus said. 'The Goldebury Bay Yachting and Sailing Club development is supposed to be Toby's project and yet he's never there, from what I've heard, and he's done nothing to get to know any of the local residents, whereas Ryan has.'

Oliver nodded. 'And Ryan's reached out to local businessmen, like us for example, about the possibility of working with them. Toby hasn't.'

'We can always say she was drunk,' Sophie said. 'I'm sure Ryan would believe that. He's seen how much we all drink at times. And despite her trying to drag Toby back to her cottage for the night, he didn't go, so at least there's no emotional fallout from that to deal with.'

'Excuse me!' Poppy shrieked. 'But there *is* emotional fallout to deal with. I'm feeling very emotional. Toby was so terrified of what that obnoxious git would do, that despite being desperate to sleep with me, he had to run home and report in! Not that you lot seem to care. All you seem to care about is how upset Ryan sodding Blackwood might be if he finds out that after he kissed me – which, by the way, makes me sick to my stomach just to think about – I still tried to sleep with his brother. And despite what you say, I don't regret for even one second, getting his number from Toby's phone and telling that bastard exactly what I thought about him. I'm just sorry I had to leave him a message – well, six messages – but anyway, I'd rather have actually spoken to him.'

168

'Oh my God!' Cleo said, peering through a stream of rain water running down the length of the bow window. 'It's Ryan... and he's coming this way! I told you we should've discussed this at one of our homes.'

Even Poppy slouched slightly into her seat, but when Ryan opened the door and shook the rain from his umbrella, there was a huge smile on his face which if anything, grew broader when he spotted them.

'Hello,' he called out in a friendly greeting as he approached their table. 'God, it's cold and wet out there. Almost cold enough for snow.' He rubbed his bare hands together. 'How are you all this morning? Is there room for one more? That's if you don't mind me joining you for breakfast. Only Poppy did invite me.'

Poppy's head shot up. 'No I didn't! Didn't you get my—?'

'Of course you can join us!' Sophie interrupted, her voice loud enough to deafen every customer in the tearoom. Beneath the table, she kicked Poppy's booted foot at the same time.

'Ow!' Poppy glared at her.

Oliver leapt out of his seat. 'I'll get you a chair.'

'Don't worry, Oliver,' replied Ryan. 'If Poppy doesn't mind budging up slightly, I can squeeze on the window seat beside her.'

What the hell was he playing at? She'd have to let him. The others were looking at her, as if to refuse would be signing her own death warrant.

She moved along the seat as far as she possibly could without falling off and even then, when he took off his coat and sat down, the sleeve of his woollen sweater still tickled her bare wrist like a naughty child trying to aggravate a grown up.

'Thanks again for the invitation to the party last night,'

Ryan was saying. 'I enjoyed myself far more than I imagined. The parties I've attended for the last few years seemed to be full of minor celebrities trying to impress as many people as possible. I'd forgotten what a real party was like.'

'We're having another one next Saturday,' Thaddeus said. 'For Guy Fawkes Night, to coincide with the firework display put on by the local council. It should be a lot of fun and virtually everyone who lives or works in Goldebury Bay will pop in during the evening. Please come.'

'Thank you. I'd love to.'

'Your family are welcome too, of course,' Sophie said. 'We didn't see Stephanie or Jules last night. Are they both well?'

'Yes. They're very well, thanks. They went to Paris with me on Friday and decided to stay for a few extra days. Stephanie really loves it. She has a very good friend who lives there. Toby flew out this morning to join them. Oh Poppy! What's wrong? You're choking. Let me help you.'

He reached out and gave her an almost playful slap on the back.

In her haste to get away from him, she fell off the seat and landed in a heap on the floor but Ryan was on his feet in a second, gently lifting her and returning her to the padded cushion of the window seat.

His face showed genuine concern. 'Are you okay?'

'I'm fine.' She looked away.

'Have you hurt yourself, Poppy?' Thaddeus asked.

She smiled and shook her head. 'No. Honestly, Thaddeus, I'm fine.'

Ryan was still staring at her when Betty came shuffling over to see if her first-aider skills were required. Poppy assured her they weren't.

'Perhaps a piece of carrot cake might help,' Ryan said,

170

smiling at Poppy.

'No. It wouldn't,' Poppy snapped.

'May I have some coffee, please Betty? And a slice of toast with some of your delicious home-made marmalade. Would anyone else like anything?'

Oliver shook his head. 'No thanks, Ryan. We've already eaten. We've been here for nearly an hour, and I for one, must love you and leave you all.' He smiled at Cleo and kissed her on the cheek. 'I'll only be an hour or so. I'll see you at home.'

'Actually, darling,' Cleo said. 'I thought I might ask Poppy and Sophie to come Christmas shopping with me today. It is the first of November, after all.'

'That sounds like an excellent idea,' Sophie said. 'Shall we go to Eastbourne?'

Poppy shrugged. 'I'm not really in the mood for Christmas shopping. You two go without me. I just want to go home.'

'Don't be such a misery,' Cleo said. 'You love Christmas and you love Christmas shopping.'

Poppy glowered at Ryan. 'Not today, I don't.' She smiled at Sophie and Cleo. 'Seriously. You two go without me. I'm just not in the mood and I don't want to spoil it for you. I'll go with you another day. And actually, I think I'm going to go home and lie down for a while.'

'Are you sure you didn't hurt yourself, Poppy?' Ryan asked again, clearly concerned.

'No,' she said. 'I didn't hurt myself. But someone else hurt me. Wait for me, Oliver. I'll walk with you.'

'Are you sure you're okay?' Cleo asked. 'We can all go shopping another day. Why don't Sophie and I come home with you, order pizza, drink loads of wine, stuff ourselves with chocolate and watch weepy movies? How does that sound? Are you up for that, Sophie?'

171

'Absolutely. You don't mind do you, Thaddeus?'

Thaddeus shook his head. 'Not in the least. When Oliver's checked everything's okay at the restaurant, we'll do something along the same lines. Only it'll be sport instead of weepy movies. Sound good, Oliver?'

Oliver nodded. 'Sounds like a plan.'

'Fancy joining us?' Thaddeus and Oliver asked Ryan simultaneously. They looked at each other and smiled.

Ryan seemed surprised. 'That sounds like a good way to spend a cold, wet Sunday. Are you sure you don't mind? Please don't feel you need to invite me out of politeness.'

'We wouldn't,' Thaddeus said. 'Believe me, if we didn't want you around, we wouldn't have made the offer.'

'Then I'd love to. Thanks.'

Poppy shook her head and glared at both Thaddeus and Oliver in turn. 'Unbelievable!' she said, completely ignoring Ryan. 'Just sodding unbelievable.' Then she looked at Cleo and Sophie. 'Are you coming then, or what?'

They both jumped to their feet.

'Yes, madam. Right away, madam,' Sophie said with a smile.

'Now who's being bossy and controlling?' Cleo added. 'No! Let's get out of here before you say another word. Have fun, boys!'

Cleo ushered Poppy out and Sophie closed the door behind them leaving Oliver and Thaddeus still talking to Ryan.

'Well, that was weird,' Cleo said. 'For someone who must have listened to six very unpleasant messages on his phone this morning, he was as bright and shiny as a new button, as Miff would say.'

'He probably gets them all the time,' Poppy said. 'He's so used to them that he doesn't even bat an eyelid. And you see I was right. He's sent Toby back to Paris. He really is determined to marry his brother off just to make more money. It is truly unbelievable.'

'Actually, Poppy,' Cleo said. 'It is unbelievable. I know what Toby told you but no matter how powerful Ryan may be, or even thinks he may be, he can't force Toby or Stephanie to marry people they don't want to. Not in this day and age. But what he can do, and I'm beginning to think this is the point, is stop paying all their bills.'

'What's that supposed to mean?'

'Oh come on, Poppy. If you weren't so infatuated with Toby, you'd be the first to say this. In all that stuff we read on the internet, not one report mentioned Toby or Stephanie having made money of their own. Even Toby admits they were poor growing up. Jules clearly didn't have any money and their Uncle Joe obviously wasn't flush so Ryan holds the purse strings because it's his purse. Obviously, he doesn't have a purse but you know what I mean.'

'Of course!' Sophie said. 'It's so obvious when you think about it. Didn't it say that Toby joined Ryan's company after trying his hand at several other things? I think that basically means that he couldn't make it on his own and Ryan's taken him under his wing.'

Poppy tutted. 'I'm not sure what you're trying to say, but Ryan should take him under his wing. He's his brother for God's sake. And as for Ryan holding the purse strings, are you suggesting that he bankrolls them? Again, why shouldn't he?'

'Because they're both adults,' Cleo said. 'They shouldn't be looking to Ryan for money. They should have careers of their own. And Stephanie's been married three times so if anyone should be paying for her rather lavish lifestyle, it should be her husbands, not her brother.'

'That's all very interesting,' Poppy said. 'But it's pure

173

speculation. We don't know whether Ryan does pay their bills, although personally I think he should. He could even give them an allowance of some sort. He's got plenty of money.'

'Perhaps he does give them an allowance. But perhaps he's sick of them wasting it.'

'I agree with Cleo,' Sophie said. 'It makes sense. Didn't Toby say that Ryan told him he could have sex with you but not with Ryan's money? Or something along those lines. Perhaps Ryan has decided enough is enough.'

Cleo nodded. 'And you said that Ryan told you himself that he'd seen the invoice for the carriage hire. You assumed Ryan had been snooping through Toby's papers. Perhaps what actually happened was that Ryan paid the bill. So when you look at it like that, Ryan paid for your entire date, whilst Toby had all the fun.'

Poppy didn't like where this conversation was going. And she definitely didn't like the thought that Ryan may have paid for her date.

She'd been furious last night when she'd phoned him and the fact that she'd got his answerphone had made her even angrier. She'd called him a mean, penny-pinching bully, a tyrant, a womaniser, a liar and a cheat and much more besides. She'd said he was a cold-hearted bastard who had no idea how to treat a woman, let alone make love to one. That he was clearly jealous of his brother's relationships and that the only pleasure Mr Ryan-arrogant-jerk-Blackwood got out of life was controlling other people's.

And that was just the first message of the six.

Perhaps her friends were right. Perhaps she really was an idiot.

Chapter Twenty-Five

Poppy felt like death warmed over. Monday morning wasn't her favourite time of the week and this Monday morning had clearly been sent from hell. With bells on. And they were ringing in her ears.

What she needed was a steaming cup of coffee, having discovered at six a.m. that she'd completely run out of the stuff. Then she needed a shower, having discovered at five past six that her boiler had decided to go on strike. After that she needed a lobotomy, having decided after an entire sleepless night, that she wasn't just an idiot, she was a blind, sarcastic, opinionated idiot of the highest degree.

The more she had thought about it, the more her friends had said made sense. Ryan Blackwood may not be a nice person; he may even have used her but he didn't deserve the things she'd said about him. And not just about him – to him, via those awful voice messages.

And yet in Betty's Pantry yesterday he hadn't seemed to want to give her like-for-like. Perhaps she really had misjudged him.

'Oh my God!' Poppy said, opening her front door and looking directly into Ryan Blackwood's eyes.

'I didn't mean to make you jump. I was about to ring the bell when you opened the door. I think we need to talk.'

From the expression on his face, her Monday morning was about to get a whole lot worse.

'What... what d'you want to talk about?'

'Well, for one thing, I'd like to thank you for your

messages. All six of them. I believe you managed to call me things I've never been called before. And I've been called a lot of unpleasant things in my time.'

'Have you only just got them? I left them on Saturday night.'

'I'm well aware of that. And no, I heard them shortly after they were left. It may surprise you to know that I've listened to them several times since then.'

'But… but yesterday in Betty's Pantry, everything seemed fine. Well, not everything, obviously, but you… you didn't seem at all bothered.'

'Looks can often be deceiving, and so can actions, as I've discovered. Besides, I try not to air my grievances in public unless I have no choice. I wasn't about to discuss the matter in front of your friends and because of the way the day panned out, I didn't have an opportunity to discuss it with you alone. Not that it seems we have much to discuss. I suppose you're on your way to work, so I'll keep this brief.'

'Um… I'm out of coffee, and my boiler's broken. I was on my way to Cleo's to beg for coffee and a shower.'

'Then it seems your day may be as bad as mine. I won't keep you. I simply wanted you to know that Toby will be back for the party on Saturday and that I've removed any obstacles in his way. The path is clear for you and he to do as you wish. I only hope you like where it takes you. I don't suppose we'll bump into one another again, so I'll wish you well.'

He turned away but this time the limo was waiting. It was only as he stepped into the rear that Poppy noticed he was wearing a suit.

'Ryan!' She called out but he didn't stop. And as the car drove off, he didn't look back.

Chapter Twenty-Six

Neither Poppy nor any of her friends really understood what Ryan Blackwood had meant on Monday when he'd told Poppy that he'd removed any obstacles in his brother's way. They all understood completely what he had meant when he'd said that Toby and Poppy could do as they wished. They all thought they understood what he had meant by hoping Poppy liked the path it took her on. What they didn't understand at all was what he had meant by being unlikely to bump into her again.

Was Ryan Blackwood leaving Goldebury Bay?

Had he in fact, left already?

There was definitely something 'final' in the way the limo had driven away and no one had seen or heard from Ryan since.

So when Poppy bumped into Timothy Richards in Betty's Pantry on Friday morning, she hoped he may know something she didn't.

'Hello Timothy,' she said. 'Mind if I join you?'

'Join me? Yes of course. But if you're hoping to have some fun at my expense I should tell you now, you'll be disappointed. Not even your sarcastic barbs can irritate me today.'

Poppy took a seat opposite him. 'I didn't think they ever did. I thought they were like water off a duck's back as far as you were concerned. Although I must admit, they gave me pleasure.'

'Looks can be deceiving.'

'Yeah. I'm hearing that a lot these days. So how are you then? You seem very pleased with life.'

Timothy nodded. 'I am. My agent called this morning and I've been offered a seven-figure sum for my book. I can't believe it. That's rarer than hen's teeth these days. Seven figures! And you know what this means, don't you?'

'That you're paying for my coffee?'

Timothy laughed. 'Happily, Poppy. I'll even buy you cake.'

'Let's not be rash, Timothy. It is only seven figures after all – and I imagine several of those will be zeros. That's a lot of zeros. Sorry. I'm being sarcastic and that's not nice.'

'Who told you that?'

'Several people but not in so many words. So tell me Timothy, what does the seven-figure deal mean?'

'It means… I'm moving to L.A. I know you suggested Timbuktu, or somewhere inhabited by aliens but the climates don't suit me.'

Poppy shrugged. 'Many people might say that L.A. is the happy medium between the two – but not me of course, because that would be sarcastic and I'm no longer doing that.'

'Of course you're not. You can't even last five minutes. I don't hold out much hope.'

'There's always hope, Timothy. No matter how bad things get, one always has to have hope. Cleo and Clara told me that. How are things with you and Stephanie Blackwood-not-Blackwood-whatever-her-name-is?'

He grinned. 'Dead in the water.'

'Oh. I'm sorry to hear that.'

'Since when have you been concerned about my love life?'

'I'm not. I was hoping for some inside information.'

'About Toby?'

Poppy shook her head. 'The other one.'

'Ryan? You want inside info on Ryan Blackwood?' He gave her a curious look.

'Did I hear you mention that handsome Blackwood chap?' Betty queried, shuffling over to their table with coffee and a selection of cakes.

'I hope my hearing's still as good as yours when I'm your age, Betty,' Poppy quipped.

Timothy leant forward. 'I think you'll find that's sarcasm.'

'Bugger!' Poppy grinned at Timothy and then smiled at Betty. 'Yes, Betty, you did.'

'Popped in here on Monday to say goodbye, he did. Lovely young man. You should find yourself a man like that, Poppy. Rich too. That always helps. But never flashed it around or put on airs and graces. Not like that sister of his. Real piece of work that one, if you ask me. Been married three times, I hear and she's younger than you, dear. But then, you're no baby in a cradle, are you? The clock's a ticking.'

'Are you sure that's not your egg timer, Betty?'

Betty shuffled round the table, cocked her head to one side and then shuffled back.

'You're a devil, you are, Poppy, make no mistake.'

'Did he say where he was going?' Poppy asked. 'Or when he'd be back?'

Betty looked thoughtful. 'No dear. And I did ask. He said he was going to be in several places but none would have marmalade like mine, he was sure of that. And he hoped that one day he'd be able to return here but it wouldn't be for the foreseeable future. Seemed rather sad to be going, truth to tell. But I heard you never liked him for some reason, so that's probably good news to your ears.'

'You'd certainly think that, wouldn't you? But oddly

enough, it's not.'

'Be back in a jiffy, dear. Table four wants something.' Betty shuffled away.

Timothy grinned broadly. 'Don't tell me you've fallen for Ryan Blackwood. I thought you were seeing Toby.'

'I wouldn't say I've fallen for him, exactly. I just... I would just like the opportunity to put something right, that's all. And as for seeing Toby, it turns out, I wasn't seeing the real Toby at all, I don't think.'

'May I give you a piece of advice? Go back to the sarcasm. Being profound isn't working for you.'

'Bugger off. So anyway, what can you tell me about Ryan or the Blackwoods in general, for that matter?'

Timothy shrugged. 'Depends what you want to know. They were poor. Ryan worked hard and is very clever. Now they're rich. Ryan's the one with all the money of course, but according to the delightful Stephanie – who is a bit of a nutcase if you ask me – Ryan gives them all an annual allowance, including the grandmother, Jules.'

'What sort of an allowance?'

'She didn't say but from the sounds of it, pretty big I would imagine. He's also set up trusts for his sister and brother which they get when they're thirty-five. Then they'll have money of their own. Although as it's from Ryan's coffers, I think that's a misnomer. It does mean they don't have to ask him to support them though or rely on the annual allowance – providing they don't waste it all. And from what I've seen and heard about Stephanie – and Toby for that matter – that's a distinct possibility.'

'Toby told me that Ryan wants him to marry Ryan's co-director's daughter. Do you know anything about that?'

'Ah... the lovely Sabine Chevalier.' Timothy nodded. 'She's not Toby's usual type. He goes for blondes like you, according to my friends in the media. Sabine's a brunette and very career-driven. She's got her own designer fashion label. She's not that well known yet but she will be. I assume Ryan thinks she may be a steadying influence on Toby. He's a bit of a runaround from what I've heard, so you're better off without him. He means well, don't get me wrong but he falls in and out of love faster than water through a colander. He's like Stephanie in that way. Rumour has it that Ryan's had to sort out a few problems over the years in relation to both his siblings' love lives. Stephanie's latest husband knocked her about, so I've heard.'

'You're joking! I thought there was something odd about that whole 'Where's Stephanie?' thing. Tell me more.'

'Sorry. I don't know much else. I do know she still 'loves' him and would go back to him tomorrow. She told me that herself the last time I saw her. But Ryan's threatened to stop her allowance and the trust fund, so for now, she's staying where she is. That's it. That's the extent of my info on the Blackwoods.'

'Thanks so much, Timothy. I never thought I'd say this but you're not such a bad guy.'

'Thanks. So is it over between you and Toby then?'

Poppy nodded. 'Pretty much. I thought he was the man for me but once again, it seems I got it wrong. I'm hopeless at this love stuff.'

Timothy leant forward and toyed with her fingers. 'You could always come to L.A. with me. Imagine it. Christmas in the sun.'

Poppy looked into his eyes. 'Don't tempt me, Timothy. The way I'm feeling right now, I might say yes, and I think we both know that would be a very big mistake. Besides, I like my Christmases cold. It doesn't seem right snuggling up in front of a wood-burning stove when it's hot enough to lounge around in a bikini outside.'

'Well, the offer's there if you want it. I'll give you my number, just in case. I'm renting a pretty snazzy house and of course, there's a pool. You'd love it there, Poppy. I know you would.'

Poppy saw the look Betty gave her and Timothy as she shuffled back towards them. This time tomorrow, everyone in Goldebury Bay would think that they were moving to L.A. together.

Oh well, it could be worse.

Chapter Twenty-Seven

'It had better not be true, Poppy!' Thaddeus demanded when Poppy arrived with Cleo and Oliver for the Guy Fawkes Night party on Saturday night.

'Oh God. What've I done now?'

'If you even consider moving anywhere with that shit, Timothy Richards, I'll have something to say about it.'

Poppy burst out laughing. 'Don't be a pillock, Thaddeus. The day he and I are picking out china patterns together will be the day hell freezes over. I don't think he's as bad as I used to but I know how you feel about him and I would never knowingly do anything to hurt you. I can't believe you listen to such nonsense.'

'So there's no truth whatsoever in the rumour?'

'No Thaddeus, there isn't.' Poppy tutted. 'And you call me an idiot. At least I know gossip when I hear it.'

'Do you? I think recent events have shown that you can be just as blind to the true facts as any of us. Sorry I shouted. But I love you and I want you to find someone who'll be good for you.'

'Yeah. That's not gonna happen anytime soon. Okay, let's get this party started.'

'Have you heard from Toby?' Sophie asked.

'This morning. He said he'll see me here tonight and that he's got some exciting news for me.'

'You didn't tell me that!' Cleo said.

Poppy shrugged. 'To be honest, it didn't seem that important. I told you, I've realised he's probably not the man for me so it doesn't really matter what his news is. I just didn't want to tell him that's it's over, via the phone. I'd rather do it face-to-face.'

'Unless it's something to do with the Goldebury Bay Yachting and Sailing Club,' Sophie suggested.

'Oh yeah. I forgot about that. We'll know soon enough. He said he'll be here at eight and it's nearly eight now.' She saw the look on Sophie's face. 'Don't start panicking.'

'Everything's ready, Sophie,' Oliver said. 'We put the chilli on when we were here this afternoon, the jacket potatoes are in the outdoor oven and all the burgers and sausages are ready to be cooked. The rice won't take long and everything else just needs to be heated up. And it goes without saying, Veronique's done all her party preparations. It's all under control.'

'Thanks, Oliver. And that's just as well because it looks as though our first guests are arriving.'

As the first guests were the Pollards, Paul Temple, Thaddeus' uncle Theodore and his wife, Precious, together with the entire Sutton family, including Ben and his new boyfriend Frank, Sophie and Thaddeus' vintner, no one was overly concerned.

'Really?' Poppy said. 'Now even Ben's got a boyfriend. Well, now I really am going to be a Christmas gooseberry. Oh joy.'

'You never know,' Cleo said, linking her arm through Poppy's. 'You may meet someone here tonight.'

'Yeah right. You seem to be forgetting that I know everyone in Goldebury Bay and there's not one potential boyfriend amongst them.'

'Is that a helicopter I hear?' Thaddeus said.

All eyes turned towards the west where the whip-whip-whip sound of rotor blades seemed to be coming from. It looked as if the pilot planned to land on the top of Summer

Hill Cliff.

'Hello darlings!' Ben called out, competing with the noise from above. 'I'll bet my last penny that's the Blackwoods arriving.'

Poppy's heart skipped a beat at the sound of that name. Was this just Toby or was the entire Blackwood family in that helicopter? She'd even be pleased to see Stephanie and Jules if Ryan had come with them. Not that she was excited at the prospect of seeing Ryan, but she did owe him some sort of apology, and she'd rather get that over and done with as soon as possible.

The helicopter landed far enough away from the house, marquee and makeshift car park, not to cause a nuisance and one by one the occupants stepped out. Toby was first and he helped Jules down. Stephanie followed and finally, Ryan Blackwood.

Poppy was just about to shout: 'Oi, Blackwood' but he was helping someone else onto the grass. It was the most beautiful woman Poppy had seen in her entire life.

As they walked towards the house, the woman's arm linked through Ryan's, her long, lustrous waves of red hair tumbled around her perfect heart-shaped face, lightly tanned and with the added benefit of being at least six years younger than Poppy's. From this distance, the woman looked around twenty-six or -seven. She was smiling up at Ryan who was laughing as he looked down at her. And that laughter seemed to carry on the breeze and dance around Poppy like children round a bonfire.

'Darling!' Ben said, tapping Poppy's arm. 'Who *is* that stunning redhead with Ryan?'

'Don't know. Don't care,' Poppy said. 'I'm going to see if anyone needs any help in the kitchen.'

She walked away, but turned as a familiar voice called out her name for the third time in a row.

185

'Poppy! Why are you ignoring me?' Toby said, looking and sounding like a petulant child.

'Hello Toby. I wasn't ignoring you. I didn't hear you call. That helicopter's making an awful racket. Will it be leaving anytime soon?'

Toby frowned. 'It was the quickest way to get here from the airport. Blame Ryan, not me. It'll be leaving any second. But aren't you pleased to see me? I told you I've got exciting news.'

'That's nice. What is it?'

'Are you okay? Have I done something to upset you? I'm not sure I want to tell you now.'

Poppy sighed and turned away. 'Fine. I'll be in the kitchen if you change your mind.'

'Poppy! Why are you behaving like this?'

She glanced past him and saw the woman give Ryan a playful slap.

'Like what? I haven't got time for this, Toby. Either tell me or not, the choice is yours. I'm going. You know where the kitchen is if you want me.'

'That's my news. I do want you. Well, I did. I'm not so sure now. Ryan's said I'm free to do as I please and he won't stand in my way. In our way. He's not going to stop my allowance or change the trust. Shit, he's even said that he'll make some sort of provision for you. Which he's never done for any of the others. Well, not whilst I was with them. Um. But you don't need to know that. That's all in the past. Sorry. I'm not thinking clearly. This wasn't how I expected this conversation to go.'

'Oh. And how exactly did you expect it to go?'

Had he just said that she was one in a long line of other women? And that Ryan had paid them off. Presumably, so that they wouldn't sell their stories to the tabloids. So it was all true. How could she have been so blind? And Ryan was

186

offering to give her some sort of payment! What did he think she was? There was no way she was apologising to that arrogant, obnoxious git now.

'I expected you to be as pleased to see me as I am to see you,' Toby said, a peeved expression on his face. 'This means that we can be together. That I can spend every night with you for as long as I like. As we like. And I don't have to worry about the money. Isn't that great?'

'Oddly enough Toby, no. It's not. And you can tell that brother of yours from me, that he can keep his sodding money. I don't want a single penny of it and what's more, Toby, I'm sorry but I don't want you. This... whatever it was, is over. What I do want is a very, very large glass of red wine.'

Chapter Twenty-Eight

It was five minutes to nine and that meant it would soon be time for the fireworks display to start. The bonfire on Summer Hill Cliff had been burning steadily for over an hour and throngs of people were standing around it drinking, chatting and laughing as if they didn't have a care in the world. The food was plentiful; drink was flowing as freely as the incoming tide in the cove below and for the third night in a row, the rain had held off.

The moon was in its final quarter and what little light it was giving was obscured by a bank of high cloud. Summer Hill Cliff would have been in almost complete darkness if it weren't for the long swathes of light thrown out by the red-gold flames of the fire, and the myriad twinkling fairy lights and larger spotlights still dotted all around, from the edge of the cliff to Summerhill itself.

'There you are, Poppy,' Thaddeus said. 'I wondered where you'd got to. I've just come in to switch off all the lights. The general consensus is that the fireworks will look more impressive if they don't have to compete with the glare this place is giving off.'

'I hope you've told everyone to stay away from the edge of the cliff then. Without the lights showing where it ends, some idiot is bound to topple over and land in a crumpled heap in the cove. And the way things are going lately, that idiot will probably be me.'

Thaddeus grinned. 'Veronique thought of that. Didn't you see the makeshift fence? It's only metal poles and rope but hopefully it'll stop anyone from getting too close to the edge. You're coming out to watch the fireworks, aren't you?'

Poppy nodded. 'I'll be out in a minute. You go on without me.'

Thaddeus gave her an odd look. 'Is everything okay? I saw Toby wandering around like a lost sheep earlier. I take it you've told him you're no longer interested?'

'I think he got the message.'

Thaddeus flicked several switches one after another and through the kitchen window Poppy could see the rows of fairy lights going out one by one; the final switch throwing the cliff edge into darkness. The only light now was from the kitchen and a couple of other rooms inside the house, the fire outside and the lights of Goldebury Bay below, to the east of Summer Hill Cliff.

'Don't trip over anything,' Poppy said.

'Come with me.' Thaddeus held out his hand.

Poppy shook her head. 'I'll be out in a minute. Honestly, I will.'

With one final look, Thaddeus smiled and headed back outside.

Poppy turned and grabbed a bottle, opened it and poured herself a glass of wine. She heard the kitchen door swing open and smiled as she twisted round.

'Thaddeus. I said I'll be—'

'Hello Poppy,' Ryan said, standing in the doorway.

Poppy couldn't speak. She couldn't move. She couldn't breathe. She couldn't do anything except stare.

'What, no sarcastic remark? No comment about me being too late to take my rightful place as the guy on the bonfire?' He stared into her eyes. 'Not even... hello?'

She breathed in deeply. 'The last time I saw you, you said we wouldn't be bumping into one another again. That

189

was five days ago, yet here we are.'

'Yes, here we are.'

'And I see you've brought along a friend.'

He smiled. 'She's not a friend, Poppy. She's much more to me than a friend.'

Poppy swallowed the lump in her throat. 'She's much younger too, from what I saw of her. I didn't think you were the type of man who'd go for bimbos. Especially redheads.'

The smile turned into a grin – a very mischievous grin that lit up his eyes like the sparklers being waved around by the children on the cliff.

'Actually, Poppy, Lucy's only a year younger than you. And she's anything but a bimbo. She's a lawyer. A damn good lawyer. As for me being that type of man, I don't know why you'd be surprised. From the messages you left me last weekend, you seemed to have a very low opinion of me. Has your opinion changed?'

Poppy ignored the question. 'You seem very close. Have you known her long?'

'Yes.'

Poppy glared at him. 'You never said you had a girlfriend.'

'You never seemed the slightest bit interested in my love life. Has that changed too?'

Now she was furious. 'I see some things haven't changed. You're still an arrogant jerk.'

'And you're still as sweet and charming as ever.'

'At least I don't pretend to be something I'm not.'

'That's very true. You're one of the most genuine people I've ever met. You and Lucy are very much alike. You must meet her.'

'I don't want to meet her! And we're not alike. I don't like her taste in men, for starters. Wait a minute. Were you

190

dating her when you kissed me?'

'Absolutely not! Um… Forgive me for saying this, but if I didn't know better, I'd think you were jealous. Are you jealous, Poppy? There's no need to be. Our relationship is not what you seem to think.'

'I'm not in the least bit jealous! I couldn't care less what it is. But whilst we're on the subject of relationships, what do you think I am? How dare you tell Toby you would "make some provision for me"! I can't be bought and sold. I didn't want *his* money and I certainly don't want yours.'

'That's good to know. And if what Toby told me half an hour ago is true, it seems you no longer want Toby either. I'd heard a rumour to that effect but I thought I'd come here tonight and ask you myself.'

'It's true. So if that large, brown envelope you're clutching so tightly in your hand is some sort of ridiculous, pre-sex or non-disclosure agreement you were about to ask me to sign, you can rip it up. Because nothing happened between me and Toby and even if it had, I wouldn't sell my story to the press. I don't kiss and tell.'

He glanced at his hand as if he'd forgotten the envelope was there. He tossed it onto the worktop next to him.

'It's not. It's something the Mayor just handed to me whilst I was looking for you.'

'You were looking for me?'

'Yes.'

'What for? To ask if it was over between me and Toby.'

'No. I believe I just mentioned. Toby told me that himself thirty minutes ago.'

'Then why? Why were you looking for me?'

'I'm about to show you.'

'Show me?' She sounded like a mouse who'd just spotted a cat.

'Yes. But purely out of interest, if that had been a

191

prenup or a non-disclosure agreement, and you were still dating Toby, would you have signed it? You said you'd happily do so the last time we had this conversation. In fact, I seem to recall it was your idea.'

Poppy cleared her throat and pulled her long, loose cardigan tightly around her. Sticking her chin out, she said: 'It was and I would but I'm not. Now as delightful as this conversation is, if you'll please stop blocking the doorway, I want to watch the fireworks.'

'Certainly. Perhaps we could watch them together.'

'Really? What you, me and your lovely girlfriend, Lucy? You're unbelievable, Blackwood. Totally sodding unbelievable.' She turned her back to walk towards the hall. 'Don't bother to move. I'll use the front door.'

'Poppy!'

He was by her side in a second.

The last time he'd grabbed her arm like this, he'd kissed her. From the look in his eyes he was about to kiss her again.

She mustn't let him. She. Must. Not. Let. Him.

'Poppy.' He said her name again but this time, it sounded like a caress. 'Lucy's not my girlfriend and I shouldn't have teased you about her but I had to know if you felt anything for me. Anything at all.'

'Oh.'

'Lucy is my cousin. She's my Uncle Joe's daughter. She's going to be spending a few days with us up at High House.'

'Oh!'

A deafening bang sent waves of vibrations through the air, temporarily distracting them both; the Goldebury Bay ceremonial cannon signalled that the fireworks would shortly begin.

'The fireworks are about to start,' she said.

She didn't want this. She didn't want him.

Did she?

She tried to back away but her feet wouldn't move.

'They've already started,' he said, slowly easing her towards him.

'No,' she said, trying to remain calm. 'The cannon always goes off a few minutes before.'

He smiled as he pulled her into his arms.

'I wasn't talking about the ones outside.'

Chapter Twenty-Nine

Poppy had no idea if the fireworks she could hear were because the ones down in Goldebury Bay had now started, or if they were simply the ones in her head, and she didn't know for how long she and Ryan kissed – although it was nowhere near long enough as far as she was concerned – but she could hear someone calling Ryan's name and he suddenly pulled away from her. When she opened her eyes, she saw Toby standing by the door. His mouth hung open and disbelief registered in his eyes, replaced almost instantaneously with a genuine display of trepidation.

She felt Ryan's entire body stiffen as if he instinctively knew something was seriously wrong.

'What is it, Toby?'

Toby blinked for a few seconds before recovering himself.

'It's Stephanie, Ryan. She's gone. One minute she was by my side, the next she was with someone heading towards a car. And it wasn't the limo. She hadn't called Doug. I've phoned and checked. It was him, Ryan. I'm sure it was.'

'Him?' Poppy queried.

Ryan briefly met her eyes and the passion she'd seen only moments before was completely overshadowed by fear.

'Enzo,' he said, his voice burning with anger. 'Stephanie's husband. I have to go, Poppy. I'm sorry but I have to get her back.'

'Um… Of course. What can I do to help?'

He was already across the kitchen and halfway out the door.

'Tell Lucy and Jules what's happened. They'll know what to do.'

'Okay. I'll—'

He was gone.

Poppy stood alone in the kitchen trying to understand what had just happened whilst the whoosh-bang-whizz of fireworks echoed all around her. He'd looked so worried. Terrified even. She had no idea where he'd gone or what he'd do. At least Toby was with him. Although how much good he'd be in a crisis she wasn't sure.

After a moment she pulled herself together. He'd asked her to tell Lucy and Jules, so that's what she must do. But how would she find them in the heaving mass of people? And in the dark? She reached for the switches and turned on the outside lights. She then rushed to the kitchen door and ran towards the crowd to find Thaddeus.

A few isolated groups of people nearby were glaring at her as if, by turning on the lights, she'd committed some heinous crime and she was just about to ask them for their help when she saw Thaddeus striding towards her.

'What's happened, Poppy? What's wrong? You've switched on the lights. Are you okay?'

'It's Ryan! He's gone after Stephanie. Someone's taken her or something. Her husband, I think. I'm not really sure. I need to find Jules and Lucy. Have you seen them?'

'They're with Sophie and the others. D'you want me to get them? What do you mean someone's taken her? What did Ryan say?'

'I don't know, Thaddeus. All I know is that Toby rushed in and told Ryan that he'd seen Stephanie heading towards a car with someone and Ryan said his name was Enzo.

195

Ryan and Toby went after them. He told me to get Jules and Lucy. Thaddeus, I'm really worried.'

Thaddeus nodded, suddenly looking almost as anxious as Ryan and Toby had been.

'Enzo is Stephanie's husband. Go back to the house. I'll get Jules and Lucy. We'll see you in the kitchen.'

'Okay, Thaddeus.'

What else could she say?

Moments later, Lucy and Jules joined her in the kitchen, together with Sophie and Cleo who told her that Thaddeus and Oliver were going to help look for Stephanie.

Seconds turned into minutes; minutes into an hour; one hour into two and there was no word from Ryan, Thaddeus or Oliver – or anyone else taking part in the search for Stephanie, for that matter.

Poppy was frantic with worry and despite everyone urging her to try to get some rest, she couldn't. How could she rest knowing that Ryan was out there somewhere chasing a man like Enzo? A man she'd never heard of before tonight but a man she now believed to be a wife-beater, and from the things Lucy and Jules had said, possibly a real danger to Stephanie, as well as to Toby – and more importantly in her mind – to Ryan.

She stared through the kitchen window at the twinkling fairy lights and the final dying embers of the bonfire and tried hard not to burst into tears. It had started raining again, just a light drizzle but enough to cause the remnants of the fire to hiss and spit, sending tiny sparks of red and gold up into the dank, night air.

All the revellers had gone home to their warm and comfy beds, many no doubt blissfully unaware that anything was amiss but others saying that the Blackwood girl had been abducted. Some believed the version that Thaddeus and Oliver had told Sophie and the others to

196

spread so as not to cause panic before they'd dashed off into the night – that Stephanie had suddenly been taken ill. Some went home immediately; some hung around to gossip; the rest soon dispersed once the fireworks in Goldebury Bay were over and it was apparent that things were winding down at Summerhill too.

Only those close to Thaddeus and his friends knew the truth. Most of them offered to help but there was very little they could do. Some joined in the search, pairing off into twos or threes and driving around Goldebury Bay and the outskirts with no idea of what they were looking for, other than signs of something out of the ordinary – a sighting of Stephanie Blackwood or Stephanie Morelzanti as Poppy now knew, was her name.

Lucy had contacted the police, more as a formality she'd said, than to ask for their assistance. It was almost certain that Stephanie had gone with Enzo willingly, and the police had neither the time nor the resources to run after people in such circumstances, especially with so little to go on. Despite Ryan's efforts – Lucy had also said – Stephanie had refused to press charges against Enzo so they didn't even have the benefit of a restraining order.

Now all they could do was wait and that was the worst part as far as Poppy was concerned. She just wanted to hear that Ryan was safe.

'He'll be okay, you know.'

Poppy recognised Jules' voice and turned to face her.

'Will he? How can you be so sure? I wish I could believe that.'

'Because I know Ryan and he knows what he's doing. He'll bring her back. He always does.'

'Always does?' Poppy nearly burst out laughing even though she was near to tears. 'Is this a regular occurrence? You say that as if there's nothing to worry about.'

Jules pulled out a chair and sat at the kitchen table, flopping against the backrest as if she were a ragdoll.

'It is a regular occurrence, I'm sorry to say. At least it seems to be. Stephanie's always getting herself into trouble and Ryan's always getting her out of it, one way or another. And not just Stephanie, either. And I am worried. Of course I am. But believe me, Poppy, Ryan is not a fool. And he's not alone.'

'Humph. I'm not sure how much help Toby will be in a situation like this.'

Jules arched her eyebrows. An affectionate smile immediately softened her expression.

'Dear Toby. He tries so hard to be like Ryan and fails miserably every time. I wish he could see that if he would just be himself, he'd make a far greater success of his life. But that's not what I meant. Ryan has Doug, amongst others and Doug would never let anything happen to Ryan.'

'Doug? The chauffeur?'

Jules shook her head. 'You're a bright girl, Poppy. You know very well that Doug is so much more than a chauffeur. Doug is ex-SAS.'

Now Poppy did laugh. A short, sharp burst of pent up nerves and incredulity.

'I'm sorry. I know that's not funny. None of this is funny. In fact it's so far from being funny, it's beyond words. But this is all so unbelievable. Nothing like this ever happened when I lived in Gibraltar but from almost the moment I arrived in Goldebury Bay, it's been one thing after another.'

Jules smiled. 'I understand. Sometimes I laugh when I'm terrified. And I've heard about Thaddeus' father and cousin... the smuggling, the trials, the prison sentences. Then there was this place.' She waved a fragile arm in the air. 'Piracy, murder and hidden treasure. You've certainly had some excitement in the last year or so.'

Poppy gave her a wan smile. 'I'm not sure I'd call it exciting exactly although...' She shrugged. 'Well, it definitely hasn't been boring.' She met Jules' eyes. 'Would you like some coffee? I can feel myself starting to panic again and I need to do something to stop myself from screaming.'

'Coffee would be lovely, thank you. And Poppy? Trust me. You'll see Ryan again safe and sound and happy. And, unless I'm very much mistaken, he's finally got something he can really be happy about. Or should I say... someone.'

Chapter Thirty

'Wow! This is all very exciting,' Sophie said as she, Cleo, Veronique and Poppy sat curled up on various chairs in Sophie's sitting room, drinking coffee and eating chocolate brownies at around eleven-thirty that night.

'I didn't think so,' Poppy said, thankful that she could finally relax a little. 'I went from elation to terror in ten seconds flat and I've never been so worried about anything – or anyone – in my entire life.'

'You know what I meant,' Sophie said. 'And now that you know he's safe and on his way back, you can breathe easily again.'

'Can I? I'm not sure I'll ever breathe easily again.'

Sophie threw a cushion at Poppy almost causing her to spill her coffee and drop the brownie. 'Don't be such a drama queen.'

'Oi. Watch it. I'm an emotionally disturbed woman at the moment. No, that's not what I meant. I meant my emotions are all over the place.'

Cleo laughed. 'I think you got it right the first time.'

Poppy placed her mug on the table and threw the same cushion at Cleo.

'What is this? Pass the parcel or something,' Cleo said.

Veronique got up and refilled their coffee cups. 'So what exactly did Ryan say when he called you? I missed that bit. I think I was in the kitchen when he called.'

Poppy shook her head. 'Not much. Only that he wanted

me to know he'd got Stephanie. That she was fine and that they were on their way home. He asked where I was and I told him I was still here and so were Lucy and Jules and we'd all been waiting for news. He said he was taking Stephanie back to High House and asked me to ask Lucy and Jules to meet them there. Then he told me to go home and get some sleep and said he hoped he'd see me soon.'

'And....?' Cleo said, grinning.

'And... nothing. I told you. That was it. He didn't say anything else.'

Cleo held up the cushion and raised her brows in a friendly mock warning. 'Don't make me throw it.'

Poppy shrugged. 'He didn't say anything else. Honestly.'

Veronique tutted. 'Don't be obtuse, Poppy. Even I know what Cleo is implying.'

'Well then, I wish one of you would tell me because I haven't got a clue.'

'I think,' Sophie said. 'What we all want to know is how much Ryan hopes to see of you "soon". You've been very tight-lipped about the whole thing. You didn't even tell us until ten minutes ago that the two of you were kissing when Stephanie went walkabout.'

'I haven't had time. So much has been going on.'

'Rubbish!' Cleo said. 'You've had plenty of time to tell us all the gory details. We've been sitting here for over two hours talking and worrying. You could've mentioned it at any moment.'

Poppy shook her head. 'There was no way I was going to say it in front of Lucy and Jules, and they've only been gone for ten minutes or so.'

'Yes. But if I hadn't asked why Ryan had called you and not them, we still probably wouldn't have known the two of you were locked in a passionate embrace and making

201

fireworks of your own,' said Cleo.

Poppy's cheeks burned and she smiled over the rim of her coffee cup.

'That was some kiss, let me tell you.'

'That's precisely what we want you to do,' Cleo said. 'Tell us! Tell us everything.'

Poppy frowned. 'But don't you get it? There's nothing else to tell. He kissed me. Toby charged in. Ryan left. I spent the next couple of hours nearly tearing my hair out. Ryan called to say he was safe – although he didn't even say that, now I think about it. He said that Stephanie was safe. As if I give a damn about her. Anyway, he called. I told Lucy and Jules. They left. Veronique made coffee. You asked me why Ryan called me. I said it was probably because we were in the middle of a rather passionate kiss and you all started shouting and bouncing around like maniacs.'

'But didn't he say that he hoped to pick up where you left off?' Sophie asked. 'Or something like that. Did he honestly just tell you to go home, get some sleep and that he hoped he'd see you soon… as if there was a possibility that he might not?'

'Really?' Poppy said. 'Thanks for pointing that out, Sophie because it had only occurred to me like a thousand times already that he might simply get in that sodding jet of his and disappear again without a word.'

'Why would he do that?' Cleo asked.

'Because that's precisely what he did the last time he kissed me, if you remember. Well, perhaps not straight away but the point is, he kissed me once before and then he behaved as if it hadn't happened.'

'Yes, but that was when you were dating his brother,' Veronique said. 'You're not now. Perhaps he felt he had to walk away the first time.'

202

Poppy shrugged. 'Or perhaps he doesn't want to get involved with a pain in the arse like me.'

They all nodded.

'Oi!' Poppy shrieked. 'You're not supposed to agree with me. You're supposed to say something comforting and encouraging like: "You're not a pain in the arse. You're wonderful, beautiful, charming and kind. Any man would be a fool not to want to get involved with you." Or at least that he must like me a little bit to want to kiss me a second time. He must, mustn't he? Because he knew that I'd stopped seeing Toby before he kissed me tonight, so he didn't do it just to try to stop me from being with his brother.'

'Sometimes I really wonder what it's like to be inside that head of yours,' Sophie said. 'But yes, of course he must like you.'

'Of course he does,' Cleo seconded.

'I think it goes much deeper than 'likes you' if you want my opinion,' Veronique said. 'I also think the reason he said what he did – that he hoped he'd see you soon – was because he's not sure how you feel about him. I think he was hoping you'd invite him round, or at the very least, ask him to call you again. I haven't known you very long but I don't suppose you did that, did you?'

'No.' Poppy shook her head. 'I... I don't think I said anything. Oh wait. I think I said something like: "Thanks for letting me know." What? What's wrong with that?'

'I don't get you,' Cleo said. 'When you think you like someone, you can be really forward to the extent of being pushy but when you really *do* like someone, you can't even ask them to call you.'

'That's not true! I asked Toby to call me. On more than one occasion, I think.'

'Yes, but you didn't really like him, you just thought

203

you did. But it's pretty clear to all of us that you really, really like Ryan, even though, knowing you, you're probably still trying to convince yourself you don't.'

'I'm not sure I do like him. He seems to think he can just grab me and kiss me whenever he... Oh! I see what you mean. You're right. I *am* a bloody idiot.'

Chapter Thirty-One

'Honey! We're home!'

'That's Thaddeus,' Poppy said, coming to and stretching her neck and back after falling asleep in the chair.

'What? Oh. We're in the sitting room,' Sophie called before yawning and stretching out her arms.

Cleo sat bolt upright with a start and Veronique, whom none of them had noticed wasn't there, walked back in with a tray of coffee. Thaddeus and Oliver were behind her, looking utterly exhausted.

'Oh, sorry, Veronique,' Thaddeus said. 'Let me take that.'

'No, no. You go and sit. I've just had an hour's sleep. You look as if you've been up all night.'

As if to confirm that statement, Thaddeus yawned, followed by an even louder yawn from Oliver.

'God, I'm shattered,' Oliver said, collapsing on the sofa next to Cleo. 'I'm getting too old for all this action-adventure stuff and staying up into the early hours. I haven't even got the energy to kiss you, darling. You'll have to kiss me.' He managed a wink.

Cleo threw her arms around him and kissed him on the lips.

Thaddeus smiled and sat on the arm of Sophie's chair. 'I wouldn't mind one of those,' he said, and Sophie seemed more than happy to oblige.

'Did Ryan go home?' Poppy asked when her friends had finished kissing.

'Yeah,' Thaddeus replied. 'Stephanie was in a right strop and Toby was trying to calm her down the last we saw of them. We did all leave at the same time though so they should be back at High House by now. Ryan told us he wanted to make sure Stephanie didn't try anything stupid, like booking a cab or something and trying to meet up with Enzo.'

Sophie frowned. 'Why on earth would she want to go back to a man who beats her? I really don't understand it.'

'Nor does anyone,' Thaddeus said. 'Except Stephanie. Ryan was telling her that she deserves someone better than Enzo but all she kept saying was that he would never understand because he had never been in love.'

'She said he'd never been in love?' Poppy asked.

Thaddeus gave her an odd look. 'Yeah. Why are you so bothered about that bit?'

'Because she's crazy about him,' Sophie said. 'She's hoping he feels the same about her.'

'What?' Thaddeus and Oliver said in unison.

'How long have we been gone?' Oliver queried. 'Or have we landed in some alternative reality? I could've sworn that when we left last night you couldn't stand the guy. Now just a few hours later, you're crazy about him? How did that happen?' His brows furrowed as he scrutinised Poppy's face.

'Don't look at me like that. A girl can change her mind.'

Thaddeus smiled and shook his head. 'So... does that mean there was something going on between you two in the kitchen last night? I remember you saying that you and Ryan were there and Toby came rushing in to tell you about Stephanie.'

'There might have been,' Poppy said, blushing.

'They were locked in a passionate embrace,' Cleo said, a huge grin on her face.

Oliver shook his head. 'First Toby, then Ryan. I suppose we should be thankful there are only two brothers in the family.'

'Oi! Watch it. I made a mistake, okay? I thought I liked Toby but it turns out I like Ryan. I like him a lot. I'm just worried he doesn't like me.'

'You really are an idiot, Poppy,' Thaddeus declared. 'If Ryan kissed you, passionately or otherwise, after those six awful messages you left him last weekend... the guy doesn't *like* you – he's nuts about you.'

Oliver nodded. 'Thaddeus is right. The guy would have to be nuts to kiss you after the things you said.'

'I'm not sure I like that, thank you very much, Oliver,' Poppy said. 'Unless you mean the same as Thaddeus, that he'd have to be nuts *about* me, not that he'd have to be nuts *to* kiss me.'

Oliver shook his head. 'I'm too tired to know what I'm saying, Poppy, let alone even begin to understand that sentence. I need to go home and get some sleep.'

Thaddeus grinned. 'I feel really sorry for Ryan. He thinks he's got trouble with Stephanie. If he's fallen for you, Poppy, he's about to find out what 'trouble' actually means. And as much as I love you all, I too, need to go to bed.'

'Well, I'll get out of your hair then,' Veronique said, with a smile. 'Would you like a lift home, Poppy?'

'We'll take her, Veronique,' Cleo said. 'She's only a couple of roads from us, whereas you'll be going in the opposite direction.'

'I'll see you all soon then.' Veronique waved goodbye as she walked towards the door. 'Call me if any of you need anything. Oh, and Poppy? Take my advice. The next time Ryan calls you, invite the guy round. Bye-ee.'

'Come on you two.' Cleo got to her feet, pulling Oliver

to his and nodded her head at Poppy to indicate she also meant her.

'So what exactly happened?' Sophie asked. 'You haven't told us how Ryan got Stephanie away from Enzo. Or where you found them. Or how you did.'

'Come to bed and I'll tell you,' Thaddeus said, getting up and holding out his hand.

Sophie winked at Poppy and Cleo. 'Now there's an offer I can't refuse. See you tomorrow.'

'But I want to know too,' Poppy said.

'I'll tell you on the way home,' said Oliver.

Poppy jumped to her feet and followed him and Cleo out.

'Ryan's okay, isn't he? There wasn't a fight or anything was there? Enzo didn't have a gun or something, did he? Well come on then, tell me.'

Oliver shook his head. 'If you'll just shut up for five seconds, I will.'

'I won't say another word. Er... When you saw Ryan, did he mention me at all?'

'Yes, now that I come to think about it. He asked me if you ever stop talking.'

'He didn't. You're... oh, I get it. Sorry.'

Cleo grinned and said: 'I'll drive, darling. That way you can concentrate on telling us the story.'

Oliver virtually collapsed onto the passenger seat and waited until Cleo had started the car.

'There isn't really much to tell. Thaddeus called Ryan to see if he and Toby had had any luck but they hadn't. A little while later, he called us back and said that Doug had discovered that Enzo arrived via the Eurotunnel yesterday, and that he had a reservation for his car for the eleven thirty-five shuttle. Ryan didn't know if they'd be there or not but it was the only lead he had. Thaddeus and I decided he might need some extra help so we went there too and met up with him at the Eurotunnel terminal. Enzo clearly hadn't realised we were on to him and he and Stephanie were calmly drinking coffee in Starbucks prior to check-in.'

'What did this Enzo guy do when he saw you?' Poppy asked. 'Did you arrive at the same time as Ryan and Toby?'

'Just a few minutes after. And it was all surprisingly civilised. Apart from Stephanie, that is. Ryan coolly told Toby to take her to the car and after she'd had a little tantrum, Enzo told her to do as Ryan said. She calmed down and went with Toby. Enzo told Ryan that it wasn't over, to which Ryan simply said that he sincerely hoped it was. Then Ryan walked up to Enzo, tossed a fiver on the table, told him that was for Stephanie's coffee and turned and walked away. Thaddeus and I were actually rather impressed.'

'Well, I suppose Doug is pretty intimidating,' Cleo said. 'I don't suppose anyone would argue with him around.'

'He wasn't there. Ryan asked Doug to wait at the car in case Enzo or Stephanie tried to make a run for it. It was just Ryan and Toby… and me and Thaddeus, although I don't think Enzo realised we were with Ryan until we all walked out together. I'll tell you something though, the guy didn't look happy and I know this may sound silly, but I've got a weird feeling that we haven't seen the last of Enzo.'

'I hope for all our sakes, we have,' Poppy said. 'It's strange that the guy would come all this way to get Stephanie and then leave so easily without her. And if Stephanie is so desperate to be with him, why didn't he just book a flight or a seat on Eurostar, or something, for her? Why go to all the trouble of driving here to get her? Jules told me earlier, when we were having coffee together, that Enzo lives in Spain, so that's a long way to come by car.'

'I heard Stephanie say that they were going to Italy,'

209

Oliver said, laughing. 'Who knows? Perhaps they were planning a little touring holiday.'

Cleo giggled. 'What? A sort of "Let's put all our troubles behind us and start again," type of thing.'

'It's not really anything to laugh about,' Poppy said. 'Jules told me that the reason Ryan brought Stephanie here was because he believed Enzo had hit her so hard that he broke her nose and jaw. Stephanie didn't tell Ryan about it, and she wouldn't press charges when he found out. She said she fell down the stairs and that it had nothing to do with Enzo. But Ryan is certain Enzo did it, and so is Jules. Ryan told Stephanie that he wants her to spend some time away from Enzo and that unless she does, he'll stop her allowance and she won't get a penny from him. He's apparently hoping the threat of losing her income will give her time to come to her senses. But Jules says that Stephanie knows Ryan would never really leave her destitute.'

'That's awful,' Cleo said.

'Yeah,' Oliver agreed. 'I think perhaps Ryan is too generous for his own good.'

'It's weird isn't it, Poppy?' Cleo said. 'We thought Toby was the nice guy and Ryan was just an arrogant, obnoxious jerk. Well, you did anyway. The rest of us weren't entirely sure. It just goes to show how wrong you can be about someone, doesn't it? And I do mean – you.'

Poppy didn't even bother to argue. 'It certainly does,' she said, as Cleo pulled up at her cottage.

Poppy was suddenly so tired that she wasn't sure she could make it from the curb to her own front door, and that was less than ten feet away. Now that she knew Ryan was safe, she would probably be out like a light the moment her head hit the pillow. She could give in to the exhaustion burning her eyes and weighing her body down like lead.

She didn't even have the energy to clean her teeth, or for that matter, get undressed. Once inside, she simply kicked off her shoes, hung up her coat and bag and crawled upstairs to bed.

But she couldn't sleep. She must be overtired. Or was it because she was still fully clothed? She dragged herself out of bed, pulled off her clothes and tossed them on the floor. She slipped a T-shirt nightdress over her head only to find it was inside out, but she didn't care as she fell back into bed.

But still she couldn't sleep.

It was time to be honest with herself and admit it was because she was hoping Ryan would call. She knew it was ridiculous. She knew it was two in the morning – or later but she wanted him to call and say that he was missing her... that he couldn't stop thinking about that kiss and that he couldn't wait to kiss her again. That he'd like to come round and tell her all about what happened... if she wasn't too tired. That he'd like to curl up in bed with her and fall asleep...

Who was she kidding? She was hoping he'd call and ask if she wanted him to come round and continue what they'd started in the kitchen. And despite her exhaustion, the answer would be: Yes.

But he didn't call and no matter how many times she checked that the battery hadn't run down or that she hadn't switched the phone to voicemail by mistake, the damn thing didn't ring.

Ryan didn't ring.

And he hadn't rung by the time she eventually fell asleep... which was five a.m. on Sunday morning.

Chapter Thirty-Two

Poppy was having the strangest dream. It felt as if she were awake but she was sure she was asleep. It was snowing outside and she was snuggled up in bed, wrapped in Ryan's arms. It was Christmas morning and there were presents everywhere but all she wanted was him. Bells of different kinds were ringing somewhere in the distance and carollers were singing, although the songs didn't sound very Christmassy. Drummers were drumming slightly out of tune and she could hear someone calling her name. Ryan was gone and she was calling for him but all she could hear was his laugh, somehow mocking her. Then... the faintest whiff of coffee made her nose twitch. Not the spicy nutmeg kind of coffee she often had at Christmas, just the ordinary kind and—

'Bloody hell, Poppy! For a minute there I thought you were dead!'

Was that Sophie's voice?

Poppy opened her eyes. The clock radio alarm was blaring out Sunday's Pop Classics from Goldebury Bay Radio and unless Sophie had an unbelievably bad case of dandruff, it really was snowing outside.

'What? Why? How did you get in?'

'I've got a key.' Sophie jiggled a bunch of keys in her hand and switched the radio off. 'That's clearly not a lot of use. You're right, Cleo!' she shouted towards the stairs. 'The silly cow was fast asleep.'

A second or two later, Cleo appeared with a steaming

mug of coffee. 'Here. Drink this. You're going to need it when you see your phone.' Cleo picked up Poppy's phone from the floor and tossed it on the bed as she handed her the mug.

Panic suddenly seized Poppy.

'Has something happened to Ryan? Is he okay? Has he had an accident?'

Cleo glanced at Sophie. 'I think that was almost word for word what he said, wasn't it?'

Sophie nodded. 'Pretty much, yeah.'

'Ah, that's really sweet. They'll be finishing each other's sentences next.'

'Oh God, let's hope not. But it is kind of romantic, isn't it?'

'What are you two going on about? I take it from those stupid grins, Ryan's safe and sound. Um… but why are you both here? You don't… oh my God! Did you say you've spoken to Ryan? When? Why did he call you? Have you seen him?'

'He didn't say any of that,' Cleo said. 'I'm a little disappointed.'

'Hmm. Me too.'

'Check your phone bed-head.' Cleo nodded towards it.

Poppy grabbed it, spilling her coffee at the same time. Sophie took the mug away from her.

Five messages and ten missed calls.

Poppy didn't know whether to be elated or miserable. They weren't all from Ryan though. As she scrolled through the calls, she could see a couple were from Sophie and Cleo.

'Ryan called Thaddeus,' Sophie explained, 'to ask if we knew why you weren't answering your phone. He said he'd called several times and he'd also left a couple of messages. He thought you might be in the shower so he tried again.

He even came round, rang the bell and banged on the door but there was no reply so he thought you were out.'

'And then he started worrying about you,' Cleo said, grinning. 'Did you hear that? The man was worried about you. Anyway, Sophie called me because we'd brought you home last night. I called, then came round and rang and banged and then I phoned Sophie to get her to bring the key.'

'I was sure we'd find you dead.'

Cleo laughed. 'I told her that once you went to sleep, a nuclear explosion couldn't wake you. Anyway, put the phone on speaker and let's hear his messages.'

Poppy held the phone to her chest. 'They're for me, not you.'

'Listen,' Sophie said. 'You almost gave me a heart attack and you've got both Cleo and me out of bed to come and check on you. Let's hear those messages or I'll kill you myself.'

Poppy grinned. 'Okay. But don't tell Ryan I let you listen. She pressed play and after the usual spiel telling her she had five messages, she heard Ryan's voice.

'Good morning. I hope you slept well. You're probably in the shower so I'll try again later. It's Ryan, by the way.'

Cleo giggled. 'And they say romance is dead.'

'Sod off,' Poppy said, playing the next message.

'Hi Poppy. It's Ryan again. I left a message earlier. And I've called back twice. Er. I'll call you later.'

'He's beginning to sound anxious,' Sophie remarked.

Cleo nodded. 'Yeah, you can hear that little—'

'Really?' Poppy cut in. 'Shut up, I'm trying to listen.'

'Poppy. It's Ryan. Look, I don't know whether there's a problem with your voicemail but this is my third message. I know this is foolish but I'm actually getting a bit worried about you. When you get this message, call me.... Please

214

'….Call me, please.'

'Did you notice he said, "please" twice?' Cleo said. 'That's almost pleading.'

Poppy smirked.

'Poppy?' That was Sophie's voice. 'Ryan's been trying to call you. Where are you? Are you okay? Call me as soon as you get this. It's Sophie.'

Sophie groaned. 'I sound awful. Do I really sound like that?'

'Worse,' Cleo said.

'Hey! It's Cleo. Where are you, you silly cow? Answer your bloody phone! Call me back when you get this. Loverboy's sent out another missing person's report – and this one's for you. If you don't call me back in five minutes, we're coming round. You'd better not be asleep. It's bloody well snowing out.'

'He does sound concerned, doesn't he?' Poppy said, hugging her knees up to her chest. 'I'd better call him.'

'You'd better— Oh hold on. That's my phone,' Sophie said. 'What's the betting it's him?' She glanced at the screen. 'Yep. Hello Ryan. Yes, she's fine. We're with her now. Hold on, I'll pass the phone over.'

Poppy grinned and took the phone. 'Hello.'

'At last! I've been worried sick,' Ryan said. 'Are you okay?'

'I'm fine. Sorry. I couldn't get to sleep last night and when I finally did, I thought I was dreaming because it was snowing and I didn't hear my… Never mind that. How are you?'

'Relieved... now that I know you're okay. I thought I was going to have to turn the jet round and come and look for you. Or worse.'

'What? Did you just say jet?'

She shot a look at Cleo and Sophie.

215

'Yes. We'll be landing soon so I can't talk for long. I just needed to know you're okay.'

'I was. Until you said jet.'

'Sorry? Until I said what?'

'Jet! This is the second time you've done this!'

'Done what?'

'Kissed me and then flown off on your sodding jet! Is this a game? Do you find this amusing?'

'I'm not finding this conversation amusing. Why are you upset? I've been calling you all morning. I hardly think that's playing games. I even came round to your cottage before I left.'

'I was asleep.'

'Apparently so.'

'Well! I spent most of last night worried sick about you, you bloody jerk. For all the good that did me. Bugger off!'

She threw the phone at the wall. Luckily she missed and it landed a few inches away, face down on the carpet.

'Er. That's actually my phone,' Sophie said.

'Oh bugger! I'm so sorry. What have I done?'

'Don't cry. It's only a phone. It's probably not even damaged.' Sophie went to retrieve it.

Cleo tutted and sat on the bed, hugging Poppy. 'She's not bothered about your phone, Sophie. She's crying over Ryan.'

'Of course she is. Sorry. What did he say then? I only heard her side. I suppose he's had to go away again. But I don't understand why she's so cross. At least this time he phoned her.'

'Nor does Ryan, I suspect. And more to the point, nor does she. Because yet again, she's behaved like an idiot. Only this time, she realised as soon as she'd done it.'

'Well, that's a step in the right direction. Oops. Wrong thing to say, obviously. My phone looks fine though.'

Cleo picked up Poppy's phone from the bed. 'Call him back. Apologise. Say you're still half asleep and you're not thinking straight.'

Poppy shook her head. 'I can't,' she sobbed. 'All he said was that he... wanted to know... I was okay. Not... that he missed me... or that he... couldn't stop thinking... about me or even... that he wanted to see me again.'

She wiped her runny nose with her hand. Cleo passed her a tissue from the box beside the bed; Poppy blew loudly into it and took a deep breath.

'All he was worried about was that he might have to turn... the jet around and come and look for me!'

'That's a good thing,' Sophie said. 'It shows he cares.'

'Yeah,' Cleo said, handing Poppy another tissue and gingerly picking up the used one between the tips of her finger and thumb. She tossed it in the waste basket near the dressing table just a few feet away. 'And if he was prepared to turn the jet around, that means he cares for you a lot.'

'Uh-huh,' Sophie continued. 'At least as much as he cares for his sister.'

'I don't want him to care about me like he does his sister.' Another loud blow. 'I want him to care about me like he's nuts about me.'

Sophie frowned. 'But he loves his sister so... I'll stop talking. I'm clearly saying all the wrong things this morning.'

Cleo sighed. 'Just call him back, Poppy,' she said. 'I'm sure he'll understand.'

Chapter Thirty-Three

Ryan didn't understand what had just happened.

He'd been so relieved to hear Poppy's voice that he wasn't sure what he'd said. But he was sure he hadn't said anything to justify her outburst. Had she really just told him to "bugger off"? And then… well, it sounded as if she'd thrown the phone across the room or something.

He dialled the number again but it went straight to voicemail. Sophie's voicemail. Of course, that was Sophie's phone he'd called. Should he leave a message? No. He'd ring Poppy's phone.

Why was she so annoyed that he was on the jet? He'd told her where he was going. He'd even told her why. Hadn't he? He was sure he'd said it in one of the messages he'd left. Or had he? He'd meant to. But then he'd started worrying about her. Perhaps he hadn't.

He should've left her a note. He knew it. Why hadn't he?

Because he'd told himself that he'd rather speak to her. To hear her voice.

He'd certainly heard it. And he didn't like what he'd heard.

He'd call her and find out what was going on.

Now her phone was engaged. Should he leave another message? What was the point?

He definitely should've put a note through her letterbox this morning.

He smiled at the thought of that letterbox and how she'd

got her arm stuck in it. He remembered the first time he'd seen her and how she was stuck on that wire by the 'Keep Out' sign.

God, she'd taken his breath away the moment he'd laid eyes on her. And he wasn't sure he'd been able to breathe properly ever since. In normal circumstances, if he'd seen a woman requiring his assistance – and not just a woman, anyone requiring assistance – he'd have given it without hesitation. When he'd first seen Poppy, he couldn't move, couldn't breathe, couldn't think, and when he could, he just wanted the moment to last for as long as possible. To be with her for as long as he could.

It wasn't just because she was gorgeous – although she definitely was. He'd thoroughly enjoyed sparring with her too. And he didn't much care about beauty, anyway. Not outer beauty. It was inner beauty that mattered to him. And he knew she had that...in spades. She just had a knack of hiding it.

It was more than that though. It was as if he'd found a missing piece of a puzzle. His puzzle. And the moment he'd seen her it had slotted into place. The picture of his future was complete and so clear for him to see that it nearly terrified the life out of him.

Then he'd discovered she was one of his brother's many women and the picture had shattered into pieces.

He wished Toby would stop falling in and out of what his brother called 'love'. It wasn't love. Much like himself, Toby had never been in love. Much like Stephanie, too. The only difference between them was that his siblings convinced themselves each new person was 'the one for them' whereas he knew better. There was no such thing. Or he hadn't thought there was... until he'd met Poppy.

Was she just an infatuation? He knew that's all she was to Toby. Sadly, all of Toby's women were just passing fancies. And all of Stephanie's men. His siblings were so much like their mother in that way.

But he wasn't like his brother and sister; he took after their dad, and Poppy wasn't going to be just a fleeting affair. Why was he even questioning himself on this? He'd never felt like this before. Ever. Whereas they said they felt this all the time. He'd never experienced this with any of the previous women he'd dated – and he'd dated several. Not as many as Toby but enough to know that what he felt for Poppy was different. It was so real that whenever he thought of the future, he saw her. He couldn't get her out of his head.

He'd never felt jealous of anyone in his life but when he'd seen the way Poppy smiled at Toby that very first night, he'd been consumed by it. She wanted Toby – not him. She'd made that very clear. But still he had to kiss her at the Halloween party. Even if it was just the once. He had to try. Had to see if the flames he felt burning up his insides every time he laid eyes on her could ever ignite just a tiny spark in her.

And he thought it had.

Until he'd got her messages.

They certainly put him in his place.

Then Jules had told him that she'd heard a rumour: Poppy may no longer be interested in Toby. So he'd gone to the Guy Fawkes Night party to talk to her and he'd seen how she'd reacted over Lucy. That had given him hope and he'd kissed her instead. Like all his Christmases rolled into one, she'd kissed him back. Really kissed him – a 'knocked his socks off' kind of kiss.

Then Stephanie had done what Stephanie always did.

And now here he was doing something he thought he'd never do – taking Stephanie to a friend's remote, private island where there was no phone and no TV. There was certainly no way in or out, save by a small boat requiring skill to manoeuvre it through a tiny gap in the reef, or by private seaplane. Neither of which, Enzo could, or would be able to afford. And without Ryan's money, nor would Stephanie.

Perhaps some time alone with his friends, one of whom had once herself been a victim of domestic violence and was now in a happy, loving, wonderful marriage would make Stephanie think more clearly. He hoped to God it would because he was all out of options otherwise.

'That didn't go as you'd hoped, did it, brother dear?' Stephanie almost spat the words at him from the other side of the jet. 'Are you going to call her back and beg and plead? She's not interested in you. I heard she's going to L.A. To Hollywood, in fact – with Timothy Richards. First Toby, then you, now him. She certainly gets around.'

'Please don't be bitchy, Stephanie. It's not a nice quality. And where could you possibly have heard such nonsense?'

Stephanie turned away from him. 'Like you, Ryan. I have my sources. I hope she breaks your heart into a thousand pieces. I really wish she would. Then you'll have just a small inkling of how I feel right now.'

When Stephanie was in one of her moods, he'd usually take anything she said with a pinch of salt. The problem was, Jules had heard a similar rumour. Well, she'd heard that Poppy was in Betty's Pantry telling Timothy Richards that Toby wasn't the man for her. That's why he had gone to the Guy Fawkes Night party. Because he thought there might be a glimmer of hope. A chance to show her that he wasn't the obnoxious jerk she seemed to think he was.

Jules hadn't mentioned the other bit. The part about Poppy going to L.A. with Timothy. It couldn't be true. Poppy had said herself that she wouldn't go anywhere she couldn't easily get back from.

Unless she didn't want to get back? Now that he thought about it, why would she be telling Timothy that she was no longer interested in Toby? Unless it was to reassure the guy that she was only interested in him. Was Poppy now dating Timothy Richards? Jules had mentioned the guy had a seven-figure book deal and possibly a film in the offing.

But Poppy wasn't interested in a man for his money. She'd told him that.

She'd also told him exactly what she thought of him via those messages the previous weekend. Was this some sort of payback? Had he misjudged her reaction to Lucy? Had Poppy only pretended to enjoy that kiss last night? He'd thought it was incredible. He'd thought she felt the same. He'd thought a lot of things. But when he'd called her last night to say they were okay, she hadn't seemed that concerned. And just now, she'd simply shouted at him and told him to "bugger off".

Was it true? Was she going to L.A. with Timothy Richards?

His phone rang and he felt his heart flip. But he recognised the number and it wasn't Poppy. Just one of the usual stream of calls he got each day.

Ryan's head fell back against the sumptuous leather seat as he answered the call.

Stephanie may just have got her wish.

Chapter Thirty-Four

Nothing had been the same since Ryan had been gone – and he'd been gone for over two weeks now. Poppy had tried to call him back that Sunday morning. Several times. But all her calls went straight to voicemail and she didn't want to leave a message. She wanted to hear his voice. Wanted to know that he accepted her apology and that he wasn't cross. She'd even tried a couple of times the following day. And the day after that. And the day after that one. Each time, it either went to voicemail or was engaged.

Well, she may be an idiot but even she could get that message. He didn't want to talk to her. He hadn't called her back. He clearly wasn't interested.

She had no one to blame but herself. Why had she behaved like such a crazy person? Okay, she was tired and worried and that stupid dream hadn't helped, but even so.

Why couldn't she have told him how happy she was to hear his voice? To ask him rationally and reasonably why he always felt the need to jump on a jet after he kissed her. Not throw a tantrum like a spoiled child. That's how Stephanie behaved according to Oliver. Ryan already had one half crazy woman in his life. He certainly didn't want another. And who could blame him?

Perhaps he'd never really wanted her. He'd kissed her a couple of times. So what? The man used a jet like most people used a car or a bus, held meetings all over the world and had enough money in the bank to buy half of it. He could have his pick of beautiful women. Why would he be interested in a barmaid-cum-waitress in Goldebury Bay? Especially one who was constantly insulting him. A man like Ryan Blackwood didn't have time for that. He didn't have time for Poppy. He definitely wasn't interested in her. She saw that now.

She was used to making mistakes in her love life – in her choice of men. But she'd never made a mistake like this one. Never felt such an emptiness inside so vast that every time she looked down at her body, she expected to see a huge hole in place of her stomach. Her heart had shrivelled and died; she was sure of that.

The weather didn't help. Getting soaked each day going to and from work was becoming a pain in the bum, apart from that one day of snow, just over two weeks ago. The day that Ryan had left, it had done nothing but rain, rain, rain.

It was the final week of November and she couldn't remember the last time she had seen the sun. The only break from the rain had been two days when there was fog. Thick, dank, cloying fog. And even on those days it had drizzled, come to think of it. Where were the cold, clear mornings and chilly, dark nights that heralded the coming of the festive season? The crisp, scrunchy leaves piled high on the pavements? The pale lemon sun by day and the star-filled skies by night? Not that she could enjoy them on her own.

She wanted to be foraging for pine cones; searching for holly bushes with the plumpest berries; making Christmas crackers in front of her wood-burning stove. Well okay, that one was straight out of Santa fantasy land. She'd never made a Christmas cracker in her life and she wasn't about to start now, but it was a nice image – and one that simply didn't go with rain, for some reason. But more to the point, every time she thought of doing anything remotely

Christmassy, she thought how wonderful it would be to be doing those things with Ryan.

'I'm bored, bored, bored,' she said, her arms stretched across Sophie's kitchen table so that she could peel the label from the front of a giant-sized, glass jar containing luxury mixed fruit.

Sophie slapped her fingers. 'Will you stop doing that. How will I know what it is without the label?'

'Really? The shrivelled up currants, raisins, sultanas and sticky-looking cherries don't give you even the tiniest clue?'

Sophie tutted. 'That's not the point. You shouldn't pick labels. They're there for a reason.'

Poppy sighed. 'I usually love Christmas but I just can't get into the spirit of it this year.'

'It *is* only the twenty-fourth of November, so there's still plenty of time.'

'But that's the problem. Christmas Eve is exactly one month away and I haven't got a boyfriend. Ryan's never coming back and even if he does, I don't think I'd want to see him because he's clearly not interested in me. I'm miserable enough now so imagine what I'd be like if I saw him.'

Sophie shuddered dramatically. 'It doesn't bear thinking about. But I still don't understand why you didn't just leave him a message asking him to call you.'

'Because then I'd be even more miserable when he didn't. I wanted to talk to him. Then it was too late to leave a message because he clearly hadn't been trying to call me. There weren't any messages from him. Besides, he's way out of my league.'

'Nonsense. Perhaps he's as big an idiot as you when it comes to relationships. Maybe he didn't want to leave a message either. So neither of you leaves a message and both of you think the other hasn't called. Crazy stuff, if you ask me. But anyway, why don't you cheer up and stop moping around? Ryan will come back, you know. He's got to. He and Toby own the Goldebury Bay Yachting and Sailing Club, so he'll have to come back. And when he does, you can talk to him. He'll forgive you and everything will be fine. You'll see.'

'What if he comes back and I don't see him? What then?'

'Let's worry about that when we get to it. I tell you what. As you're clearly not in the mood to sit and make mince pies, let's call Cleo and the three of us can go Christmas shopping.'

'I suppose so. But don't expect me to get all Christmassy and happy just because we'll be spending money. It'll only help a little. It'll take more than that to mend my broken heart… this time.'

Suddenly, the kitchen door at the side of the house burst open and Cleo stood in the doorway looking as if she'd just won the lottery or something.

'We were just about to call you,' Sophie said. 'We're going Christmas shopping. You, me and misery guts here. I see Clara's with you. Clara, would you like to—'

'Forget Christmas shopping!' Cleo cut in. 'Well, no. We can do that too. But mostly we'll be… ta dah! B – A – B – Y shopping!'

'B.A.B… Oh my God!' Poppy screamed. 'You're pregnant!'

Cleo nodded frenetically.

'Are you sure? Because last time you—'

'I'm sure, Poppy. In fact I'm positive. The test was positive but I went to the doctor's in case and she did another one and that was positive too. We're going to have a baby Oliver! Well, it may be a baby Olivia, we don't

226

know yet of course but—'

'Oh Cleo, that's wonderful!' Sophie exclaimed.

Poppy ran to Cleo, hugged her and burst into tears.

'Are you okay, Poppy?' Cleo asked.

'I'm more than okay. I'm going to be an auntie! Well, not technically of course but in every other way. I'm so happy for you, Cleo!'

Sophie joined in the hug and all three of them jumped up and down, screaming. Cleo reached out for Clara who also joined in, although she didn't jump up and down.

Thaddeus burst in from the hall.

'Oliver's just… but I see you already know. Congratulations, Cleo!' he yelled above the din. 'I'll get the champagne.'

Before he could make himself heard any further, he'd poured four full glasses and one containing just a sip, knowing full well that Cleo wouldn't drink it now she was pregnant but would want to take part in the toast.

'Congratulations!' Thaddeus said again.

'Thanks, Thaddeus,' Cleo beamed.

'So when did you find out? And how many weeks are you?' Poppy asked, after their toast to Cleo, Oliver and the baby.

'This morning. I did a test yesterday because I'd been feeling queasy for a couple of days but I thought it was probably nothing – like last time. Then… and I can't explain this but I just felt… different somehow. So I did the test. It was positive but I wanted to be absolutely sure this time, so before I said anything to anyone, I went to the doctor. And you won't believe this but it must have happened just after I did the last test on that night of the Blood Moon because according to the doctor, I'm eight weeks pregnant.'

'Oh my God!' Poppy screamed.

'I know! I told Oliver straight away. Then Mum and Oliver's parents, and now you. Oliver wanted to come here too but he had to go into the restaurant. He wants us all to go there for lunch if you're free.'

'We'll make ourselves free,' Thaddeus said, wrapping his arm around Sophie and giving her a very odd look. Almost as if he wished they had similar news to share. 'Oh, and Poppy? Right after Oliver called me, I had a call from Ryan.'

The room suddenly went quiet.

'Sorry,' he added. 'It's not the right time to talk about that. I'll tell you later.'

'No,' Cleo said, taking Poppy's hand in hers and squeezing it. 'Tell us now.'

'Okay. Um. You'll probably have a go at me, Poppy but someone had to do something. None of us like seeing you so unhappy.'

'What did you do, Thaddeus?' Sophie asked.

He shrugged. 'I'd called him a couple of times over the last two weeks but it was always engaged and I didn't want to leave a message.'

'I know that feeling,' Poppy said.

'Well... I called again yesterday and this time I did leave a message. He's just got back to me. He said he's been unbelievably busy which is why the phone's almost constantly engaged and that I should always leave a message because he will call back as soon as he gets it.'

'Fascinating. Is there a point to this?'

'Yes, petulant Poppy, there is. I told him you'd been trying to call him too, but you were too pig-headed to leave a message.'

'You did what!'

'Oh, don't worry. I didn't come right out and say it like that. Wait a minute. I think I did. But first I asked how he was and if he was coming back here. He said he had a lot going on, so not for the foreseeable future. So I said that I knew it was none of my business but I loved you and don't want to see you hurt and if he didn't mind, would he be man enough to tell me the truth about something. Did he have any interest in you or was whatever happened in our kitchen at the Guy Fawkes Night party, before it all went up in flames – no pun intended – just a passing fancy?'

'Thaddeus!' Sophie said.

'Don't get cross. It was good. All good.'

'Good? Good how? What did he say?' Poppy's heart was thumping in her chest.

'He said that he couldn't see why that mattered because you'd be on your way to L.A. fairly soon, if you hadn't gone already.'

'L.A.?' Cleo said. 'You didn't tell me you're thinking of going to L.A. When did you decide this? You can't go there. You can't go anywhere. I'm pregnant!'

'I didn't. I'm not. Why on earth does he think I'm going to L.A.?'

'Because Stephanie told him you were.'

'Stephanie? Why the hell would she say that? The only person I know who's going… Oh God! Timothy Richards and I were discussing it in Betty's Pantry two weeks ago. That was even before Ryan kissed me that night. Please don't tell that somehow Ryan – or Stephanie – heard that gossip and jumped to conclusions.'

'That's exactly what must've happened,' Thaddeus said. 'It took me a little while but I eventually managed to convince him that you had no intention of going anywhere. Especially not now. Oh, he sends his congratulations by the way, Cleo.'

'Thanks. That's nice of him.'

'That's bloody marvellous,' Poppy said. 'Sorry to be so

self-centred but can we get back to what he said about me, please?'

'I realised that was probably why he hadn't called you. So I asked him the question again and this time he said he could assure me it was no passing fancy and that yes, he did have an interest in you.'

'Oh my God!' Sophie said. 'That's excellent news. Thaddeus you're a genius.' She kissed him on the lips.

'Oi. Break it up you two. What else did he say? Was that it? Is he coming back?'

Thaddeus grinned. 'I asked him if that interest was likely to lead to anything because again, I said I don't want to see you hurt. And he said that it wasn't really up to him. It was up to you and you hadn't called, so he took that to mean you weren't interested. That's when I said the bit about the calls and about you being pig-headed. I also said that he could take it from me that you were nuts about him because you were driving us all nuts going on about him and how you'd screwed things up.'

'Oh. My. God! You didn't? Please tell me you didn't.'

'Sorry, Poppy, but I did.'

'And?' Clara piped up. 'Don't stop there, Thaddeus. What did Ryan say then?'

'He said that in that case, he would definitely be coming back to Goldebury Bay.'

Poppy's scream nearly shook Summerhill's foundations and once again, she hugged Cleo and the others and they all jumped up and down on the spot.

This time, even Clara and Thaddeus joined in.

Chapter Thirty-Five

If Poppy checked her phone once, she checked it a thousand times and finally, at seven o'clock that evening as she was curled up in a chair beside the wood burner, drinking hot chocolate, she got the call she'd been waiting for. The only thing was that now she was so nervous she was almost too afraid to answer. But she so wanted to hear his voice. His laugh. She would try to sound light-hearted. She pressed 'call answer'.

'Hello Poppy.'

'Hello. I hope this isn't one of those calls where you're going to tell me that if I'll just give you all my bank details, you'll be able to fix the computer problems I don't even know I have.'

And there it was. That wonderful, marvellous, sexy laugh. She'd like him to bottle it, wrap it up and give it to her for Christmas. Then she could hear it whenever she wanted.

'No Poppy. It isn't. But it is one of those calls where I ask you if you'd like an all-expenses paid trip on a private jet. And before you say no. It's only to Paris and it'll only be for the day. For lunch actually. There's someone I'd like you to meet. Plus, I'll even arrange for an open ticket back on a commercial flight – or Eurostar – or both – so that you have choices, just in case you want to leave at any time. I'm in the Caribbean at the moment but I'm leaving tomorrow. I've got a couple of urgent meetings in London but if you'd like to come – and assuming you're happy to take the time off work – I'll have someone pick you up and take you to the airport and I'll meet you there. That way the next time I kiss you, we'll be jumping on the jet and leaving together.'

Poppy was shaking. She was actually shaking. But it was with excitement at the thought of kissing Ryan again. Sod the jet and the trip to Paris. Although it was clear that he now knew why she'd been so upset two weeks ago.

'That sounds… perfect. But there's just one thing.'

'Yes?' Now he sounded nervous. Or perhaps anxious was more like it.

'You can forget the open ticket because once I'm on that jet, there's no way I'm coming back unless it's with you, Ryan Blackwood.'

After a moment's silence, he said in a raspy voice: 'Then I'll see you on Thursday, Poppy Taylor.'

'You can count on… wait! Thursday? As in, *this* coming Thursday? Thursday the twenty-sixth?'

'Yes. Is… is that a problem? Please tell me it isn't.'

'Oh Ryan! I wish I could tell you that, but it is. We're all going to The Dead Llamas, Horse or Hamster. Sorry, I mean The Dalai. Never mind. We're all going for curry on Thursday at lunchtime. There must be something in the water in this town because after Cleo and Oliver's news today, the Reverend popped the question to Clara. Paul asked Clara to marry him, I mean.'

'Yes, Poppy. I know what popped the question means,' he said, the hint of laughter in his voice almost covering the tone of disappointment.

'We were going to go tomorrow but Paul's got four funerals and a wedding. Who on earth wants to get married on a Wednesday is beyond me but the dead don't choose when they die, so those you can sort of understand. Anyway, that's why it had to be Thursday. And we can't go in the evening because Cleo says now that she's pregnant, if she eats spicy food in the evening it'll keep her up all night. Although God knows how she knows that because she's only known she's pregnant since this morning. Well, technically yesterday because she... Sorry, I'm rambling, and you must have far more important things to do than listen to me going on and on.'

'Actually Poppy, I don't think there's anything I'd rather be doing than listening to you, no matter how important they may be. Although that's not strictly true. There is one thing I'd rather be doing than listening to you.'

'Oh?'

Should she be offended? No. He was a busy man. She had to accept that.

'I'd rather be picking up where we left off on the night of the fireworks. And this time, I'd rather we didn't have any interruptions.'

Oh. My. God. How could she be so turned on just by a few little words?

'I... I can ask if they'd have lunch another day. Or I could ask if they'd mind if I didn't go.'

'No. That wouldn't be right. You go to the lunch. I'll... Actually, Poppy, d'you think they'd mind if I came to the lunch with you? I can re-arrange the Paris trip for Friday – if that's okay with you, of course.'

'Okay? It's better than okay, Ryan. It's... wonderful. Of course they won't mind.'

'Great. Then I'll see you on Thursday.' There was a momentary pause then he continued: 'I've really missed you, Poppy. More than you would ever believe.'

'I've missed you too, Ryan. I've been miserable since you left.'

He laughed. 'Yes, so Thaddeus told me. And thank God he did.' Another brief pause after which he said: 'I've

233

behaved like the jerk you kept telling me I am. I thought you'd gone off to L.A. with Timothy Richards. I thought you really meant all those things you said in those messages and that you just wanted to teach me a lesson. To put me in my place. I should've called and made sure I spoke to you. Hell, I should've turned the bloody jet around and come and kissed you over and over again. I'm sorry Poppy, I really am. I'll be counting the hours until I see you again, you do know that, don't you?'

It was as if he wasn't used to expressing such emotions and suddenly it had all come pouring out.

'Same here,' she said, swallowing the lump in her throat. 'And if anyone's been behaving like a jerk, it's been me. I'll be counting the hours too.'

She very nearly said that she'd be counting the hours until they had sex – but perhaps that wasn't really the sort of thing a girl should say to a guy before they'd even been on a first date.

Chapter Thirty-Six

'I'm so happy I could cry,' Poppy said. 'Yesterday morning I was miserable because I thought I'd be spending Christmas alone again this year – well, not alone, I know I'd be with you – but you know what I mean.'

Cleo and Sophie nodded. 'We know,' they said in unison.

'But today, exactly one month to the Big Day itself, I think there's a very good chance that I'll be spending it with... the radiant Ryan Blackwood.'

'Unless you behave like an idiot and screw it up,' Cleo said. 'And *radiant* Ryan? Are you sure? Can't you do any better than that? Pass me another mince pie, please.'

Sophie passed Cleo the plate of mince pies. 'It's better than *repulsive* Ryan,' she said. 'But what about... rich Ryan? He's definitely rich. No one can argue with that.'

'That's awful,' Poppy said, topping up two large glasses already half full with Baileys and ice and waving her glass in front of Cleo's nose. 'You can sniff it but you can't drink it.'

Cleo beamed. 'I'm high on love and life. I don't need alcohol.'

'You're high on hormones,' Sophie chipped in. 'What about rambunctious Ryan?'

Poppy tutted. 'What about ravishing Ryan? He's definitely ravishing and I'm hoping he's going to ravish me.'

'Er. I don't think you are,' Cleo said. 'In that context,

ravish means 'to take by force'. And that's not a good thing, however "ravishing" he may be.'

'Oh! Perhaps I'll just call him Ryan from now on then. God, I'm really nervous. It's been so long. What if I can't remember how to do it?'

'Now you're being an idiot again,' Sophie said. 'That's one thing you don't forget. Ever.'

'I think we need to talk about something else,' Poppy said. 'Ever since he called me last night, all I've been thinking about is him and what it's going to be like. Will he kiss me when he comes here to pick me up to go to the restaurant? And if so, will I be able to keep my hands off him? Is it really wise to have your first night of sex with someone after curry?'

Cleo burst out laughing. 'Now that is actually a very serious consideration. Especially as you insist on eating the phaal.'

'That's true,' Sophie agreed. 'Hot sex could have a whole new meaning after phaal.'

'I'll have the korma then.'

'Still not a wise move,' Cleo went on. 'If I were you, I'd seriously consider postponing the sex bit. Just stick to kissing and cuddling.'

'Really? Have you seen this guy? Now that I know he likes me there is no way on this earth that I'm going to be able to be in the same room as him and not want to rip his clothes off.'

'They're expensive clothes, Poppy,' Sophie said. 'Perhaps try undressing rather than ripping.'

'Nah,' said Cleo. 'He's rich. He can afford it. Rip away. But not after curry. You said he's taking you to Paris for lunch on Friday. Why not wait until then. I mean, Paris and sex just go together somehow.'

'You could do it on the jet. Sex on a jet would be really

hot.' Sophie looked as if she were imagining it.

'Hello!' Poppy said. 'Okay, I'm serious. We need to change the subject. Let's talk about Christmas. Ooh! I can buy him a Christmas present, assuming we're still together. Oh God! What if he dumps me before Christmas?'

'He's not going to dump you,' Cleo said. 'But what you can possibly get a man as rich as him for Christmas is beyond me.'

Sophie nodded. 'Yeah. Me too. Good luck with that, Poppy.'

'Thanks. Now I've got something else to worry about. That's just great. Was that the doorbell?'

'Yeah. It's probably Oliver. I told him to come and get me when he took Cleover out for her final walk this evening. It'll do me good to walk a little and get some fresh air at the same time. Especially as it's such a lovely evening.'

Poppy and Sophie walked to the door with her and kissed Cleo goodnight and Oliver, hello and goodnight.

'See you tomorrow,' Cleo said. 'And stop worrying. It'll all be fine. You'll see.'

'Yeah, you're probably right. Gosh, it's really cold out. I hope it's not going to snow. That would be just my luck. His jet will probably get snowed in or something and he won't be able to get here.'

'Stop panicking, will you?' Cleo said. 'Get back inside. We'll see you tomorrow.'

'Bye,' Poppy and Sophie said, and Poppy closed the door.

'Thaddeus will probably be here soon,' Sophie said. 'This evening has gone so quickly. I can't believe it's ten-thirty. You will get an early night, won't you? Don't spend the whole night panicking because then you'll wake up looking tired and drained and you'll be worrying about that.'

'It's funny,' Poppy said. 'I thought having a boyfriend again would be wonderful but there's just so much to worry about.'

'And it'll only get worse from here. You'll be worrying about whether he'll ask you to marry him or whether it's far too soon. You'll be wondering if he even wants to get married. Your friends will be having babies and you'll want one too. You'll wonder if he wants one and you'll worry if it's too soon to discuss it. And then you'll remember that you love one another and there really isn't anything to worry about as long as you're together.'

'Hmm,' Poppy said. 'Were we just talking about me or you?'

Sophie laughed. 'It's ridiculous, I know. But I love Thaddeus so much and even though we've only been together for a few months, it feels so right that I just want us to get married and start a family.'

'That's not ridiculous, it's lovely. And if I know Thaddeus, I wouldn't be at all surprised if he's thinking exactly the same. Why don't you just ask him?'

'What? Ask him if he wants to marry me? Perhaps I should be more like my namesake Sophia Summerhill and take matters into my own hands. Perhaps I should propose to him.'

Poppy smiled. 'I don't think that's a bad idea. I know this sounds silly – and it is silly, but knowing Thaddeus, the one thing that would hold him back from proposing to you is the fact that you're the one with all the money now.'

'Bloody hell! I hadn't even thought of that but you know, you may well be right. I know he loves me. I mean *really* loves me. And he's such a romantic but I was the one who suggested he should move in with me. I had to tell him that there was no way I wanted to live in Summerhill on my own. And I remember how weird he got when I suggested reopening Beaumont Boats. It was as if I was offering him charity or something.'

'All I can say is that there's no harm in asking. And it would make a change for one of us to do the proposing. Although I'm not sure you should get down on one knee.'

Sophie beamed at Poppy. 'I think I'm going to do it. I'm actually going to do it.' She shivered.

'Are you cold?' Poppy asked.

'A little. I knew I should've worn a jumper over this blouse.'

'I'll nip upstairs and get you one. The heating's still on although the wood burner is dying down now. I won't be a second.'

Poppy dashed upstairs and grabbed her favourite, thick, wool cardigan. She heard what sounded like the doorbell and then a muffled shout, followed by a thud like something solid falling against the wall. What was going on downstairs? Had Thaddeus arrived and tripped on that stupid boot-scraper? She'd done it herself more than once. But Thaddeus knew to step over the raised iron bar which protruded a little too far onto the main doorstep.

Oh God! Had he hurt himself? Or was it Sophie? Poppy ran down the stairs in her stockinged feet and raced towards the hall. Sophie was sprawled on the floor with Thaddeus leaning over her.

'Sophie! Oh my God, Sophie! What's happened, Thaddeus?' Poppy screamed. 'You're not Thaddeus! Who the hell are you? What've you done to Sophie?'

The dark-haired man bending over Sophie looked up, shock and confusion etched on his face.

'Sophie?' the man said, his voice heavy with a foreign accent. Suddenly, his eyes sparkled as if realisation had dawned. 'You're Poppy.'

239

It was a statement and one that sent fear into every fibre of Poppy's being. Instinctively she backed away and raced for her phone but the man was right behind her. He grabbed her by her hair and yanked her back towards his solid body. Her foot flew up in the air as he pulled her backwards, knocking the small table and her glass of Baileys onto the floor. She screamed and then a smell of ether invaded her nostrils as a cloth was placed and held firmly over her face.

'Ryan!' she mumbled before blackness engulfed her.

Chapter Thirty-Seven

Poppy opened her eyes and shivered. This was no dream... or nightmare, to be precise. This was real. She had been abducted and although she'd never seen her kidnapper before last night she somehow knew his name was Enzo.

She searched around the window-less room for Sophie but she was completely alone. Slowly and painfully getting to her feet, she staggered to the door and tugged at the handle but it was locked. She screamed for help over and over again but only her echo came back to her.

She looked around but other than the mattress on the floor, there was nothing in the room and certainly nothing that might help her escape.

Why was she here? Why had he taken her? It was clearly her he wanted. She could tell that by the way he had said her name. The way he had looked at her when she had first dashed into the hall. He'd been astonished. He had no doubt assumed Sophie was her.

What had he done with Sophie? He had obviously used chloroform or whatever that awful smelling substance on the cloth was, to knock her out too. But what had happened to her then? Did he just leave her? Or did he do something worse? Lucy and Jules had said that they and Ryan believed Enzo was merely a petty criminal, prone to violence but the fear was that one day he'd go too far. Surely that meant Sophie was okay. Didn't it?

What could she do? She thumped her hands against the door with all her might. She tried with her stockinged feet and then hurled her entire body weight at the door but all she did was cause herself more pain.

She leant against the door and slowly slid to the floor. For now, there was nothing else she could do. What time was it? How long had she been asleep? Was it still night or was it now day?

Thaddeus would've arrived at her cottage not long after she had been taken. She prayed that he would have found Sophie passed out but otherwise okay. He would've contacted the police immediately. Then he would've contacted Oliver and then he probably would've contacted Ryan. Would any of them have guessed that Enzo was the culprit? Would they have any idea where she was? What was Enzo planning to do? But more importantly, would Ryan and the others find her before he did anything?

Chapter Thirty-Eight

Ryan was beside himself with worry. And not just worry –
fear. The minute Thaddeus had called him, it was as if his
heart had stopped.

Thaddeus' voice had been filled with a mixture of shock
and relief as he had briefly told Ryan that he had found
Sophie unconscious in the hall of Poppy's cottage and that
he was waiting for an ambulance. That there was no sign of
Poppy.

Ryan immediately knew that this had something to do
with Enzo. That was both a good thing and a bad. He knew
Enzo didn't want Poppy. This was about Stephanie, and it
was about Ryan. Somehow Enzo had discovered how Ryan
felt about Poppy – which wasn't difficult in a place like
Goldebury Bay. Even those with the kindest hearts and best
intentions would happily divulge information to a friendly
face. And Enzo could be friendly. Enzo could be charming.
Stephanie could vouch for that.

Perhaps it was even Stephanie who had told Enzo about
Poppy. Perhaps she'd guessed Ryan's feelings and
mentioned it to Enzo on their journey on Guy Fawkes
Night. This was clearly Enzo's way of putting Ryan in his
shoes. This was him saying: "You took Stephanie from me.
I've taken Poppy from you."

Ryan had no idea what Enzo planned to do next. Did he
intend to ask for a ransom? Did he want Stephanie in
exchange? Ryan would willingly hand over any sum of
money for Poppy's safe return, but would he be prepared to

risk his sister?

Had he underestimated Enzo? He believed him capable of manipulating Stephanie; of hitting Stephanie and breaking bones; of one day, possibly even worse, which is why he knew he had to keep Stephanie away from that man. But this? This he had never imagined. Or had he?

Why had he been so worried that day when he couldn't reach Poppy on the phone? Had something deep down told him that she may be in danger? Why hadn't he listened to that feeling? Why had he dismissed it the moment he knew she was safe?

It was too late now to worry about that. All that mattered now was getting Poppy back and he would do anything to achieve that. Anything. And yes, he would even use Stephanie if that was what it took.

But he knew it wouldn't come to that. Enzo was a bully but he wasn't very bright. The man might have Poppy now but he wouldn't have her for long. Ryan had money and powerful friends as well as contacts and influence. Ryan had Doug. And he would use them all to find Poppy. If he knew one thing, it was that money could buy anything.

He smiled wanly at that thought. Poppy wasn't interested in money. She had shown she couldn't be bought. But the people he needed right now certainly could. He was just relieved that he was back in England when this happened. His important meetings could wait. All that mattered now was finding Poppy. As worried as he was, he knew that with his resources, it wouldn't take him long.

Chapter Thirty-Nine

Why couldn't she think of anything other than mince pies? Here she was, held captive without food, water, or even basic facilities other than a mattress and all she could think about was mince pies.

Was it just because she was hungry? She must have been here for several hours. She was definitely thirsty. Why wasn't she thinking about water? Or even coffee? Or wine? Why was it just mince pies?

Well, not just mince pies. Sitting curled up on the sofa in her cottage, eating mince pies. Ryan's arms wrapped tightly around her, logs crackling in the wood burner, fairy lights twinkling on the Christmas tree, it's pine scent filling the air. Snow falling outside and glistening in the moonlight... and carol singers who also seemed to have a penchant for mince pies.

Would that picture become a reality? Would she feel Ryan's arms around her once more? Would she ever have sex again? Would she...

What was that noise? Was that someone coming? Was that Enzo? That was more than one person. That was several people. And they were running and shouting. Was that Ryan?

She scrambled to her feet and thumped her fists against the door calling out his name repeatedly.

'Ryan! Ryan! I'm in here! Ryan!'

'Poppy! Are you okay? Stand away from the door, Poppy.'

Poppy burst out laughing and started crying at the same time as she stumbled towards the centre of the room.

Seconds later, the door burst open and Ryan stood before her. The fear in his eyes subsided as he rapidly scanned her body; a smile replaced the tight line of his lips and his worried expression diminished.

'You've come to my rescue again,' Poppy said, unable to move.

He beamed at her. 'It was a quiet day. I had nothing more important to do.'

In three long strides he met her as she ran into his arms. He kissed her face, her hair, her mouth, repeating her name over and over again.

'For a moment I thought I might never see you again,' Poppy said. 'But somehow I knew you'd find me and I was just being a drama queen.'

He laughed into a handful of her hair. 'I was sure he wouldn't harm you, and yet... I was terrified he would. But you're safe now and I'll make sure nothing like this ever happens to you again.'

'I don't think it's really sunk in yet. I'm not in shock or anything. I'm just so happy to see you, Ryan,' she said between his kisses.

'Are you really okay?'

Poppy nodded. 'I'm fine. Tired, thirsty and hungry, but fine.'

'Then let's get out of here.'

He swept her into his arms and encircling his neck with her arms, she rested her head on his shoulder. He carried her past several other people including Thaddeus and Oliver and, noticeably, the uniformed police. One of them had Enzo face down on the floor and was applying handcuffs.

Safe now, exhaustion overcame her as Ryan gently

placed her on the rear seat of the limo.

Before getting in beside her, he smiled down. 'Do you need anything?'

She shook her head and smiled back.

'Then I'll just be a minute. I need to have a very quick word with the police.'

'Oi! Blackwood!'

Her voice was little more than a whisper but he was back with her in less than a second.

'Yes,' he said, half anxious, half smiling.

'I don't suppose anyone has a mince pie, do they?'

Ryan laughed and glanced at someone by his side.

Doug said: 'I'll find one.'

Poppy was content. If anyone could get her a mince pie it was Ryan Blackwood and his 'spies'. She smiled and closed her eyes.

Chapter Forty

'I'm going home and I don't care what anyone says.' Poppy was adamant. 'I'm feeling fine now and I've got to go home some time. I've got to face it. You know the saying: "When you fall off a horse, get back in the saddle." Well the cottage is my horse and I'm going back in. No arguments.'

'Just stay here until Ryan gets back,' Sophie pleaded, sitting in the chair opposite the sofa on which Poppy was curled up under a Christmassy-looking throw. 'He'll kill us if he finds you've gone back while he's away.'

'He won't kill anyone. He's not a violent man.' Poppy sipped her hot chocolate and scooping out a teaspoonful of marshmallows from the whipped cream on the top, held the spoon up to her mouth. 'Although Thaddeus told me that on the day Ryan rescued me, he punched Enzo pretty hard just before the police arrived. He told them Enzo fell down the stairs leading to the hallway and the cellar I was being held in. I don't think they really believed him but I don't think they were too bothered about it. Enzo really isn't very bright, is he? Ryan said it only took Doug about an hour to find the house the guy had rented… in his own name!' She popped the marshmallows into her mouth and closed her eyes, savouring their gooey texture.

'I know. I really don't understand what Stephanie sees in that guy… apart from his looks. He's definitely handsome, from what I saw of him that night – and charming when he wants to be, so Ryan says. Anyway, don't try and change the subject. Please don't go home. The doctor said you need rest. You went through far worse than I did and I'm still a little shaken.'

Poppy shook her head. 'No, I didn't. Not really. I agree the doctor said I needed to rest, but only for a few days. You and Thaddeus have been wonderful but I've been here for over a week now and I want to go home. It's the fifth of December tomorrow and I haven't got any decorations up at the cottage. I need a tree, lights, holly – the whole shebang. I want to do it. I love Christmas and I want this one to be special.'

'It will be special. You'll have Ryan. You've got Ryan.'

'I know. But I want to make the cottage look special too. Please don't argue with me, Sophie.'

Sophie shrugged and sighed as Cleo walked in.

'What's going on?' Cleo asked. 'Veronique let me in on her way out. She's gone to look at trees, apparently.'

Sophie nodded. 'Poppy is insisting on going home. She won't listen to me – or to Veronique. And Thaddeus is at Beaumont Boats. Perhaps you could try.'

Cleo shrugged. 'If she wants to go home, I think she should go.'

'What? Ryan will go mad.'

'Let him. Anyway, he won't go mad. He must know she's fully recovered. He's been virtually living here for the last week.'

'For all the good that's done me,' Poppy said. 'Which is another reason I want to go home. All the while I'm here, he seems to think I'm some sort of invalid. The most he'll do is kiss me. And as wonderful as his kisses are, I want more than that. If I go home, he'll see I'm fine and maybe then we can move this relationship along. And if he thinks I'm not fine, then he'll stay the night with me. It's a win-win situation.'

249

Cleo laughed. 'And let's be honest, Sophie, if he didn't think she was okay he wouldn't have gone away this morning.'

'But that's the point,' Sophie said. 'He went, knowing she'd be safe here. If he comes back tomorrow evening and find she's gone back to the cottage, he'll be furious. She said she told him she was going back, but he didn't mention it to us this morning, so I don't believe her.'

'Excuse me,' Poppy said. 'Are you calling me a liar?'

'Yes,' Sophie replied.

'Fair enough. But I'm still going. Look, it's only for one night. Ryan will be back tomorrow evening. And besides, there's that new alarm thing fitted at the cottage, plus a security lock that Ryan says is virtually impossible to break into. And let's not forget, Enzo himself is under lock and key at the moment. What could possibly go wrong?'

'Knowing you, a lot,' Sophie said.

'Well, I'm going, so that's that.'

Sophie sighed again. She must have known she couldn't win. 'Okay. But we're coming to help you decorate and you're calling Ryan to tell him. Deal?'

'Deal,' Poppy said. 'I'll call him right now. I don't suppose I could have another mince pie, could I? I've really become addicted to them.'

'Fine,' Sophie said. 'But you're calling Ryan first.'

Poppy pulled a face and rang Ryan. Fortunately, it went to voicemail.

'Hi honey,' Poppy trilled into the phone. 'I'm going home to put some Christmas decorations up and Cleo and Sophie are coming with me. I feel absolutely fine so please don't worry about me. I'll see you tomorrow night. Missing you already.'

'Why didn't you say you love him?' Cleo asked.

Poppy blushed. 'We haven't said the L word yet,

although he nearly did the other day. He said: "I really love... being with you. It's much more fun than working." I think he was going to say that he really loved me. But he didn't. And that's another reason why I want to go home. Perhaps if we're alone together he might say something more about his feelings.'

'Why don't you just tell him how you feel?' Sophie asked.

'I don't want to put any pressure on him. If I say it, he might think he has to.'

'That works both ways,' Cleo said. 'Perhaps he feels if he says it, you'll have to.'

'I hadn't thought of that. Perhaps I'll tell him this weekend. Under the mistletoe we're going to put up today. And the sooner we get started, the sooner I can say it.'

Chapter Forty-One

The cottage looked magical by the time the three of them had finished decorating. A huge wreath made of pine boughs entwined with glittering red and gold ribbons and studded with slices of dried orange and apple, pine cones and cinnamon sticks hung on the dark oak door. Multi-coloured fairy lights danced around the door and window frames, both outside and in. A pine tree, heavy with twinkling lights and ornaments stood in front of the sitting room window, and the holly and baubles displayed on the mantle-piece over the wood burner added the finishing touch.

Poppy glanced around the room. 'I think we've done it!'

'It does look really Christmassy,' Sophie said. 'And very cosy too. I hope Summerhill looks like this when we've finished decorating. Thaddeus wants us to have two trees, one outside the house, and one inside. I have visions of Silas racing up and down both of them, and of smashed ornaments and fairy lights being an everyday occurrence.'

'That's all part of Christmas.' Poppy said. 'I think Summerhill will look absolutely fabulous, and a tree outside would be really special.'

'I assume those are the trees Veronique went to look for this morning,' Cleo said, with a smile. 'It'll be a lot of work to decorate Summerhill even if we all pitch in but I guess Veronique will organise the whole thing.'

Sophie nodded. 'Yes. She texted me this afternoon to say she's found the perfect trees and they're being delivered today. We've been picking the decorations online all week, which Poppy helped with. I didn't have any and nor does Thaddeus. Everything is new and that'll make it even more special somehow.'

'Are his mum and Mercedes definitely coming home for Christmas?' Poppy asked.

'Yes, and I'm really looking forward to meeting them, especially Mercedes and the children. Even Turner's coming because he's on leave this Christmas. And Mum and Hugh will be coming back too, so it'll be a packed house. I know you and Oliver are going to Mary and Christopher's for Christmas lunch, Cleo, but you are still coming to us on Christmas Eve, aren't you? All of you, including Mary and Christopher. And you and Ryan, Poppy.'

Cleo nodded. 'Yep, that's all still as planned. I'm really excited about this Christmas. Mary's well, my mum's engaged to a Reverend, and Oliver and I are not just engaged but also expecting our first child. It's going to be a wonderful Christmas. I can feel it.'

'What you can feel is probably just wind from the baby,' Poppy said, grinning. 'And yes, Sophie, Ryan and I will definitely be there.'

'And what you'll be feeling is a slap of my hand around your head if you're not careful,' Cleo said.

Poppy laughed. 'Right. Anyone for a mince pie?'

'You and those mince pies!' Cleo shook her head. 'Are you sure you're not pregnant?'

Poppy tutted. 'In case you've forgotten, you have to have sex to get pregnant and I'm still waiting for that.'

'Er. I'm not sure you'll have to wait much longer,' Sophie said, looking back from where she was standing near the window. 'It's fairly dark outside, but the coloured Christmas lights in the street are making rather pretty patterns on a black limo heading this way. Unless I'm very much mistaken, I think it could be Ryan's.'

'Very funny,' Poppy said. 'You know as well as I do that he only left this morning and he won't be back until tomorrow evening. The only way that could be him is if he turned the jet around in mid-flight and he wouldn't... Bloody hell! You don't think he did, do you?'

Sophie walked towards her, grabbing her handbag on the way. 'Seeing that it's just pulled up outside, that's a question I'm going to leave you to ask him. I think it's time we left, Cleo.'

'I'll get the coats,' Cleo said, dashing towards the door. 'Don't forget to stand under the mistletoe, Poppy! See you tomorrow. Good luck. And if you do have sex, we want to hear all about it.'

'Wait a minute!' Poppy shrieked.

'Oh hi Ryan,' Cleo called out as she opened the front door. 'Sophie and I were just leaving. Don't get mad at us. You know what Poppy's like. She's in the sitting room. Bye.'

'I'm not mad at you. But I do have a few words to say to Poppy. Bye Cleo. Bye Sophie.'

A few seconds later, Ryan marched into the sitting room, stopped and looked around him.

'This looks wonderful. But why couldn't it have waited until Saturday? I couldn't believe it when I got your message. I was going to call back but I realised there was probably little point. You'd have done it anyway, wouldn't you?'

'So... you turned the jet around and came back?'

'The pilot did, but yes. There was no way I was going to let you stay in this house on your own.'

'I'm not going back to Sophie and Thaddeus'. I've been there for too long. I know they don't mind but I want them to have some space. Sophie wants to propose!'

'To Thaddeus?'

'No, to Silas the cat. Of course, to Thaddeus. She thinks he's too worried about the fact that she's so rich to ask her, and Cleo and I agree. And don't say that perhaps it's too early because they haven't been together very long. They're crazy about one another so there's no reason why they shouldn't get engaged.'

Ryan nodded. 'I wasn't going to and I can go along with Sophie's thinking. Money can sometimes seem like an obstacle. Okay. You can come to High House.'

'I don't want to go to High House, Ryan. Well, not tonight anyway. I know you think you're doing what's best for me but I want to stay here tonight. Is everything okay? You haven't even kissed me hello.'

'I'm cross. I'm also rather worried.'

'Why? I'm fine. Honestly, I am. And I'm safe here. You've made sure of that. Please don't be worried. And please, please, don't be cross.'

'I'm not worried about your safety at the moment, although I was for the entire journey. I'm worried because I've been thinking of nothing else but holding you in my arms again, all the way here and if I come over there and kiss you, I think I know what that will lead to. In fact, I know it will.'

'And that's a problem, why?'

'Because I'm not sure you're well enough for that yet. I just need a few moments to regain my equilibrium, that's all.'

Poppy smiled, leant to one side and grabbed a sprig of mistletoe. She held it in the air above her head.

'Oi. Blackwood,' she said, in the sexiest voice she could muster. 'I'm well enough for anything. Can't you see I need a kiss? A very, very long, slow but ultimately passionate kiss. In fact, I'm going to need several. And then I'm going to need you to take me upstairs to bed, where I'll definitely need a lot more than kisses.'

He was pulling her into his arms before she had finished the sentence.

'Are you sure you're ready for this?'

'Oh yes,' she said. 'I've been ready for days. I think my Christmas is going to come early this year.'

He smiled down at her. 'And mine. You know I love you, don't you, Poppy Taylor?'

Poppy beamed at him. 'I do now, Ryan Blackwood. And just so there's no doubt, I'm pretty stuck on you. And this time, I'd rather like to stay stuck, if it's all the same to you.'

'You know me,' he said. 'Always happy to help you… in any way I can. Now what were you saying about those kisses?'

He didn't give her time to answer.

Chapter Forty-Two

'So what do you think of this tree?' Veronique asked.

Sophie and Thaddeus stood outside the front of Summerhill, arm in arm, admiring it as one of Veronique's assistants flipped the light switch in the house.

'I think it's beautiful,' Sophie said, watching as hundreds of wildly twinkling lights chased each other from the bottom of the fifteen-foot tree to the very top where a bright, white star perched, shining down on them.

'I do too.' Thaddeus looked from the tree to Sophie, and smiled at Veronique. 'Even more so because I helped decorate it.' He winked.

'Right then,' Veronique said. 'I'll get my staff together and we'll be on our way. Tony is taking me to a special late night Christmas shopping event in Hastings. And I know exactly what I'm going to get him to buy me. See you soon.'

'Thank you,' Sophie said. 'Have fun.'

Within minutes, everyone had gone. Sophie was alone with Thaddeus and she could think of no place she would rather be. She had thought of nothing except proposing to him since she had left Poppy's cottage yesterday evening.

Well, that wasn't strictly true. Once or twice she had thought of Poppy and Ryan and smiled to herself. If she knew Poppy – and she did – it would be at least a couple of days until anyone saw Ryan or Poppy again.

'I love you, Thaddeus.' Sophie turned to face him. 'I love you with all of my heart.'

'I love you too,' he said, with an adoring smile.

She looked deep into his eyes. Now was as good a time as any.

'There's something I want to ask you.'

She fiddled with the buttons of his coat. It was freezing out here. Perhaps this wasn't the right place.

'There's something I want to ask you too,' he said.

'Oh?'

'I wonder if it's the same question.'

'Question? You want to ask me a question?'

He nodded. 'A very important question.'

Her heart thumped in her chest and she held her breath. Was he going to propose to her?

She smiled. 'You go first.'

'Are you sure?'

She hesitated. What did he mean by that?

She nodded. 'Yes, I'm sure.'

He beamed at her. 'Okay. Sophie?'

'Yes.'

'Sophie Summerhill…? What on earth can I give you for Christmas?'

Sophie blinked several times.

'That… that's your question?'

'What were you expecting?'

'Nothing,' she said. 'Nothing at all. And that also answers your question. I don't want anything for Christmas. I've got everything I want.'

'You have? Does that mean you don't want this?'

He got down on one knee, pulled a small, velvet covered, antique box from his pocket and held it out to her.

'You don't need a dagger or a rapier to open this box.'

She couldn't believe her eyes. She took the box in trembling hands and opened it to reveal a stunning sapphire and diamond ring.

'It was my grandmother's. My mother passed it down to me. It may not be quite as spectacular as the rings in the Summerhill treasure, but my grandparents were happily married for seventy years. I'm hoping we can beat that because seventy years with you is nowhere near enough. Will you marry me, Sophie, even though I have nothing to offer you but this ring?'

'Oh, Thaddeus you idiot! You have everything to offer me. You are everything to me. And the ring is far more beautiful than any I have ever seen. Of course I'll marry you! Yes, yes, yes, I'll marry you.'

She flung herself into his arms and neither said a word for at least five minutes. Finally, Thaddeus slipped the ring onto Sophie's finger.

'What were you going to ask me?' he said, his smile full of love.

'Oh. The same as you asked me.' She returned his smile. 'What on earth can I give you for Christmas?'

His eyes gave the twinkling lights on the tree a run for their money.

'Well… it's too late for this Christmas,' he said. 'But possibly for next Christmas, a baby Summerhill-Beaumont would be pretty fantastic.'

'A baby! Oh Thaddeus, yes! But… I think Beaumont will be fine.'

'If we have a girl, we could call her Summer Beaumont. And maybe Silas, if it's a boy.'

'Let's go and talk about that… inside,' she said. 'And I don't just mean talk about it.'

Chapter Forty-Three

Poppy could honestly say that she had never been so happy. Ryan hadn't jumped on his jet once since he had kissed her on that Friday night over a week ago and the only time he'd mentioned it had been on one occasion when he had said that they must go to Paris before Christmas. He wanted her to meet his friend and co-director, Lucien Chevalier and Lucien's daughter Sabine. But then he had kissed her again and said that it could wait... possibly until the New Year.

Instead, they had curled up together on the sofa, the wood burner eating through logs as fast as he and Poppy were eating mince pies. They talked about the things they both loved doing – Ryan about his life, his work, his interests and Poppy, her travels through Europe and all the places she hoped to visit; her love of the simple life; her friends. Both of them getting excited about spending Christmas together; drinking wine; eating even more mince pies; sharing long, slow kisses with the taste of the wine and the fruit still fresh on their lips, followed by slow, gentle love-making leading to the most incredibly passionate sex.

It was exactly as Poppy had imagined her perfect Christmas would be – and it wasn't even Christmas yet.

'I still can't believe this,' Poppy said, snuggling closer to Ryan.

'Nor can I,' he said, as he wrapped his arm tightly around her.

'So much has happened in such a short space of time.

Cleo and Oliver's plan for a January wedding is going well despite the rush. I know Cleo wanted to be married several months before their baby is due but I didn't think they'd manage it. It seems with Veronique's help, and Sophie's money as a wedding present, anything is possible.'

Ryan smiled. 'When we were in The Dead Llamas, Horse or Hamster yesterday, Paul told me that he and Clara are hoping to get married in the spring. So that's two weddings next year. Then there's Sophie and Thaddeus, of course. That makes three.'

Poppy nodded. 'Sophie has asked Veronique to see if she can get Saturday the twenty-fifth of June. That'll be just over a year after Sophie came to Goldebury Bay. A summer wedding at Summerhill. That's *so* romantic.'

'Speaking of romance. Toby called me this morning to tell me he's asked Sabine to go on a date with him. To quote his very words, he said: "I don't know why I hadn't ever done it before. Sabine is perfect for me." And this time, I agree with him wholeheartedly. He'll finally be in a relationship I won't have to bail him out of.'

'Or blackmail him not to get into. I still can't believe you told him that he could have sex with me whenever he liked, but not with your money!'

Ryan squeezed her tighter. 'It was the only way I could think of to make sure he *didn't* have sex with you. I'm sorry but I knew that to him, you were another infatuation whereas to me... well, even then I couldn't bear the thought of you being in another man's arms. I knew he'd choose the money over you. It was only when I thought it was really what you wanted, that I capitulated.'

'And decided to give me some sort of allowance too! To ease the pain of him dumping me later, I suppose.' She gave him a playful slap.

Ryan shrugged. 'What can I say? A man in love doesn't

think rationally. I didn't want you to be hurt. I thought having money to fall back on would help. Plus, it meant I'd still be in touch with you and perhaps… well, perhaps in the future, you'd see me in a different light.'

'You'd have been happy to have me after your brother cast me off?' She looked deep into his eyes.

'Absolutely. Do you really need to ask that? I love you, no matter what.'

Poppy smiled then kissed him.

'Have you heard from Stephanie?' she asked, several minutes later.

Ryan nodded. 'Yes. First Jules called me this afternoon to say they're enjoying their cruise and Stephanie has finally come to her senses after her stay with my friends in the Caribbean. Then Stephanie phoned me half an hour later. She told me that Enzo was definitely history. She said she'd never have forgiven herself if anything had happened to me, or to you for that matter. Oh, and I forgot. She also said she thinks she owes you an apology for the way she behaved to you. What did she mean by that?'

Poppy smiled. 'Nothing. We just didn't hit it off at first but I've got a feeling everything's going to work out perfectly.'

'Funnily enough, I feel the same way too. And talking of working out perfectly, Toby is really getting things together with the Goldebury Bay Yachting and Sailing Club project. Handing over the reins to him has worked wonders on his work ethic. I should've done it sooner. We should have some definitive plans before the New Year.'

'I've got some "definitive" plans of my own,' Poppy said. 'But they involve just you and me, a bottle of wine and a very early night.'

Ryan grinned. 'Who needs wine? I'm already intoxicated by you.'

Everything was perfect. Poppy knew she wouldn't be alone this Christmas – or any Christmas... if she got her wish.

Chapter Forty-Four

Poppy couldn't believe her eyes as she opened the door of her cottage on Christmas Eve. It had been snowing almost every day for a week and tonight, the waxing gibbous moon shone down on a glistening white layer of fresh powder. Ryan stood before her, looking sensational in a tuxedo, white shirt and a Christmas bow tie with reindeers on it. Behind him, blocking the road, stood a sleigh, drawn by six reindeer with a coachman dressed as Father Christmas at the reins.

'It was good enough for Toby!' Ryan winked. 'But this does have a folding roof, you'll be pleased to hear.'

Poppy giggled. 'This is really romantic. There's nothing quite as magical as a sleigh ride on Christmas Eve. Is that a sack of presents in the back?'

'Yes. But they're not all for you,' he said, escorting her to the sleigh. 'I just thought this would be fun as there's so much snow on the ground.'

He helped her into the sleigh after she had spent several minutes petting the reindeer, and he wrapped her in a faux fur throw. The sleigh, complete with jingling bells on the reindeers' reins headed towards Summer Hill Cliff as she snuggled into his arms.

'There's something I need to tell you before we get to Summerhill,' he said, after a while.

'That sounds serious. Has something happened?'

'Yes and no. Don't worry – it's all good. At least I think it is. When Stephanie and Jules were on their cruise, one of the places they went to was Sydney. I have a few friends out there through one of my companies and I asked one of them – Gary – to spend some time with Stephanie and Jules.'

'Don't tell me. Stephanie's fallen in love.'

Ryan smiled. 'Again, yes and no. She has – but with the country. No, it's Jules who's fallen in love. It seems she and Keith, Gary's grandfather, hit it off and they've been phoning and texting every day. She's planning on going out there for an extended vacation in the New Year and Stephanie wants to go too. Jules says she can.'

'Wow! That's amazing. Good for Jules. And... that means you won't have to worry about Stephanie?'

'I suppose it does. I know she'll be fine with Jules, and with Keith and Gary to watch over her.'

'And...? There's something else, isn't there?'

'It got me thinking about next year – and about holidays – and I remembered you saying that Oliver had been saving to pay for his parents to go on a safari, so... and this is just a suggestion – if you don't like the idea, we can do something else. I thought that, as part of our Christmas gift to Cleo and Oliver, we could pay for that. And for Cleo and Oliver to go too. In fact... for us all to go... as a group. We can use the jet to go anywhere they choose and of course, we'll pay for everything. I thought it would be good to do something with all of us together before their baby arrives.'

Poppy twisted round to look him directly in the eye. 'Oh Ryan! That... that's a wonderful idea. But... when you say "we", you do realise that, as a barmaid-cum-waitress, I can't afford to contribute much to this present. I might be able to stretch to safari hats or binoculars or something, but that's about it.'

'That's not a problem,' he said, as the sleigh came to a halt beside the derelict Goldebury Bay Yachting and

Sailing Club. 'This is where we first met, three months ago tomorrow. I thought we should have our own little celebration tonight.'

He pulled out a bottle of champagne and two glasses. Handing the glasses to Poppy, he popped the cork and poured the champagne. They clinked glasses.

'To us,' he said, smiling. 'To fairy tales coming true and to me finding my very own princess.'

She smiled back. 'To my frog – who turned into the most handsome and wonderful prince.'

He turned away as she emptied her glass and when he turned back, he offered her a basket full of bread.

'I'm not hungry, thanks,' she said, a little disappointed that it wasn't chocolate brownies... or mince pies.

'So you don't want it then?'

'Bread? No thanks.' She laughed suddenly. 'The last time you offered me a bread basket was when...'

It couldn't be. She was being ridiculous. He wasn't..., was he?

His smile grew wider and there was something in his eyes that told her he was.

'...there was a ring in it,' she continued. 'Are you...? Is there...?'

He reached inside and produced a magnificent diamond solitaire ring between his thumb and forefinger and held it out to her. 'And this does mean we're engaged... if you take it, that is. Will you take it?' he asked, looking a little anxious now. He got down on one knee on the floor of the sleigh whilst the coachman sat staunchly looking out across a silver sea. 'Will you marry me, Poppy? I'll even say please.'

She couldn't speak for what felt like minutes but was only a second or two. Holding out her left hand to him, she nodded repeatedly.

'Yes, yes, yes! Oh Ryan! Yes, please!'

He slid the ring on her finger and pulled her into his arms.

After several passionate kisses he eased her away from him and leant to one side. He pulled out a brown envelope and handed it to her.

'I need you to sign this,' he said. 'Lucy drew it up for me. I hope you'll find it's in order but you're welcome to ask Tony Hardman to check it over for you.'

She blinked several times. 'A prenuptial agreement?' It took the edge off the romance slightly but why should she be surprised? He was a millionaire after all, and a shrewd businessman. What did she expect? She was a virtually penniless barmaid-cum-waitress. 'Do you have a pen?'

He produced a gold fountain pen and handed it to her as she removed the document from the envelope.

What? She turned it over but it was only one page and on that one page it read: *I, Ryan Tiberius Blackwood agree to share my entire fortune, both present and future, with Poppy Taylor.* It was followed by his signature. Then it read: *I, Poppy Taylor (also known as Cinderella) agree to share my entire fortune, both present and future, with Ryan Tiberius Blackwood.* Followed by a space for her signature.

'It only seems fair to share,' he said, grinning. 'I forgot to ask if you have a middle name.'

'I don't,' she said, half laughing, half crying but completely blissful. 'Is yours really Tiberius?'

He nodded. 'Don't ask. So anyway, once you sign that, you'll be able to pay for your half of Cleo and Oliver's Christmas present. Speaking of which, we'd better get going or we'll be late.'

'I think you should have a real prenup drawn up,' she said, as the coachman headed the sleigh towards Summerhill.

267

'No need. I know a good deal when I see one. I'm very happy with this. And…,' he said, wrapping her in his arms again, 'unless you have any strong objections, I was thinking that, maybe after Christmas we could jump on the jet and get married in Las Vegas. I don't want to wait and we can have a real wedding next year… along with everyone else in Goldebury Bay, it seems.'

Chapter Forty-Five

Summerhill was full to bursting and Sophie and Thaddeus – with Veronique's help, of course – had made the house, the cliff and the gardens into a virtual winter wonderland. Fairy lights danced on the trees both inside and out, casting rainbows of colour all around and there were fires in the sitting room, dining room and even the Great Hall.

Holly, mistletoe and a variety of decorations, hung from several of the beams throughout the ground floor and the banisters were wrapped in pine boughs, holly and ivy. Heavenly spices filled the air, wafting out from both the kitchen and the sitting room where mulled wine and spiced cider filled the punch bowls.

Even Silas the cat wore a Christmassy collar and didn't seem at all bothered by it – or the fact that Cleo and Oliver had brought their daft dog, Cleover with them. Silas didn't go as far as curling up with Cleover by the fire but he did sit on the arm of Sophie's chair without hissing or snarling, so he was clearly also full of the Christmas spirit. Perhaps it had something to do with the fact that GJ had given him a saucer of eggnog when Sophie wasn't looking.

'It's snowing again,' Poppy said, as she and Ryan walked into the sitting room, hand in hand.

'Did you just arrive in a sleigh… with reindeers, darling?' Ben asked. 'Or have I had too much of this delightful, spiced cider?'

'Yes,' Poppy said. 'Both, probably.'

'Hello Ryan,' Sophie said. 'Come in and sit by the fire.

It's freezing out there. We're going to open some presents tonight. Is that okay with you?'

'I've already opened one of mine,' Poppy said, unable to contain her excitement any longer. She held out her hand and little beams of light from the sparkling diamond on her finger reflected all around the room.

No one heard the carollers who had just arrived and were singing *Silent Night*. It was far from a silent night inside Summerhill but it was definitely a spectacularly happy Christmas Eve.

THE END

MERRY CHRISTMAS!

Thank you so much for reading, *Ninety Days to Christmas.* I do hope you enjoyed it.

COMING SOON

A Christmas Hideaway

You can't hide from Love

Holly Gilroy was devastated when her long-term boyfriend, Paul ran off with Naomi, her best friend. Now Paul and Naomi are back in Hideaway Down for Christmas but Holly has no intention of bumping into the happy couple. Cooking and cleaning for the guests at her Mum's holiday cottages is one way to avoid that. Because she can't let Paul see she's still in love with him… can she?

Gabriel Hardwick is desperate to finish his novel… and avoid his agent, Bryony Dawes – who also happens to be his girlfriend. At least that's what Bryony's still telling everyone. Will Gabriel's decision to spend Christmas alone in a rented holiday cottage finally make Bryony see that it's over between them? And is that really what Gabriel wants?

But they're not the only ones with problems this festive season. It's the coldest winter for years and the villagers and visitors in Hideaway Down are finding warmth in the most unexpected places… and not just from the roaring log fire in the hearth of The Snowdrop Inn.

***

To see details of my other books, please go to the books page on my website or scan the QR code, below.
http://www.emilyharvale.com/books.

***

Scan or tap the code above to see Emily's books on Amazon

To read about me, my books, my work in progress and competitions, freebies, or to contact me, pop over to my website http://www.emilyharvale.com. To be the first to hear about new releases and other news, you can subscribe to my newsletter via the 'Sign me up' box.
Or why not come and say 'Hello' on Facebook, Twitter or Pinterest. Hope to chat with you soon.
Love,
Emily xx

14231115R00159

Printed in Poland
by Amazon Fulfillment
Poland Sp. z o.o., Wrocław